HEART

Conditions

HEART

Conditions

SARA LEWIS

Harcourt Brace & Company

New York   San Diego   London

Lyrics from "Fourth of July" written by Dave Alvin,
© 1987 Blue Horn Toad Music (BMI). Administered
by Bug. All rights reserved. Used by permission.

Library of Congress Cataloging-in-Publication Data
Lewis, Sara.
Heart conditions/Sara Lewis.—1st ed.
p.   cm.
ISBN 0-15-139805-4
I. Title.
PS3562.E9745H4   1993
813'.54—dc20   93-19355

Designed by Camilla Filancia
Printed in the United States of America
First edition   A B C D E

*For my mother
with love*

Acknowledgments

I WOULD LIKE to thank several people for helping me with this book. In a daring leap of faith, editor Claire Wachtel of Harcourt Brace & Company bought the book when it was just a fraction of an idea. Edie Soderburg read several drafts and commented, as always, with both truth and kindness. Melinda Knight of the University of San Francisco supplied excellent suggestions on writing that always worked. Matthew Perl, M.D., of Sharp Cabrillo Hospital in San Diego, California, advised me on medical matters.

I am especially grateful to my agent, Robert Colgan, for the way he always seems to be right here with me, even from a distance of three thousand miles or more. Because of all the things he said that got me started, kept me going, and straightened me out, this book is also his.

Contents

HEART
Conditions

AN OPEN WINDOW

ONE EVENING after a long, difficult period in our relationship, without anything in particular leading up to it, Nick and I made love in the living room. I had been looking through a pile of magazines for a picture of a short haircut I remembered from some weeks or months before. I was considering doing something drastic to try to get Nick's attention again when suddenly he was behind me, one of my breasts in each of his hands, breathing hotly onto the back of my neck. He pulled my sweatpants off fast, as if sliding the paper wrapper down a drinking straw. Then he pulled me to the floor. Next, I knew from years of experience, he would want to open my bra under my shirt, not to take it off yet but for now just to give his hands more room to move around. It was a brand-new bra, with the clasp in front, unlike my old ones, which had fastened in back. For a moment, I panicked, afraid that he wouldn't be able to find the clasp. I worried that fumbling to get my bra open would distract him, break the mood, and he would lose interest in making love. Swearing or possibly laughing, he might wander to the kitchen for ice cream or popcorn or to the phone to make a call. But this was not what happened. To my surprise, he did not fumble. His fingers went immediately to the front clasp, clicking it open deftly, as if he had undone me there hundreds of times before. A minute later, I was the one who fumbled—with the top button of his jeans, which were snug in the waist, making it difficult for me to get a grasp. Nick came to my assistance, popping the button open with one hand as the other slid my underpants off in one smooth, practiced motion.

Afterward, it felt a little embarrassing to be naked on the living room floor with the TV on, even with someone I had lived with for five years. The rug needed to be vacuumed. This was my fault. We had divided household chores years before, and vacuuming was mine. It had been at least a month. On TV, there was a commercial about some kind of new laundry detergent, concentrated, more powerful than ever before. The sound was muted, but the two of us looked at the screen, as if expecting it to explain something important to us, something we needed to know right away.

I felt relieved then, believing that now things would get back to normal. It had been months since we had made love anywhere. This evening in the living room had finally broken the spell. It just shows you, I thought, how things can change completely in a single moment.

"Nick," I said later, in bed, "I love you."

"Thanks, Alice," he said sleepily. He was going on tour the next day. He had a big part in a comedy. He would be gone for ten weeks.

"I was really worried," I said.

He started; he had fallen asleep since I last spoke. "Hm?" he said. "About what?"

"It hasn't been going very well between us," I said. "And I was afraid that we were going to break up."

"You were?"

"You weren't? Well, anyway, we're OK now."

"Sure." He fell asleep.

I felt so grateful about the way the relationship had turned around that I made plans to change. From now on, I wasn't going to drop my clothes on the floor. And I was going to take a cooking class. Anyone could learn. All you had to do was practice following recipes and what steps to take when things went wrong.

Just as I was starting to drift off into sleep, an alarming image came into my mind. It was the picture of my diaphragm in its turquoise plastic case and the tube of spermicidal jelly next to it, both at that very moment quietly gathering dust on a bathroom shelf. I hadn't even thought about the diaphragm until that moment. My eyes sprang open, and I was instantly as tense and alert as if I had just seen a stranger climb into my home through an open window.

Two

THE STORM

EFORE I WENT to Hollywood," my grandmother was saying, "I had hardly ever eaten in a restaurant, never gone swimming in an ocean or slept in a house without my parents. I had never seen a man naked."

I wasn't really listening. I had heard all this before. And at the moment I was trying to keep my grandmother's huge maroon Buick on the Long Island Expressway during the worst blizzard in fifteen years. I was going twenty miles an hour, because it was snowing so hard I could barely make out what was the road and what was not. There were hidden patches of ice under the snow. I had the headlights on at eleven in the morning. In the past ten minutes we had seen six other cars. Luckily, we only had to go two exits. We were on our way to my grandmother's weekly hair appointment. One of the few reasons she would go out in a snowstorm was to get her hair and nails done.

"My life had not prepared me for Hollywood. The year I was born, my father bought a house in town that's still there to this day if you care to visit Drinkwater, Iowa. But who would? I had taught school at home, but I had no common sense. Within the first month of my arrival in Hollywood, a producer asked me to come to his office," Gram went on. "He said I was a perfect Pollyanna for the new movie he was working on. I was twenty-six years old, but I believed him and I went. Of course, there was no such movie. I was lucky I got out of his office without being raped. I lost a shoe trying to hurry out the door and had to go home on the streetcar without it. That's when I learned the most important lesson of my career: You can't trust anybody who has anything to do with movies or the theater. They are all a bunch of lying cheats, no matter how good and kind they appear. And how is your friend Nick?"

"He's fine, Gram," I said. "He's not a lying cheat."

"Yes, well," she said. Then she went on with her story. "Shortly after that little episode, I went to work at Winnie's. A lot of movie people had their hair done at Winnie's. If I close my eyes, I can just see the place." I didn't dare look away from the road, but I knew she was closing her eyes. "The telephone, the leather appointment book. I can smell all the different things they used on people's hair. I got my hair done there for free, and it changed my life. I mean that. That's how I got into the movies, moved to a better neighborhood, and met Walker Kincaid, who became my lover." She stopped. "You should be getting all this down."

"Pardon?" I said.

"On videotape," she said. "I saw this on the *Today* show. Fellow wrote a book about people telling the stories of their lives, oral histories. Just your regular video camera you'd use for home movies is all you need. I won't be around forever, you know."

"I don't have a video camera," I said. "Let me just

concentrate on getting us there, Gram. This is very scary driving." We passed a car on its side in a ditch. "I shouldn't have let you talk me into this. It's much worse than I thought, really dangerous."

"Shall I ask Mary Lou if she has any ideas about your hair?" Mary Lou was my grandmother's hairdresser.

"No," I said. My hair was brown, unstyled, not curly and not straight but bumpy, falling just below my shoulders. I was always trying to figure out what to do with it and then, in the end, doing nothing at all. When I was a little girl, my mother had told me, "You have lovely hair, Alice, and someday you will be a very pretty lady." I had waited and waited for some kind of transformation to occur, for many years believing that my mother had known something about me that no one else did. Nothing happened. I was as plain grown-up as I had been as a child. To some people, maybe, appearance was not important. But to my grandmother, a person's worth was measured first by looks. Intelligence, wit, kindness, sense of humor—to my grandmother, these were only resources to fall back on if you failed to be beautiful. "I like my hair," I lied.

Gram said, "That's unfortunate."

I almost missed the exit because I didn't see the sign until I just about ran into it. The temperature was seven degrees, and I was sweating. My heart was thumping in my chest. "You don't drive much, do you?" my grandmother said. "I can tell you're not comfortable behind the wheel."

I managed to get my grandmother's car to Mary Lou's Beauty Spot, a small hair salon in a house. As we pulled up, Mary Lou peered out the kitchen window. I went around to my grandmother's side of the car and opened the door. Holding on to the back of the seat with her right hand, she worked her body around until she was facing me. First she took her right leg out, lifting it with both hands, and put it on the ground. Then she took her left leg out and put it down.

Mary Lou appeared beside me in her bathrobe and boots. "What? Are you kidding?" She held my grandmother's left elbow while I took her right one, and together we pulled her to her feet and steered her toward the back door of the house. "It's a blizzard, Mrs. Williams. Don't you listen to the radio? I'm sitting here in my robe drinking coffee," Mary Lou said. "I'm thinking I'm going to have a Saturday off for once in my life."

My grandmother said, "This is my granddaughter Alice, my houseguest this weekend."

"Nice to meet you, Alice." She gave me a sympathetic look behind my grandmother, bent in concentration on the icy ground. "Mrs. Williams, you must be out of your gourd coming here on a day like this. You could slip out here and bust a hip."

"Just look at my hair," my grandmother said. "It looks like a bird's nest. I can't let anyone see me like this."

"You look like a million bucks," Mary Lou said. "As always. I should be coming to *you* every week. Look at *my* hair."

My grandmother stopped, straightened, and examined Mary Lou's hair, which now had big lumps of snow resting on it. "I've seen you look better," my grandmother said. "I think you've got the color too dark for your skin."

"Oh, shut up. Who asked you?" Mary Lou said. "Alice,

you going to stick around? Come on, where you going to go, weather like this? You can have the coffee I was going to drink with my feet up."

I stayed and listened to the two of them talk. My grandmother was getting color today. "Last time it was too red," she said to Mary Lou. "But I don't want it too blond, either." My grandmother had been dyeing her hair for about sixty years. If she didn't, she said, she would look as old as the hills. She was eighty-nine. She slept in a terry-cloth turban and used a special satin pillowcase. During the day, she wore a hair net made of human hair to hold it all in place.

"Golden," Mary Lou said. "Don't tell me. You want it 'golden.' We go through this every six weeks," she said to me. Mary Lou was the kind of person who could call my grandmother an old bag and get away with it. I wished I could do that.

"My daughter, Bonnie, was going to come out for the weekend too, but she canceled because of the weather," Mary Lou said, slowly lowering my grandmother's head into the sink. "You know, I hate to say this, but I'm just as glad. Lately we're always arguing, and it gets me down—you know what I'm saying."

"Yes, I do," Gram said. "I surely do. You don't like Bill, and she knows it."

"I guess that's it," Mary Lou said. They went on, talking about why Bill was wrong for Bonnie.

My grandmother probably knew more about Bonnie's life than she knew about mine. I didn't often visit Gram. We didn't get along. But the day before she had called me at my office in New York, where I was an editorial assistant for a publishing company, to invite me for the weekend. I hadn't heard that a snowstorm was coming, and I didn't know that Eleanor, her maid/cook/chauffeur/gardener/house-keeper, had walked out on her just moments before. When I got there, she had me drive her to the Shopping Basket to buy a hundred and fifty dollars' worth of groceries (including over twenty frozen diet entrées), carry them all inside for her, and put them away—while she barked at me for putting the milk on the wrong side of the fridge and the peanut butter behind the box of crackers, where she couldn't see it. Then she wanted me drive her to the video store and pick a movie for her while she waited in the car.

My grandmother wasn't supposed to stay alone. She didn't drive anymore, since she had flattened a stop sign once on her way home from the dentist. About twenty years before, she had had a heart attack, and she was supposed to have someone around to make her take a walk every day and keep her on her low-salt diet. This was not humanly possible, but my aunt and uncle felt better believing that there was someone there trying. My grandmother did not cook, so she also needed someone to do that for her. I didn't cook, either. The best I could do was put little frozen food trays in the toaster oven. Aunt Louise and Uncle Richard came from Connecticut about once a month to pay the bills that Gram crammed into drawers; to chop away at the bushes and trees in her yard, which always seemed to be either growing or dying too rapidly; and to take care of hazards like frayed electrical cords and scatter rugs on slippery wood floors. My aunt and uncle were giving a big dinner party this weekend, or they would be here now. And they were about to leave on a trip

to Europe, I expected my aunt to go into high gear trying to hire someone to look after Gram while they were
away.

I wouldn't have minded if Gram had asked me to help
her over the weekend. But my grandmother was not that
direct. She didn't ask me to come out to help her. Instead,
she said she just thought I might like a change of scene, a
weekend in the country.

For dinner, I had scrambled eggs and rye toast, two
things I knew how to make. My grandmother had a frozen
diet spinach soufflé that I had heated up and carried out to
her in the living room, where she was watching television.

I put the video I had rented into my grandmother's
machine. It was *Broken Promise* (1938), which had been a
Cheapo Chestnut at the video store, two nights for two
dollars. "I've seen this a thousand times," Gram said.

"That's why I got it. You told me it was your favorite
movie. But we don't have to watch it if you're tired of it.
We can see if there's something you like better on
television."

"No, no," Gram said. "You're the guest. We'll watch
your movie." I pushed Play. "Walker Kincaid almost got
this part," she said.

She had told me this at least a hundred times. Walker
Kincaid, her married lover, was a movie actor she knew
before she met my grandfather. "You're kidding," I said.

"He was too old to play romantic leads by then. The
rejection nearly killed him. He left his wife and took up
with an eighteen-year-old extra he met on a studio lot. This
was years after my time. His wife tried to commit suicide.
Have you heard from Nick?"

"I left your number on our answering machine, in case he tries to reach me," I said. "Why do you always ask about Nick after you've told some awful story about creeps you knew in Hollywood? Nick isn't like that."

Walker Kincaid had been a classic leading man type—tall, with chiseled features and a deep, resonant voice, a big phony. Nick was a character actor—short, dark, and funny. I had met him at a party five years before. As soon as I met him, I knew I wanted to spend the rest of my life with him.

"Nick? Like Walker?" My grandmother laughed. "Certainly not. Walker was an overnight success. For twenty years, he was never out of work. You know yourself how rare that is for an actor." Nick had had a hard time getting acting work for a while. For almost two years, I supported us both. But lately Nick was getting a lot of acting jobs.

Halfway through the movie, my grandmother said, "If you're still hungry, put some of those frozen cookies in the toaster oven and get yourself some ice cream."

"Do you want me to get you some cookies?"

"If you're having some yourself, you might as well," she said.

"Do you want some ice cream too?"

She looked at me. "Oh, no." I pushed Pause. "You wouldn't be able to find the chocolate syrup," she said.

"Tell me. I can find it."

"In the icebox, on the middle shelf on the door. But you won't put enough on." She shuffled her feet around, pretending she was about to stand up and do it herself.

"Gram, I'll get it. Cookies and ice cream with gobs of chocolate syrup, right?"

"Get yourself some ice cream," she yelled after me. "I bought it for you."

In the kitchen, I took the box of cookies out of the freezer. I opened the lid and put two cold lumps of dough in my mouth. I could barely close my lips around them. Lately I did things like this. At an office party the day before, where I had had to put out the food, I had hidden behind a door and put a whole brownie in my mouth, practically swallowing it whole. Then, after stuffing myself at the party, I had a bagel with butter and a hot chocolate on the train on the way out here, really enjoying it, as if I were eating something unusual, delicately prepared, as if I had been very hungry for a very long time.

When the cookies were done, I reminded Gram that you were supposed to wait a few minutes until they cooled slightly, or they wouldn't have the right texture. She stuffed them into her mouth, one after the other, without waiting for anything. With her mouth full, she said, "Hot." Maybe this was what I was becoming.

I pushed Start on the VCR.

The phone rang, and my grandmother picked it up. "Hello?" she said. I pushed Pause again. She smiled the way she always did when she was having her picture taken and pushed her chin out so that her neck didn't sag. "Well, how *are* you? . . . Oh, how *won*derful. I wish I could be there myself." She tilted her head, doing a flirtatious look that she had probably practiced in the mirror as a teenager. This was how I knew she was speaking to a man. "Yes. She's sitting right here. Just a moment." She put her hand over the receiver and hissed at me, "It's *Nick*. Run up and take it in my room."

I took the stairs two at a time, thinking he might be right in the middle of a rehearsal or something, he might not have much time. "Hi, honey," I said, breathless. I sat down on my grandmother's bed.

"Hi," Nick said. He cleared his throat. "I have something to say. I know you can't stand dishonesty," he said. There was a familiar tone in his voice. He was speaking the way he did when he practiced his lines, before he really had them down. "So I'm just going to come right out with it. I want to split up." In the pause, I pictured him looking down at a script. "Our relationship has been over for a long time. You know that as well as I do. I know you won't be surprised when I tell you that I'm involved with someone else."

I said, "What? No. I don't believe you."

"Now, don't tell me you haven't known for months. Please. I couldn't stand that."

"You're sleeping with someone else? Why?" I had this weird feeling. I was hot all over, as if I were about to burst into flames. "You're having an affair?"

"Don't call it an affair. I love her. When you meet her, I think you'll really like her too. I hope we can all be friends."

I said, "Friends?" I was standing up now, gripping the phone tightly. My mouth was open. My brain scrambled for a way out, a reason not to believe any of this.

"I was hoping you wouldn't make a scene. I thought you were above that kind of thing," Nick said. "Please don't disappoint me, Alice."

"Disappoint you? Say you're kidding."

"Stop," he said. "Don't be childish."

I didn't say anything.

"When you've thought about it for a while, you'll see

that it doesn't make sense for us to stay together. I wasn't happy."

"I was," I said lamely. "What about that? I was happy."

"Alice, I'll tell you what. You can stay in my apartment until I get back. I'm sure you can find another place in six weeks."

"I have to move?" Only Nick's name was on our lease. "Six weeks? The vacancy rate in Manhattan is less than one percent. And even if I could find a place, I've only got seven hundred dollars in my checking account. What about the first and last month's rent, the security deposit, the broker's fee? You can't do this. You're not that kind of person."

"I'm sure you'll think of something. You're a survivor. I mean that. I'm not just saying it to make you feel better. I've got to go now. So long." There was a far-off click. I sat there frozen for a few seconds, still holding the phone to my ear, a lot of little clues coming to me now, too late. I would bet just about anything I had that Nick's lover's bras opened in the front. I was wondering if I should call him back and scream or cry or something. Then I realized that he hadn't said where he was calling from. I heard another click, close and loud—my grandmother hanging up.

I went downstairs, trying to keep my face still. I didn't want her to know that I knew she had heard everything. I didn't want to talk about it.

"I was listening," she said. "The son of a bitch."

I stared at the television without trying to make sense of what I saw. My grandmother didn't say anything comforting, but she didn't mention Walker Kincaid again, either.

"Your ice cream melted," said Gram after a while.

"I forgot about it," I said. She was looking at the bowl on the coffee table. "Do you want it?" It was soup. I handed it to her.

"Well, if you're not going to eat it." She took the bowl and spooned in a few mouthfuls. Then she drank the rest straight out of the bowl.

When the movie was over, my grandmother put her arms out and waited. I took both her hands and pulled her to her feet. She stood still in front of the couch for a moment, getting her bearings. "I just can't believe I'm an old lady. Inside, I feel the same as when I was thirty-three or seventeen or eight. Isn't that stupid? Sorry about your boyfriend. Good night, Alice."

" 'Night, Gram," I said. "See you tomorrow."

"Don't count on it," she said, slowly making her way to the staircase. "I'm eighty-nine, you know. I could go like that." She snapped her fingers and laughed, as if she had made a good joke.

I put the video back in its box and the dishes in the dishwasher. I was going to wait until I was sure my grandmother was in bed before I called my sister to tell her what had happened with Nick. As I was closing the dishwasher, all the lights went out, a power failure. This happened almost every time there was a big snow. I heard a small thump, and my grandmother said, "Shit. *Alice!*"

"Coming," I said. Upstairs, I said, "Gram?"

"Here," she said from somewhere near the bathroom. I walked slowly with my arms out to keep from bumping into anything. "The damn light cord is wrapped around my foot." I untangled her. "Now get the flashlight. It's next to my bed."

I groped around. "I can't find it. It's not on your bedside table."

"Oh, it is so," she said through gritted teeth. "You're as bad as Eleanor. You can't cook, you can't drive, you can't even find a simple flashlight." As soon as it was light in the morning, I decided, I would call for a taxi to the train station. I found the flashlight in the bathroom, on the back of the toilet. "Well, I certainly didn't put it there," she said, grabbing it from me. "I'll be fine now. You go along to bed."

By the time I called my sister, it was after eleven. I woke up her husband, Mark. "Alice?" he said hoarsely. "You OK? Let me get Laura."

"What's the matter?" Laura said when she came on.

"I'm at Gram's."

"Oh, God. And something happened."

"No, no, nothing like that. Eleanor left, and she needed some help over the weekend."

"Oh. You scared me for a minute."

"Nick called. He's dumping me."

"What? Nick? No."

"Yes. He has another girlfriend."

"Nick? How could—? Who would ever—? Are you sure?"

"Yes. I have to find a new place to live before he gets home. Six weeks."

"He's throwing you *out*?" Then she said to Mark, "Nick's dumping Alice, and he's throwing her out *on the street*. He has a new girlfriend."

I heard Mark say, "Nick? *Nick*? You're kidding."

Laura said to me, "You can sleep on our couch, Alley. I mean, I know it's not much, but you'll never find a place to live in six weeks. And where are you going to get the money?"

"That's OK," I said. "You guys are cramped enough."

"When are you getting back to the city?"

"Tomorrow," I said.

"Call me, OK? Don't get isolated."

"Right," I said. "Maybe I'll stop by in the afternoon."

"OK. 'Night," she said.

" 'Night."

Our parents were dead. They died when I was thirteen and Laura was fifteen. We lived in a suburb of Chicago then. On the way home from a movie during an ice storm, their car slid through a red light and smashed into the trailer of an eighteen-wheeler. I finished high school and Laura got through a year of college while living with our aunt and uncle and their children in Connecticut. The two things that were important in their family were clothes and academic performance. Our own parents had left these matters to us. As soon as we moved in with them, our aunt Louise got rid of most of our clothes and bought us new ones that were more like what our cousins wore. Our uncle Richard looked at our homework before we turned it in and often had us do it over his way. Laura, who had never been good in school, got a lot of lectures from Uncle Richard, who believed that all she needed was to be pushed. Laura froze in school and had to repeat eleventh grade. I was always being taken to have different things done to my hair—body waves, layering, highlighting—expensive, time-consuming treatments that did nothing to improve my hair and left me feeling ugly.

My cousin Candace and I shared a bedroom because we were close in age. Olivia and Laura shared another room.

When I was in ninth grade and Candace was in tenth, she went on a diet and lost some weight. Then she went back to eating what everyone else in the family ate, but managed not to regain the weight. In fact, she seemed to be losing more. The skin on her face appeared to have shrunk, so that her teeth started to look too big, like the teeth of a skeleton. She was always cold and wore many layers of clothes, which she took off only in the bathroom with the door locked, never in the bedroom in front of me. Her mother called her Beanpole and Skinny Minnie, but otherwise no one mentioned anything about it.

One night, I helped Candace study for a French test she was worried about. When we were finished, she was relieved and grateful for my help. She said, "Do you want to see something?" Her eyes glittered with a secret. I followed her into the bathroom, where she showed me how she could vomit her entire dinner into the toilet easily, almost without a sound. She had been practicing, she said, and I could learn to do it too, so that I would never get fat. She said that at first I would have to put my finger down my throat and try several times, making myself gag over and over again before I actually vomited. Red spots might appear on my face. But once I had done it a lot, my food would come up right away, anytime I wanted it to, and no one would ever know. That night she undressed in front of me. I had seen bodies like hers before, in haunting black-and-white photographs of concentration camp victims.

People told me things. There was something about my face or personality that caused people to confide in me. A stranger on a bus would start talking about the hot weather and end up telling me that she was in love with her boss, who was a woman. An acquaintance at work would tell me he had had an affair ten years ago that his wife still didn't know about. Even when I was a child, people told me things.

The next night, when Candace was taking one of her endless showers, I found Aunt Louise and Uncle Richard in the living room, watching the news. They looked up from the TV at me. I said, "Candace needs a psychologist."

Aunt Louise said, "Alice! What a hideous thing to say."

"What do you mean, Alice?" Uncle Richard said.

"I mean, she is trying to disappear. I mean, if somebody doesn't help her, she might die."

"Honest to God, Alice," Aunt Louise said. "I don't know what gets into you. Here we've taken you girls in, done everything in the world for you, and this is what we get in return—vicious attacks on our children." She was crying.

Uncle Richard snapped, "Louise, stop. The girl is trying to help." He looked at me. "You think it's really that bad, Alice?"

"Yes," I said. "I got some names of psychologists from the counselor at school. Other girls have this too, Aunt Louise, not just Candace." She wouldn't look at me. I handed Uncle Richard a list.

"Thank you," he said. "I'll look into it."

Candace started seeing one of the psychologists and going to a group once a week. Uncle Richard thanked me again for bringing the situation to his attention. "You saw a problem and were not afraid to come forward with it. Many kids would not have been so clearheaded." He asked if there was anything else I wanted him to know.

I said, "Yes. We're grateful for your help and everything, we really are, but Laura needs to do her own homework or she'll never get out of high school. We want to choose our own clothes, and do you think you could ask Aunt Louise to give up on my hair?" After that, Uncle Richard always asked my opinion on family problems, and Aunt Louise always treated me as if I had caused them.

When I was ready for college, Laura and I shared an apartment in Manhattan. I went to Barnard, where I qualified for financial aid, and Laura went to City College. At Christmastime we got ourselves invited home to friends' houses. Laura got married before she graduated. She was worried about being on her own without the social possibilities of college; she didn't want to be alone. And the marriage worked. Fourteen years later, Laura and Mark were still together.

Part of our inheritance went for tuition and living expenses when we were in college. The money had come from our parents' life insurance and savings and the sale of our father's dry-cleaning store and our house. There would have been more money if I had agreed to sell off our mother's costume shop. But I insisted on keeping the costumes. I had them put in storage. Our aunt and uncle agreed to it because Laura said it was all right with her and because the costumes were all we had left of our mother.

After college, Laura and I still had a little money. I used the rest of mine when Nick was unemployed and my salary was not enough to support us both. Then I had four impacted wisdom teeth pulled. I developed an infection, which required additional surgery. My money was gone. Laura and Mark used hers as a down payment on their apartment. Unlike my sister, I didn't have much to show for the money I had spent. Besides this regret, there was another, unexpected effect of not having the money anymore. Since our parents had died, I had felt unanchored, as if gravity some-how did not apply to me the way it did to people with living parents. When the money was gone, I realized that it had seemed like a counterweight to me. Not having it, I felt I might float away and vanish like a released helium balloon. The costumes were still ours, and that helped. The quarterly storage bill made me feel slightly grounded. But I needed more to hold me down. Up to now, I had seen Nick as my anchor. Waking up in the morning, I would find myself clutching the sleeve of the T-shirt he wore, as if the slightest draft could blow me away while I slept, while my guard was down. When Nick was out of town, I held on to his pillowcase. I had looked forward to marrying him, to finally loosening my grasp.

As soon as I hung up the phone from talking to Laura, I went to my grandmother's powder room. I put my hand over my mouth, breathing through my nose, feeling as if I might throw up. Lately so many things made me feel queasy: the sight of the slick sheen of grease on a pepperoni pizza or the smell of broccoli cooking. When the nausea passed, I went to the kitchen and took a spoon from a drawer. I opened a jar of peanut butter, shoved the spoon in deep, then put it straight into my mouth. I thought I might be pregnant. Gram would notice about the peanut butter—it was a new jar—but I would be home by then.

Sunday morning, in Gram's guest bathroom, I used a home pregnancy test that I had brought with me. All I had to do was pee on a little plastic wand, put it into a holder, and wait three minutes, the box said. But it didn't take that long. It seemed the stick glowed pink almost immediately: positive. I put all the parts of the test into a brown paper bag before I took it outside to the garbage can. I pulled some used paper towels out of the can, put the bag in, then put the towels back again. I pushed the lid down tight. I was grateful for the fifteen inches of snow on the ground, which severely curtailed my grandmother's ability to get around.

I didn't get back to Manhattan that day. When I called for a cab to the train station, the woman said, "What? Are you nuts? You're going nowhere today, miss." The Long Island Railroad was out of service. And many roads had not been plowed. I waited for the phone to ring at Gram's, for Nick to call. All day, I kept picking it up to see if it was out of order, but it seemed to be working fine.

Three

THE MOVE

$\mathcal{B}$Y MONDAY morning the trains were running again. My aunt Louise was driving out from Connecticut to take over with Gram. From home that night, I called six abortion clinics. They all asked me when my last period was and then said that I would have to wait at least a week before I had "the procedure." I wasn't far enough along, they said. I made it through work by avoiding everybody all week, going to the research library on Forty-second Street a lot—part of my job was to look up facts for the six editors in our department—and pretending I was having lunch with my sister a couple of times. I didn't call my sister or stop by, as I had said I would. I wasn't going to tell anyone that I was pregnant. Soon this would be over; there was no need to discuss it with anyone and have people feeling sorry for me. Nick didn't call.

Saturday morning, I was trying to get up the stairs with two bags of groceries. The nausea had increased. Walking

up the three flights of steps to our apartment, which I had
never given a moment's thought, had turned into a big deal
in the past week. Becoming even slightly winded made me
gag, and I did not want to vomit again today. With the
groceries, climbing the stairs without breathing hard was
almost impossible. I went up three steps and stopped, inhaling deeply through my nose. I did another three steps,
stopped, breathed in. I thought of my grandmother. This
was the way she went up stairs—unbelievably slowly—
since her heart attack twenty years before. She did this once
a day only, coming downstairs in the morning and not going
back up until evening, and in between having someone else
get whatever she needed from upstairs.

I waited, then climbed another three steps. I heard a
door open. It sounded like George's door, on the floor above
our apartment. I heard him locking up, then his footsteps
thundered down the stairs with speed that seemed impossible to me now. I would try to be in motion when he got
to my level, between the first and second floors, so that he
would not guess that anything was wrong. I arranged a
smile that would appear as a neighborly greeting. When he
was almost there, I lifted a foot, putting it on the step, and
I moved up as soon as I saw him. I went up one more step,
then another. I had to stop. I looked at him, ready to lie
about what was wrong with me: I had twisted an ankle this
morning; I had the stomach flu. George was in his running
clothes. "Hi, George," I said as he sped by.

"Alice, hey," he said and kept going past me to the front
door. He opened it, it slammed, he was gone.

I put my foot on the next step, went up. This was going
to take all day, I thought. I went a little faster, up six steps.
My hands grew hot, my face sweated. I pressed my lips

together hard but gagged anyway. I ran the rest of the way up the steps and struggled to unlock the door before I threw up. I did not make it to the bathroom but got only as far as the kitchen sink. After vomiting the first few times, I was able to turn on the water, rinse everything down, and put my hot hands into the cool water. When my stomach stopped heaving, I put my wet hands on my face, cooling it, took some more water, and wiped my face again. Now I would be all right for a little while. I dried my hands and wiped the cold sweat off my neck with a dish towel. This would be over on Monday, I reminded myself again. Then I started to put the groceries away. Before I had finished, I had opened a box of Triscuits and eaten many of them. After that, I had some yogurt and made a piece of toast.

When the groceries were put away, I lay down on the bed for a minute. I had a newspaper and planned to look at the apartment rental ads. I was going to start looking for a place to live as soon as the abortion was over. But before opening the paper, I closed my eyes for a minute. I was exhausted at eleven in the morning. The apartment was a mess. I was going to pick up as soon as I rested for a second and had a look at the paper. All the clothes I had worn in the last five days were either on the floor or on a chair next to the bed. There were empty cups all over the place and plates with crumbs on them. I would take care of this. Maybe it would lift my spirits to have the place straightened up.

The doorbell rang. I jumped to my feet, thought I was going to vomit again, breathed in slowly through my nose, didn't throw up after all. I walked to the window to see who it was. There was no intercom in this building. If it's Nick, I thought, how much time would I need to clean up this mess and put on makeup? Four and a half hours, I calculated. But it was probably my sister. She would understand and accept my mess. I looked out the window and didn't see anybody I knew. "Yes?" I yelled. A middle-aged female figure backed out of the doorway and onto the sidewalk and looked up. "Hi. Open the door, honey. It's Aunt Louise." She smiled at me.

I had a clutching feeling in my stomach, not nausea this time but fear. I didn't want her up here. Aunt Louise had never seen this apartment, which was full of unfinished attempts to improve it. The bathroom walls were studs, wiring, and tar paper. The kitchen floor was rotten planks patched decades earlier with flattened coffee cans. The bedroom walls were scraped, pitted plaster in a variety of colors. To someone from Connecticut not used to this neighborhood, the place would look like a bombed-out home in some developing country that had been at war for many years. Besides, she might guess that I was pregnant. "I'm sick," I said.

"That's too bad." Aunt Louise waited to be let in.

"I'll have to throw a key down." I found the extra key, tied it into a bandanna, and tossed it down to her. "No buzzer," I said. The key landed beside an open garbage can. She picked it up from the sidewalk, waved at me, and went to the door. While she climbed the stairs, I brushed my hair, which was all I could manage to organize in the time I had.

Aunt Louise was panting from the stairs as she walked in. She took off her coat. She had on gold clip-on earrings, a red knit dress, a string of pearls. She looked too dressed up for my run-down neighborhood, for my messy apartment. I was wearing sweatpants with a hole in the knee and a shapeless white T-shirt that had turned gray with age. "Oh, you poor thing," she said. "You're green! You look awful! Lie down right now." I sat on the edge of the bed. "What's wrong, dear? Do you have the flu?" She put a hand to my forehead.

I said, "Food poisoning, I think. Maybe something weird I ate at a party last night."

"Oh, you went to a party?" she said, brightening. "That sounds like fun." Then, remembering, she said, "I'm sorry. You look miserable. Shall I make you some weak tea?"

"No, thanks, Aunt Louise."

"Good Lord," she said, surveying the apartment. "How do you find anything?"

"What are you doing in New York?" I said.

"Before we go on this trip to Europe, I have to get Gram squared away. Laura told me about Nick, so I thought I'd better peek in on you too. And it's a good thing I did, it seems to me."

"I'm fine," I said. "Really."

"I see. Now. What are your plans?"

"Plans?" For a moment, I was afraid that she somehow knew, that she had found out I was pregnant.

"Laura said you have to move. I thought I might be able to help you start getting organized."

"Oh, that's OK. I'm fine. I can manage."

"Sweetheart, you're not fine at all."

"I am. Really."

"You will be," said my aunt. "But it will take some time." She tried to say comforting things, which only made me feel worse. "You're going to put this all behind you sooner than you think. You may not believe it now, but if he's the type who has affairs, it's better that he leaves you now. He wasn't right for you anyway, Alice. He always seemed too quiet to me, sort of moody. Now that you're on your own, you'll find someone more suitable. Maybe Candace and Olivia know someone nice for you." My cousins lived in Manhattan too, but we never saw each other. "When you're feeling a little better, you can go shopping, buy yourself something really pretty, get all that hair cut off, and before you know it, you'll forget all about Nick." She looked around the room again. "I'll just start picking up a few things here."

"Thank you, but that's all right. I can clean up my own apartment."

"No trouble," she said. "You're sick. I can understand that you might let things go a little when you're feeling down and a bit under the weather. But you shouldn't let things go completely," she said. She shook a finger at me. "It's not good for your mental health. Before you know it, you'll be out of circulation completely, and that's not what you want, is it?"

She was fast. She had all the clothes folded, in the hamper, or hung up in about ten minutes. She washed the dishes and straightened the clutter. "Where's your yellow pages?" she said. I got the phone book for her. Good, I thought, she has an errand to do; she's leaving. She wrote something on a scrap of paper and put it in her purse. "Where's Delancey Street?" she said.

I took her to the living-room window and showed her.

"Fine," she said.

"What do you want to go there for?"

"I'll be right back," she said.

While she was gone, I took a shower and washed my hair. I put on jeans and a different gray T-shirt. I got out the vacuum cleaner. I sat down on the floor next to the vacuum and stared at it. The doorbell rang again. I looked out the window and saw my aunt getting out of a taxi, struggling with a big pile of cardboard cartons, the kind you buy flat and assemble yourself. She held up her hand. "Don't come down," she said. "I can manage this. Just throw the key." I tossed it down again. She made three trips. "These weigh nothing, of course," she said, in case I felt guilty for not helping. "They're just a little bulky."

"What are the boxes for?" I said.

"I thought we could get your things packed for moving."

"Now?" I said. "Today? But I don't have anywhere to go. I haven't found a place yet. I haven't even looked."

"Why not take advantage of me while I'm here to help you?"

"Oh," I said. "I guess. Thank you." But I had this feeling that I was about to do something I didn't want to, like missing my exit on a highway, realizing that there wouldn't be a way out for miles and miles.

We started filling boxes with my belongings. My aunt kept holding things up and saying, "Yours or his?" and "Do you still want this?" I kept feeling sick and having to sit down.

With minimal participation from me, all my things were getting packed up faster than I would have thought possible. "Now," she said. "These boxes are for storage, so I'll just put the blankets in here." She folded two blankets, stuffed them in a box, taped it, and labeled it. This was when it hit me that she had someplace specific in mind for me to go, somewhere I wouldn't need blankets.

Two months after our parents died, Aunt Louise signed Laura and me up for ski camp for spring vacation. We cried and told her we didn't want to go. But she thought she was doing the right thing, forcing us to be with other kids, to do something active. She thought it would snap us out of the doldrums. "You'll meet people, you'll have fun," she said. We didn't know how to ski, and all the other kids did. Most of them were younger than we were and knew each other. Our parents' death was still an open wound, and we were not ready to spend all day falling down in the snow and smiling at a lot of people we had just met. Laura hurt her ankle on purpose the first day—we planned it together—and after it was taped up, we stayed in our room, reading and playing board games that we brought upstairs from the lobby. Besides feeling miserably alone and out of place at a ski resort, we felt guilty about the money Aunt Louise and Uncle Richard had spent for something we didn't do.

"Where am I going?" I said. "What are you going to do with me?"

"To Gram's," she said and smiled at me. "You're going to Gram's. It's perfect. You can look after each other, while she finds someone else to work for her and you get over Nick."

"No. I'm sorry. I can't. That just would not work. We don't like each other. She thinks I do everything wrong. I would give her a heart attack the first time I made salad dressing. She doesn't like me."

"Nonsense. She loves you. She's crazy about you. You're her granddaughter. Who owns the bed?"

"Nick."

"Good. That's one thing we won't have to deal with. Shall we tackle the kitchen?" Aunt Louise crumpled newspapers and put them in the bottom of a box. "You know, getting old has been very hard for Gram. She's lost her independence. Imagine how she feels not being able to drive herself where she wants to go, not being able to see well enough to know if she's wearing a clean dress. The people she's been most dependent on in the last few years have been women I've hired to look after her. I think it would do her a world of good to feel that a granddaughter cared enough to come and stay with her, to get to know her better, to do things for her—not because she's being paid to but because she wants to. She said you both had such a nice weekend together, making cookies, watching a movie, talking. She said she told you all about her Hollywood days. You know she loves that. It's been a long time since she had so much fun, she said."

"She said she had fun with me? Really?"

"Yes." There was a pause while we crumpled newspapers around plates. Then my aunt said, "But I can understand how you feel. You're young, after all. You don't want to spend your time with an old lady."

"It would take me an hour and fifteen minutes each way on the train to work. And that's under ideal conditions, which never happen."

"Terrible. We'll think of something else."

"How long would I have to stay?"

"You don't *have* to do anything, Alice. It's entirely up to you. A week, a month, whatever. But I don't think you want to do it. So forget it. Dumb idea. It wouldn't be good for either of you if you felt obligated to be there."

"No, I'll go," I said. "I guess I can do it. For a while." What had gotten to me was the idea of my grandmother, with her perfect golden hair all fluffed up just so, walking around in a dirty dress.

Aunt Louise drove me out to Gram's with two suitcases and four boxes in the trunk and on the back seat of her car. She took Gram and me out to dinner at an Italian place. I ate a whole basket of garlic bread. "I see you've got your appetite back," my aunt said. "That's a good sign." After dinner, Aunt Louise dropped us off at Gram's before driving home to Connecticut. As soon as she left, my grandmother and I argued about where I was supposed to put my things. She didn't want me to use the dresser and closet in the guest room, which were full of ancient bathing suits, nightgowns, evening bags, and other old junk. She said that if I started rearranging things, she would never find anything she needed. "You can use the drawers and closet in Eleanor's old room downstairs," she said. "They're all empty."

"Fine," I said. "I'll sleep downstairs, then." That room had its own bathroom and TV. The bathroom for the guest room was down the hall, and there was no TV.

"You absolutely will not!" my grandmother said.

"Why not?"

"Because it's the maid's room," she said. "And I'll hear no more about it!" She went to her own room and closed the door.

I sat down on the bed in the guest room. It was lumpy and bouncy. The wallpaper—pink roses on a gray background—was peeling and torn. Someone had put Scotch tape on it in several places to hold it together, and the tape had turned yellow. On the bureau was a ceramic ashtray with a little shepherdess figure attached to it. The shepherdess had been missing her head for at least five years. Next to her was a little bowl of dusty, artificially scented plastic flowers. I could hear something scratching above my head. I hoped it was branches blowing against the roof and not a family of rodents. I'll just stay for a little while, I told myself; a few weeks, maybe. After the abortion I could look at apartments on my lunch hour.

I plotted the way I would get to and from the clinic on Monday. I would take a 5 A.M. train to the city. Gram would not be up yet to ask questions. I would be back by early afternoon and tell her that there had been a bomb scare in the building I worked in. Without trying to decide where to put my things, I stretched out on the bed in my clothes. I was almost asleep when my grandmother opened the door.

"Don't think I don't know how you feel," she said. I sat up. "When Walker Kincaid left me for that singer, it was just about the end of me. Do you know how I found out about it? I went to his apartment all dressed up, with a birthday present for him tied with a big red bow. *She* opened the door, wearing his bathrobe. For two weeks I wandered around the streets of Los Angeles with tears streaming down my face. People thought I had lost my mind. I had. I went crazy. I had to go home to Iowa on the train. I caught rheumatic fever. I was in bed for three months. My heart was damaged, which was just right because I felt as though he had torn it out of me. I mean that. It was a physical pain." She came to the side of the bed, took my hand in hers, and squeezed. Her hand felt good, warm and dry and softer than I expected, around my cold, clammy one. "I know all about it," she said. "Good night." She walked slowly toward her room, her slippers scuffing against the wood floor.

"Good night, Gram," I said.

I heard her bed creak and paper rustle as she sat down to read an assortment of magazines and novels late into the night.

Four

THE ABORTION

*T*HE CLINIC was called the Women's Health Center, Inc. On the phone, the woman had given me instructions: "Don't eat or drink anything after twelve midnight. Get here no later than 7 A.M. We fill up very early, and it's first come, first served. Be prepared to see some people out front handing out anti-abortion fliers. We recommend that you bring someone with you and that you do not return to work or do any strenuous exercise for the remainder of the day that you have the procedure. We take cash, Visa, and MasterCard. Only. Most important, do not eat or drink anything after twelve midnight. Any questions?"

"I got it," I said. "Thank you."

I left my grandmother's before five and arrived at the clinic at a quarter to seven. There was a man out front of the building, all bundled up in a down jacket, gloves, and a ski hat. He was holding a stack of fliers with pictures of fetuses on them. "Do you know your baby can already suck its thumb?" he said.

"Pardon?" I said. "Oh, I'm not pregnant. I work in a dentist's office on the fifth floor."

"Oh," he said. "Sorry. Cold enough for you out here today?"

I said, "Terrible. You want me to take those fliers inside for you?"

He hesitated, looking over his shoulder, as if someone might be watching him. "Well, yeah, if you would. This is pretty early for me, and I'm cold." He handed over the fliers. "Thanks a lot."

"No problem," I said. I went inside and put the pile of fliers in a garbage can near the elevator. I pushed the button for the clinic's floor. There was an ashtray next to the elevator door, and the smell of the old cigarettes in it made my stomach lurch. The nausea was worse on an empty stomach. I stepped back from the smell and put my hand over my mouth. The elevator came. I held the door for a girl and her mother. The doors closed, and we went up. I took off my coat and wiped sweat off my face with the sleeve of my shirt. At the fourth floor, the door opened and the three of us got out.

The waiting room was enormous, like one in an airport, with rows and rows of chairs. Two televisions, at opposite ends of the room, were turned on at low volume. I walked up to a huge U-shaped desk and had to wait behind three other women before I gave my name. A woman checked me off a printed list. "Have you had anything to eat or drink this morning?" she said.

"No," I said.

"Please fill this out." She handed me a clipboard with a pen attached. "How will you be paying today?"

"Visa," I said.

She took my card, ran it through a machine, and handed it back.

I sat down. Across from me, a man was leaning against a woman, watching her write. I filled in my full name and medical history. I wasn't allergic to anything; I had never been pregnant before. When I returned to the desk, the woman there gave me a little cup with my name on it to pee into. I had to wait in line. The two women in front of me were talking about their children. "My kids were all slow to start walking," one said. "Fourteen, fifteen months."

"Mine were early. Nine and a half months, all three of them. It's nothing to wish for. It just makes your life impossible sooner. But the youngest is just fourteen months. I just can't see . . . I can't imagine . . . I mean, starting all over again with a tiny newborn would be . . . we can't afford the kids we've got. I had to quit work because we couldn't afford the day care. Can you imagine that? Day care for three kids cost more than I was making."

The other woman shook her head. "You don't have to tell me."

They were silent. The first woman looked at the bathroom door. "Hurry up," she whispered. A few seconds later, the door opened. A very young girl came out. Another girl was waiting for her. They took her cup and put it on a tray with others on the counter. They walked together to the waiting room and sat down to watch television.

I began to wish I had somebody with me, and I went over a list of people I might have asked. Not Nick, not the way things had turned out. And my sister would be wrong too. She would go on and on about what was the matter with Nick. I pictured my grandmother in this place. She would have talked endlessly about girls she knew in

Hollywood who had "got into trouble." Eric, from the office, might have been all right. He was always sympathetic. But of course, I worked with him, and I wouldn't want him knowing I was pregnant. Dan, my other friend from work, was out of the question, too. Besides being a co-worker, he didn't talk enough to be good company in a situation like this. I thought of several other friends, but most of them had moved out of the city for some reason or other, and we had lost touch. In the end, I couldn't come up with anyone I would have liked to have with me.

A nurse, arriving at work, strode past in her hat and coat. The hat was white, with shiny spangles on top. My mother had a sweater with those things on it that I had almost forgotten about. Laura and I had given it to her for her birthday. We had put all our money together to buy it at Woolworth's. She made a big deal about how beautiful it was. Of course, it was not. We were seven and nine; we had bought the brightest color we could find. It was purple. The sequins sewn all over it were as big as quarters. The collar flared out in a sort of ruffle, like a clown's. She wore it a lot. She claimed to love it. Every time she went out to dinner or a party, she would put on that horrible sweater with a black skirt or velvet pants. Maybe she changed in the car, but it was possible that she actually wore it in public, telling people proudly that her daughters gave it to her. She stopped wearing it only after many of the spangles had broken and fallen off.

After she died, I found the sweater folded up in a plastic bag in the top of her closet. She had saved it. I kept it for a long time. It still smelled like her. For years, whenever I felt miserable I would take it out and press my face into it, breathing in her fading scent. But the sweater made me cry deeply and without stopping for hours. In college, I asked a friend to throw it away and not tell me where. It worked. I hadn't cried like that since then.

I didn't go to nursery school. My mother had me enrolled in the one Laura had loved and tried to leave me there once. I cried. I said, "Don't go. I want to stay with you. Take me home."

My mother said the teachers told her that I was being manipulative; many children did this, they said, and some of them could keep it up for an hour or more. "Just go," they said. "She'll be fine. Go." One of the teachers made a sweeping motion with her hand to usher my mother out. I was screaming.

"Alice, come on," my mother said, walking back into the room to pick me up. She carried me past the teachers, out to the car. "These people are heartless," she said. Until kindergarten, I went with my mother everywhere—coloring while she sat under the drier at the hairdresser, licking stamps for her at the post office, drinking a cup of hot chocolate while she had her coffee and talked on the phone. As late as sixth grade, I still missed her when I was at school.

Now it was my turn for the bathroom, which smelled slightly of fresh urine. This made me gag, though not much came out of my empty stomach. I ran cold water over my hands and wiped it over my face, then I peed in the cup. That was the last time for morning sickness, I thought with relief.

I turned in my cup and took my seat again, picking up a magazine. But I was distracted. One woman had a really loud voice. "I mean, diapers," she was saying. "Cheapest you can get the large package is about nine bucks. Then there's formula and baby food. Shoes. Little-bitty sneakers about as long as your thumb—thirty dollars. I'm serious. I just love kids, but I want a life. You know what I'm saying? So I hurried in here as soon as they'd take me. Because once I feel that baby kick, people, nothing and nobody can take that rascal away from me. But right here, eight or nine weeks, we're OK."

I forced myself to read an article about the cosmetic surgery of a lot of famous people and not to listen anymore. I preferred not to think just now about tiny shoes or babies kicking.

A young woman came over, her coat in one hand and her clipboard in the other, looking for a seat. "Anyone sitting here?" she said, pointing to the chair next to mine.

"No," I said. "Go ahead."

"Thanks." She sat down to fill out the form. When she was finished, she left her coat draped over the chair to save it and took her form to the front desk. "This your first time?" she said to me when she came back.

"Yes," I said.

"You're lucky. This is my third," she said. She shook her head. "I swear to God I have the worst luck in the world. The woman behind the desk recognized me. I mean, I could work here, I know the routine so well. 'Did you eat or drink anything this morning?' I'm putting this on my MasterCard, and I'm going to be paying for it for a year." She shook her head. "I'm Penny."

"Alice," I said.

"You came by yourself too?" I nodded. Penny said, "This time, I didn't tell anybody, not even my mom, who would have cried. I didn't tell my boyfriend, either. I just started going out with him a couple of months ago. You married or anything?"

"No."

"Did you tell the guy?"

"No," I said. "We just broke up."

"Ah," she said. "Poor kid. And now here you are. Darn." She put a hand on my shoulder. "You'll be OK," she said. "This is the worst part, the waiting. This and just before they give you the anesthesia. That's pretty lonely. Then you wake up and start to feel relieved because it's all over and you can have your life back."

A young woman came out from behind the desk to call some names. We listened, but we were not called.

"How long does it take?" I said. "How soon can we get out of here?"

"A couple of hours from when they call you," she said, "depending on how fast you recover. Some places you can just get a local and get going pretty quick. But I always come here because I really don't want to be awake during the procedure, you know? It's bad enough imagining it." She looked at her watch. "I hate the waiting."

We sat there for a long time. I got a headache and wished for some toast and, since I was off coffee because of the morning sickness, a Coke with a lot of ice. Several groups of women were called, but Penny's and my names were not among them. Almost all the chairs were filled. I counted them—two hundred and forty.

Finally, it was our turn. We were in the same group. I was relieved to at least be going somewhere else. We joined the women standing next to the reception desk and waited. She counted us. "OK," she said, and we followed her down a long hall to a locker room. "Please take off everything, ladies, and put on a gown. Paper slippers are on the bench. Locker keys are in the locks. Choose a locker, place your belongings inside, lock it, and put the elastic around your wrist to keep your key with you during the procedure. After you've undressed, please take a seat next door here, and someone will be by shortly to pick you up."

We undressed. No one spoke. I was pretty fast and one of the first to go to the next room. It was cold in the room with just the skimpy gown and paper slippers on. My feet were freezing. Before long the room filled up with women in gowns, keys hanging from their wrists. "Maybe we should tell someone how cold it is in here," said a woman with blond hair.

"I guess we won't be here long," said another woman, who appeared to be in her early forties.

Penny said, "We might. We could be in here an hour."

"Maybe we could get our sweaters until they call us," said a girl who had kept her socks on.

Just then a woman in green scrubs came in. "Is it cold in here?" she said. She turned a dial on the wall. A blower turned on, and warm air blasted out from a vent on the wall. "If it gets too warm, just turn this off," she said. "OK, I need Erica Faber." A tall woman with very short hair got up and left with her.

The warm air from the blower hit me in the face and made me nauseous again. "I'm going to throw up," I said, and someone handed me a wastebasket. Nothing came out but a string of saliva; I wiped it on my gown and heaved some more. My stomach hurt a lot from these spasms, and I thought, Stop, stop, please be over. The sides of the wastebasket became wet with the sweat from my hands, but there was no water to cool them. After what seemed like a long time, the nausea stopped, and I leaned back against the wall. Someone took the wastebasket away. That had to be the last time, I thought. After a minute, I felt better.

The nurse came back for someone else. "Brittany Johnson," she said, and a teenager stood up.

"What kind of work do you do?" I said to Penny.

"I work in a jewelry store," she said and shrugged. "In high school I had all these plans about being a fashion designer. I didn't get too far."

I said, "You might still do it."

"Oh, no," she said. "I've been in this job two years already. I'm stuck."

"Two years is nothing," I said. "Listen, things can change in a second. You know how it is. You think your life is going in one direction, and all of a sudden something happens and you're going another way altogether."

Penny looked at me. "That never happens to me. And hey, it's not like I hate my job or anything. I mean, it's OK."

"But if you want to do something else, you can," I said.

The older woman was nodding. The nurse returned. "Pamela Beal," she said, and the woman stood up. "You're too young to give up," she said to Penny.

"I didn't say I was giving up or anything. I just said I worked in a jewelry store. *God.*" Penny shook her head.

One by one, all the women were called, until only Penny and I were left. We didn't speak for what seemed like a long time. I started thinking about my mother again. At thirteen, she pushed me to go on a five-day trip to Chicago with my school. I didn't want to go without her. The night before we were to leave, I said, "You can come too, Mom. They need more parents to help out. Please. Why don't you?" She said, "No, Alice. It will be good for you to get away from me for a few days. You need to be a little more independent." I felt a sharp pain in my chest, as if she had physically injured me.

I went with my class. When I came back I punished my mother for hurting me. I began to have secrets from her. When she asked me what I did at school, I said, "Nothing," the way a lot of my friends did. I spent the night at friends' houses every chance I got. When she invited me to do special things with her—go shopping for Laura's birthday presents or go to a movie, just the two of us—I refused.

One night after several months of chilly silence between us, she sat on my bed and said, "Enough, Alice. I hurt your feelings when I said you needed to be more independent, and I'm sorry. I made a mistake. I miss my special girl, and I want you back." She had tears in her eyes, and there was a choking feeling in my throat too. I turned over onto my stomach. She sat there a long time, rubbing my back, waiting. But I had gone too far. To my junior-high mind, there was no way back, no matter how much I missed her.

Then my parents died, and besides experiencing the immense loss, I felt crushing regret for being mean to my mother, wasting what had turned out to be my last year with her. I felt guilty as well for causing her pain, making her sad. It was Aunt Louise who told my mother that I wasn't independent enough, that I was too old to be so attached to my mother. Laura had overheard the conversation, and she told me about it after our parents died.

It must have been a burden for my mother to feel that I would be miserable whenever she wasn't around. I could imagine that when I was small, she probably felt terrible all the times she had to leave me screaming for her and also that sometimes she must have felt desperate to escape from all that dependence and overpowering love. But I couldn't remember her objecting to my clinginess until that time when I was thirteen. I had a picture of her holding me when I was a baby, my fat little arms locked tightly around her neck. She was kissing my nose. She always looked so happy to see me when I came home from school or ballet lessons or swimming, as though she had missed me while I was away.

Finally, the nurse came back for one of us. I said, "Excuse me." I raised my hand, as if I were in school. "I want to go."

"You mean you need to empty your bladder?" Being a nurse, she thought this way. I shook my head. "Oh, you want to be next?" she said.

"No, no," I said. "I mean I want to leave." I hadn't known I was going to do this.

Penny turned to look at me and said, "Alice, you're kidding."

"You've decided you don't want to have the procedure after all?" said the nurse.

"That's right," I said. "No procedure for me. I'm going to have the baby."

"Your name?" the nurse said.

"Alice Hammond," I told her.

She made a line through it on her list. "We offer counseling," she said, "if you'd like to talk to someone."

"No, thank you," I said. "I'm all set."

"Fine," said the nurse. "Make sure you stop by the front desk to get your money back."

"OK," I said. "Thank you."

Penny said, "Hey, good luck, Alice. Nice meeting you."

"Good luck," said the nurse. She winked at me. She led Penny out of the waiting room.

I didn't go to work. I still had the day off. I went into a health food restaurant and had an enormous lunch at a little after eleven. Boys' names and girls' names came to mind. I was happy.

CINDERELLA

ỴOU DON'T ALWAYS have to do everything people ask you to," my sister, Laura, was telling me. "You don't always have to say yes." Laura was a paralegal for a big law firm in Midtown. We had just eaten pizza at a place exactly halfway between our two offices, and now we were walking into the Discount Cosmetics Superstore to find a certain kind of mascara that Gram wanted. I had planned to tell Laura that I was pregnant and then decided not to. She was lecturing me on what a good thing it was that Nick was out of my life. She said it was an opportunity to change, to do things differently. "What you need to do is have an answer ready so that you don't automatically say yes. Something simple but strong, like 'No. I'm sorry. I can't help you.' " Laura, who was shorter than I was, looked up at me, tucking her straight, dark hair neatly behind her ears. She had a pretty face like our mother's, with a lot of points: a widow's peak, perfectly centered on her hairline; a sharp little nose; two small peaks beneath it on her upper lip that she was careful to preserve when she put on lipstick; and a softly pointed chin like the bottom of a birthday balloon, just above the knot. Often, standing beside her, I felt that my own features were blurry and dull.

I looked around the store for the area we needed and pointed to the far wall. Following me, my sister went on. "In my opinion, this was one of the problems with Nick. You did everything for him—shopping, running lines, taking messages. You stayed up late until he got home from his shows so he could go over every laugh he had gotten, every compliment, not to mention all his worries and insecurities. I bet he never once cleaned the bathtub or took out the garbage in the whole time you guys lived together. Why should he? You were always there to do it for him. And the same goes for work. These editors ask you to do things that are not part of your job or that you're too busy for, just tell them you can't do it: 'No. I'm sorry. I can't help you.' Go ahead, let's hear it."

I tried it. " 'No. I'm sorry. I can't help you.' Hm. Maybe it would work." I stood in front of two rows of mascara hanging on hooks. Laura picked up a card of mascara and held it up to me. I shook my head. "She wants a wand, not a brush."

"A wand?" she said. "What do you mean, a wand?"

"It looks like a metal stick with grooves in it."

"For a woman with less than ten eyelashes, she sure is picky about what she puts on them," Laura said, scanning a row of mascara. She took one card off a hook, then put it back. "So how is it?" Laura said. "Is she driving you crazy?"

"Yes," I said.

"Whoa, look at this one. Hot pink. It says it glows in the dark. I'm getting it." Laura held it up. "How did you know about this place?"

"I used to buy Nick's false eyelashes here. Remember when he was in *Some Like It Hot*? He was so good in that."

"This?" Laura said, walking over to me.

I looked. "That's not a wand." She put it back.

"Have you heard from Nick?"

"No. I called him once. I talked to about fifteen people to get the number of the hotel—his agent, other actors, friends of ours. I finally got it from the travel agent who booked the tour."

"What did you say?"

"Nothing. A woman answered. I hung up. Do you think he'll change his mind?"

"Oh, God, Alice. Would you really want him to? Look what he's put you through. And all of a sudden. I mean, no warning at all."

"I guess it was partly my fault too. It always is in a relationship."

"Sure, that's what I'm telling you. You were too nice to him."

"You just don't like Nick," I said. "You never did. He wasn't that bad. A lot of people do like him, Laura. He's sweet and funny and smart."

"Alice, don't do this," Laura said. "Just put it behind you. Forget. Find someone else. He did."

When Nick and I first started seeing each other, Laura assumed it wouldn't last and told me exactly what she thought was wrong with him. "He's kind of short for an actor, isn't he? Aren't they supposed to be tall? He seems quiet to me. I bet he's moody. How many actors ever make any money acting? One of the most depressing things about New York is seeing these pathetic middle-aged losers waiting on tables or, worse, pouring coffee into cardboard cups in some deli and telling everybody that they're actors. It's the best cover they can come up with for the way they've wasted the last twenty years of their lives. Alice, I'm saying this because you're my sister and I care about you: I think you can do much better."

Nick didn't like Laura, either. What irritated him most was the way she promised to do things for me and then didn't or made plans with me and canceled at the last minute. "What happened to the curtains she was going to help you make three years ago? And what about the time she said you could borrow her car to come out to Westchester to see me when I was working on that stupid play that bombed? She had to go pick up a rocking chair she ordered. Give me a break. And how many times have you stood out in front of a movie theater, waiting for her, only to find out that she changed her mind without telling you? I mean, who does she think she is, treating you that way? She's always criticizing you, and you let her get away with it. You get a new job and she says they're underpaying you. You buy a sweater, she says it's out of style or a bad color and that's why it was on sale. I don't see why you put up with it."

"Because she's my sister," I always told him, "and our parents are dead."

"So tell her off every once in a while. She'll still be your sister."

Now I said to Laura, "Do you know of any apartments?"

"No. But I put up a sign for you by the coffee machine at work. Something might happen. Who knows? Look, the bristles on this brush are really short. It's sort of a wand."

"Keep looking," I said.

"This is exactly the kind of thing I mean. Gram asks you to do these impossible things, and you do them. I bet this isn't the first place you've looked. Is it?"

"It's the fourth," I said. "But the others were just two small drugstores and one department store. No selection."

"She's going to keep increasing her demands until there's nothing left of your life."

I said, "Look, she's eighty-nine and can't drive. How else is she supposed to get her makeup?"

"But can't you just get her normal mascara, the kind everyone else uses? You don't have to go crazy looking for some really obscure thing. You see what I mean?" she said. "She wouldn't have asked me. She knows I would get the wrong thing or just give up after the first store and tell her it didn't exist. Meanwhile, she also knows that you'll make it your personal quest to get the perfect mascara, even if it's the last one left in the universe." Laura looked at me closely. "By the way, are you feeling all right? You're awfully pale."

"I'm fine," I said. "I might be getting a cold or something." Now I was absolutely certain this was the wrong time to tell her that I was pregnant. She would give me another lecture about Nick and how irresponsible he was or about how careless I was to let this happen. I would wait to tell her when it was absolutely necessary. "I found it! Here it is." I held up a card.

"Eight dollars," Laura said. "Brother."

"She pays me back. Oh, look, refills. Maybe I should get three or four."

"Alice," Laura said. "Stop."

"You're right. OK. One. I'll just get one refill."

Outside the store, we said goodbye and took off in opposite directions for our offices.

When I got back, Eric and Dan were sitting in Dan's office, across the hall from mine. Dan didn't like the fluorescent ceiling light, so the room was dimly lit by a small reading lamp pointed at his desk. Photographs with yellow slips stuck to them were stacked on his desk and work table. The room smelled of pickles from their sandwiches. Eric was a production editor, and Dan was a photo researcher. The three of us always ate our bagels and coffee together in the morning and then, later, our lunches. We talked about things that happened to us inside work and out. But lately I had been not telling more than I was telling. "Hi," I said now. "How was lunch?"

"Did you go to that falafel place again?" Eric said. "I hate that place." Eric was always a little sulky if one of us made other plans for lunch. Eric and Dan had worked here a full year and had barely spoken to each other before I came. They were different types. Dan was tall and thin, with long, dark hair that he always wore in a ponytail. He wore jeans and sneakers to work. Eric was plump, with thinning, light brown hair that he kept very short. He wore no-iron shirts and slacks, and his neckties had pictures on them: dogs and horses, a sunset-over-the-ocean scene. Eric talked a lot, and Dan didn't talk much at all. They worked on opposite sides of the office and had barely noticed one another before we all found ourselves in the same pizza line one day. We took our food back to Eric's office and got hysterical about his impersonation of his sister's boyfriend eating a hot dog. After that, lunch together became virtually mandatory, each of us counting on it as a bright spot in the workday.

"Are you OK?" Eric said to me now. "You don't look too good."

I said, "I think I'm coming down with something."

"What's in the bag?" Eric said.

Dan said, "Eric, it's none of your business."

"I'm a curious guy," Eric said. "She doesn't have to tell me if she doesn't want to. What's in the bag, Alice?"

"Mascara for my grandmother," I said.

"Your grandmother wears mascara?" Eric said. "My grandmother doesn't even shave her mustache." He pulled a chair out for me. "My sister's spending over ten thousand dollars on her wedding. Do you know how many commas I would have to delete to earn that kind of money? It's disgusting. I'm wearing a maroon tuxedo. I asked her, 'Why maroon?' She said because it will be fall. What? I'm supposed to blend in with the leaves or something?"

"Do you guys know of any apartments that might be available?" I said. They both looked at me.

"What happened?" Eric said.

"Oh, nothing. We just need to move, that's all."

"Geez, you scared me for a second," Eric said. "I thought you meant you and Nick were having problems or something. Are you?"

Dan said, "Eric, Jesus."

I looked Eric straight in the face. "No," I said. "Everything's fine. It's just that we've been living in a sublet. Now the woman wants it back right away." I didn't plan to lie about it, but I knew Eric would never be satisfied with just the fact that Nick and I were breaking up. He would want to know why, whose idea it was, all the emotional details. "In fact, I've already moved out to my grandmother's," I said. "Just temporarily. Until I find something."

Eric did an exaggerated double take. "You don't even like your grandmother. What does Nick say?"

"Nick is still on tour," I said.

"You never mentioned your place was a sublet," Eric said.

"We've been in it so long," I said, "I almost forgot myself." For a minute, I thought he was going to challenge my explanation.

"And now all of a sudden, she wants it back." Eric looked at Dan. "Can you believe people? No consideration. I don't know of anyplace, Alice. I wish I did. Dan, you? Any vacancies in your building?"

Dan said, "Nobody has moved out of my building since 1989. Sorry, Alice. If I hear of anything I'll let you know."

"Thank you. I have to get to work," I said. "I have to look up statistics on the status of different jobs for Jim's sociology book," I said. "He wants it right away."

"Dan has to find a photograph of a baby playing dress-up," Eric said. "And I have to go over Jane's glossary. It's all extremely urgent." He picked up the camera on Dan's desk and looked at me through the viewfinder. Dan started leafing through a magazine.

I went to my office and found the table I needed, photocopied it, wrote the bibliographic information on the bottom, and put it on Jim's desk. When I came back to my office, Eric was waiting near my door. "You want to do something after work?" he said. "Have a drink or dinner or something?"

"Thanks," I said. "But my grandmother's expecting me, and I really don't feel very well." Without thinking, I put a hand over my stomach.

"Are you sure?" he said. "You seem kind of . . . I don't know. I just thought you might want to talk for a while."

"I'd like to, Eric. I just can't tonight."

"All right. I tried," he said and left.

There was a new note on my desk, marked "URGENT! ASAP!" It was from Mary, who was doing an intro-to-marketing book. It said, "How many cut flowers sold in the U.S. annually? Please, Alice, I need it *right away!*" I had to make four phone calls, but I found out and took the information to her.

"Here it is," I said. "I got it."

"What's that?" Mary took the slip of paper. "Oh, I don't need that anymore." She let the paper fall into the wastebasket. "Sorry. Thanks, though."

When I got back to my office, I practiced the line Laura had suggested: "No. I'm sorry. I can't help you." Then I added, "I am extremely busy now. That will have to wait."

I worked my way through the rest of the pile of notes on my desk undisturbed, until Katharine, another editor, knocked on my door. "Excuse me, Alice. Sorry to bother you." She was holding a manuscript chapter of the book she was working on, seventy pages or so, held together with a rubber band. "I wonder if you would mind just photocopying these few pages for me and popping them into the express mail box downstairs."

It was 3:31. Express mail had to be downstairs by four. Photocopying was not supposed to be part of my job. I thought, No, I'm sorry. I said, "Oh, sure. No problem."

Next time, I really am going to say it, I told myself. I

took the chapters to the copy machine down the hall. Some-one from another department was using it: a stack as large as mine was sitting on the sheet feeder. He was talking to another man from his office. The machine stopped. The paper-jam light was on. The two of them kept talking. I said, "Excuse me. You've got a paper jam."

"Oh," said the man making copies. "So I have. I'll have to call someone. Whom would I call?" He looked at me and then at his friend.

I stepped between them. I opened the machine, pulled out the stuck sheet of paper, reset it, and pressed the green button on top.

"Oh. Well, you're a good person to know around here." It was 3:49 when he finished.

I pulled the rubber band off the chapter. The machine copied three pages and stopped. It was out of paper. I got a package from the shelf above the machine, tore it open, pulled out the empty cartridge, put in the paper, inserted the cartridge, and waited for the green button to light up. After making two copies, the machine jammed again. I kicked it, opened the door, and pulled out the jammed sheet. I wasn't going to make it by four.

When the copies were made, I shoved them into an envelope, addressed it from the scrap of paper Katharine had given me, ran to the elevator, and hit the button. I got to the box at 4:12. The driver from the post office had just arrived. I handed the package to him and went back up-stairs.

Jim was waiting for me in my office. "Could I ask you something?" he said. He was holding a thick chapter of his sociology book. "Could you check the tables in this for me? I need it first thing Monday."

"Jim, it's after four," I said.

"Oh, there aren't many. I just want you to make sure we have the most recent figures before my author comes in for a meeting at nine Monday morning. If not—and I'm sure most of them are fine—just update whatever needs it."

I took a deep breath. "No. I'm sorry. I cannot help you with that," I said. My hands became sweaty, and my heart started pounding. "I would have to work on it over the weekend. I can't do that. I'm sorry."

"You're right," he said. "Of course. I have no business asking you to give up your weekend for my book. Oh, Alice," he said. He sat down on my extra chair, defeated. "What am I going to do?" He sighed and rubbed his face with his hands.

"Jim?" I said. "Are you OK? Do you want some water or something?"

"Oh, I'm just under a lot of pressure," he said. "I think I'm going to get fired," he whispered. "The last two books I worked on have sold badly." He bit his lip.

"But that's not your fault. They assigned you those books."

He shook his head. "Tell that to Jane," he said. Jane was head of our department. "She's already called me into her office to talk about my 'performance' as an editor. She tried to make it sound as if it was coming down from someone above her, as if it wasn't her idea to give me the boot but just something she would be forced to do if I didn't shape up. I don't know what I'm going to do. This book is a mess. It's not going to be any better than the other two. Why do I always get these authors who can't write and are slow about it too?" He looked at me. "You won't tell anybody they're thinking of firing me, will you?"

"Me?" I said. "Of course not."

"You're a good person," he said. "You're not like all these other people around here at all. I didn't mean to dump all this on you. It just came out."

"Don't worry about it," I said. "I'm sorry you're having such a hard time. I wish I could help. I might be able to do a few tables before I leave, but—"

"No, no," he said. "That's all right. I need it finished by Monday morning early. You don't have time for this." He sighed again and started to get up to go.

"OK," I said. "Give it to me. I'll do it over the weekend."

"Really?" Jim said. "You'd do that for me? You see what I mean? You're different. You care." He handed me the chapter. "There's not much here. Thanks, Alice," he said, backing out of my office. "A lot. Have a nice weekend." He smiled broadly and waved. I heard the hanger banging around in the hall closet for a few seconds after he yanked his coat off it and went out the front door. It was 4:32. There were twenty-three tables in the chapter, and they were all out of date. Jim had written Update under each one. I went to the bookcase and took down the sources I would need to do this job over the weekend: four books of government statistics and two almanacs. I put them in two shopping bags. I straightened my desk. The phone rang. "Alice Hammond?" I said.

"Ice cream."

"Oh, hi, Gram. You want me to get some ice cream for you on the way home? OK. Anything else?"

"I bet you forgot my mascara."

"No I didn't. I got it. Laura went with me. She says hello."

"Good. I'll see you later." She hung up.

At twenty to six, I went to Eric's office to see if he was ready to leave. Maybe I would tell him now about Nick breaking up with me; maybe we could go out and have something to eat, after all. But his light was out, and his coat was gone; he had already left.

I put on my coat and my headphones, turned on a Laurie Anderson tape, and started walking to Penn Station; the bus would be too crowded now for me to get a seat. The books were heavy. I felt my arms lengthening. People kept bumping into me and not saying excuse me. I got hot in my coat and out of breath from the walk and felt nauseous for the first time since morning; I was hungry again. I stopped for a minute next to a garbage can just in case I had to throw up, but I did not look into it. If there was anything disgusting in it, I would throw up for sure. Then, just as I began to recover, I saw a flash of a familiar coat go by fast: Nick. I started to walk faster than before, then I was running. What was I going to say? What if he was with someone? The coat appeared and disappeared in the crowd, but I was getting closer. I was right behind it. The coat was Nick's, all right, but someone else was wearing it, a teenager with a shaved head. My eyes filled with tears. I was out of breath. I threw up in the gutter, recovered, wiped my face with a Kleenex, then started to walk again.

"Alice," I heard behind me after a block or so. I turned around. It was Dan.

I stepped to one side near a signpost to keep from being trampled and took my headphones off. "Oh, hi," I said, hoping that he had not witnessed my vomiting into the street. "Where are you going?"

"Meeting a friend," he said. "What's all this?" he said, pointing at my shopping bags of books.

"Jim. He left me with a chapter with twenty-three tables to check before Monday." My eyes filled with tears. I hoped he wouldn't notice. "I know, I know. It's my own fault. I should have said, 'No. Absolutely not. I am not going to work for you over the weekend.' I guess I did say that, as a matter of fact, but then I caved in. And you know what? He left early. He was smiling. I'm a jerk."

Dan said, "Your eyes are watering."

"Allergies," I said.

He pulled a handkerchief out of his pants pocket. It was plain white, ironed and folded and ironed again, the kind my grandfather would have had in his pocket. Without unfolding it, I wiped my eyes. I didn't want to mess it up. Then I changed my mind, opened it, and blew my nose. I felt a little better. "I'll wash it for you," I said.

Dan picked up the bags. "Let's go," he said. "What time is your train?"

"I guess I could make the 6:14."

He walked me the rest of the way to Penn Station, eight blocks, without saying anything else. I kept trying to think of ways to start a conversation, but the longer I waited, the more awkward it felt. I realized that Eric was the one who usually kept us all talking. Dan stopped in front of the escalator and gave me back the two bags of books. "I hope your eyes get better," he said.

"Me too," I said. "Thank you." I ran down the escalator steps, pushing past people and not saying excuse me. I didn't want to miss my train.

On the way to Gram's, I stopped by the little store where she liked me to buy her ice cream, and the video store. When I got to her house, she was sitting in her usual place on the couch, with the TV tuned to the news and the sound off. She was reading the *National Enquirer*. She glanced at me. "Cher and her bosoms," she said. "What's that in the bag?"

"Hi, Gram. Fine, thank you. How are you?" I put the bags down. "This? It's work I have to do. One of the editors came into my office way after four—"

"No, the other bag."

"Oh, English toffee and chocolate sauce. And here's your mascara."

"Thank you. When are we going to eat? I'm starved."

"What do you want?" I went to the kitchen.

"I'll take the lasagna. You have whatever you want."

"OK." Without taking my coat off, I went to the freezer and got out two frozen lasagnas. I read the package. I should be eating something better than this now that I was pregnant. I put the trays in the oven, took off my coat, and made a salad.

When we started eating, she said, "What's that you're having? Lasagna? Well, I guess you can buy some more tomorrow."

"There are six more of these in the freezer."

"We're going to have some visitors on Sunday," Gram said. "Candace and Peter and Olivia and Matthew." These were my cousins and their husbands. "They're coming out for a wedding, and staying overnight with friends. They'll be here for tea on Sunday."

"Tea? What do I have to do?"

"You don't have to do anything. You can boil the water if you want. Nothing much." She pushed her plate away.

"You didn't eat any salad."

"I'll just have some ice cream."

I heated the chocolate sauce for Gram's ice cream and put her dessert on the coffee table so she could eat it while watching the movie I had rented. I turned on the TV, and there was Nick, getting out of the shower. I couldn't breathe for a minute. I didn't know he had made a commercial. Nick was smiling because not only was he clean but he *felt* clean, too, after using some green soap, Seafoam. With a towel around his waist, he did a little twirl. Stepping out of the shower, he looked just like the Nick I used to see every day stepping out of the shower. And now everyone who happened to be sitting at home watching Channel 7 knew just what Nick looked like wet and smiling, with his hair all flat.

"Oh, my God," Gram said. "Look who found work. How much do you suppose he got paid for that?" She picked up her spoon and took a big bite of ice cream and chocolate sauce. "A lot, I bet," she said with her mouth full. "He probably got a bundle for it. They do, you know. And the more it's on television, the more they get."

I shoved in the movie and pushed Play.

I corrected tables all day Saturday, except when I was taking Gram to get her hair done, when I did her grocery shopping, and when I forced her to take her walk with me to the stop sign at the end of the road.

Sunday morning, I found my grandmother standing at the kitchen sink in her Christian Dior nightgown. The lace in front was torn and hanging. She had the silver polish out and was scrubbing away at a large tray.

"What are you doing?"

"For tea today. Candace and Olivia. I knew you'd forget."

"I didn't forget. Do you have to use this fancy tray for them?"

"I want things to be nice, and you don't know how to polish silver."

"Of course I do," I said. "What's to know?"

She handed it to me. "Rub in a circular motion," she said, leaning over my shoulder. "Harder."

My grandmother had me make a dozen watercress and cucumber sandwiches on white bread. I had to cut the crusts off. She said this was what they had in England the time she went to visit some costume designer she had met in Hollywood. "That was the time I saw Olivier. You wouldn't have known him offscreen. He looked like nothing, nobody. You really should get all this on tape," she said. "I won't be around forever."

"Sure, Gram," I said. "I'll tape your stories for you. Anytime." After I made her lunch, she had me vacuum the downstairs and clean the powder room. I set the silver tray with Gram's Wedgwood tea set, her fancy spoons, and cloth napkins. I had to scrub the insides of the pot and cups with Brillo to get the brown stains off. Neither Gram nor Eleanor had very good eyesight, and the kitchen was too dark. She used forty-watt bulbs. My cousins were coming at three. At two-thirty, I started making brownies, which I happened to be very good at. I was mixing the batter when a cloud of perfume hit me. I sneezed. A few minutes later, Gram came shuffling through the dining room to the kitchen. She was wearing a heather-colored wool suit, pearls, gold earrings, and dark-red lipstick in place of her everyday coral. "You look nice," I said. "Hold it. You've got a streak of foundation on your chin." I blended it in with my thumb. "There's a spot on your sleeve too. Looks like peanut butter." I scratched this off.

"Thank you," she said. "Notice anything?" She blinked at me.

"What? Oh, the mascara. Gorgeous." There were a couple of globs on her eyelids, but I let these go.

"What's that?" she said, peering into the brownie bowl.

"Brownies."

"Looks awful."

"You'll like them. They're chocolate."

"Eleanor always made scones. Maybe we have some old cookies or something we could give them." Gram started opening the cupboards, peering inside.

I said, "Gram."

"All right, all right," she said. She went to the living room and sat down on the couch to wait. She had to wait a long time. They were late.

At three-thirty, she sent me to get her lipstick. While I was upstairs, I got my tape player, which could also record. I found a homemade Tom Petty tape that I didn't mind taping over because it reminded me of Nick. I gave Gram the lipstick and she put it on without a mirror. "We could make a tape if you want to. Why don't you tell me how you got to Hollywood." I pushed Play and Record.

Gram looked out at the driveway. "Do you think they forgot?"

I said, "They probably got into heavy traffic somewhere."

"On a Sunday?" The corners of her mouth drooped; she slumped. She glanced at the tape recorder. "What's that for? I meant *video*tape. And I can't do that now. We're having guests."

When they finally pulled into the driveway, Gram changed her face. Suddenly she wore the glowing, superior smile of a movie star greeting a throng of adoring fans, though my cousins were still outside. She put out her hands. I pulled her to her feet.

I opened the front door. "Hi, you guys," I said. "Long time no see."

Candace said, "Alice!" and smiled at me hard. "My mother said you were out here staying with Gram, helping out. I think that's so sweet."

Olivia said, "Hi, Alice," and hugged me briefly.

Peter and Matthew came in behind them, scraping their clean shoes vigorously and removing their coats. One by one, the four of them handed their coats to me and headed for the living room. It must have been their habit to give their coats to the person who opened the door. I dumped the pile of them over the banister.

Gram was standing where I had left her. "Hi, Gram," Candace said. "You look so pretty! Doesn't Gram look pretty, Olivia? Good thing she's in the family, or we'd have to worry about her stealing our husbands!"

"Gorgeous suit. Keep your hands off my man, Grammy," Olivia said.

This was the reason Gram had gotten all dressed up, this stupid flattery about her clothes and the dumb teasing about her stealing their husbands. She didn't find it condescending; she liked it. "Oh, this is just an old rag," she said, waving her hand in dismissal. "I've had it for years. Adolfo." She smoothed her front, puffing herself up and smiling at them like a beauty queen.

"I wish I had an old rag like that," Candace said. She was wearing black jeans, expensive ones that looked brand-new, with a gray cashmere sweater and gold earrings similar to Gram's. Olivia had on a short black skirt, a white shirt, and a cardigan with thin black and white stripes that pulled the outfit together. I was wearing black sweatpants and one of my formerly white T-shirts. I had to keep reminding myself to pull my stomach in.

Peter said, "You're looking radiant as ever, Gram," and kissed her on the cheek.

"Well, you're just as handsome as you can be," Gram said. "And Matthew, sweetheart, come here, you." He kissed her too.

I went to get the tea ready. Gram had brought a special box of tea down from her bathroom, where she had kept it hidden from Eleanor. I filled the teapot with hot water and took the tray to the living room. I brought out the sandwiches and the brownies and set them down. I sat in the one empty chair. Gram made a pecking motion at me with her head. I was supposed to pour.

Candace was saying, "We're going to France on a wine tour next fall. Peter is getting to be such an expert that I thought it would be the perfect vacation for him. He's got an album just full of the most beautiful labels from wine bottles. He gets so much pleasure out of it."

"A really fine wine gives me a great deal of pleasure, yes," Peter said. "Oh, thank you, Alice. Just a bit of lemon for me, please. Oh, are those brownies? Yes, I will. Thanks so much."

Matthew said, "Yes, Peter, we've all seen you getting a great deal of pleasure out of a bottle of wine. Out of more than one sometimes." Everyone laughed.

Candace was telling about the hotels they were going to stay in on their vacation. Matthew said, "No tea for me, Alice, thank you." Then he whispered, "Could you possibly get me some coffee? Thank you." He winked at me.

I thought of the prepared answer Laura had given me: "No. I'm sorry. I can't help you." I went to the kitchen and made the coffee.

As soon as Matthew tasted it, he said, "Is this instant?"

"Oh, Gram," Olivia was saying, "these brownies are scrumptious."

"I'm so glad you like them," Gram said.

"I bet you told Alice exactly how to make them," said Candace. "Gram is a genius at instructing people. Or did you have her buy them?"

I said, "I got the recipe off the box of chocolate. She wanted scones." But they didn't hear me. Peter was making some joke about Gram's way with people. The people he meant were those who worked for her, the people she counted on to do things for her. I was one of them, a reliable drudge.

Candace said, "We saw your friend on TV the other night."

I said, "The soap commercial? I saw it too."

"No, this was for Home Away from Home," she said. "The motel chain."

"Yes," said Peter. "He was lying on a bed with his arms crossed under his head, looking pleased with himself. You haven't see it?"

"No," I said. "I'll have to look for that one."

"Don't do that," Olivia said. "Don't make yourself miserable about all the money he's finally making."

"Why don't we change the subject?" Candace said. "Alice, you just turned green. Are you OK?"

"Yes," I said. "I've had a little stomach thing. But I'm fine."

"Say, Alice," Matthew said, "we saw that picture of you. In the gallery?"

I said, "Pardon? A picture of me?"

"Yes. What? You didn't know about it. Photography show? It was in one of those little galleries downtown. What was that place called, sweetie?" Matthew turned to Olivia.

Olivia said, "Which one? Oh, you mean that one on Avenue B? I forget."

"Well, anyway, the photographer's name was Donald something."

"Barton?" Olivia said. "Donald Barton? No, it was Daniel, I think."

"Daniel Bennett?" I said. "I work with him."

"There you are," Matthew said and snapped his fingers. "Daniel Bennett. That was it."

"Are you sure it was me?" I said. "In the picture."

Olivia said, "Yes. It was you looking up at a traffic light. It was called *Alice Waiting*. Quite honestly, I didn't recognize you at first. I actually thought, What a pretty young woman, and so unlike anyone I know. She looked so— so—oh, what was it? Original, striking. Then I read the title, and that's when I thought there was something familiar about her. It was the hair that gave you away. And I said, 'Matt, you won't believe it, but that's Alice. Alice Hammond, my cousin.' He said, 'No, it isn't.' He thought you were that Irish playwright—what's her name? Then he thought you were someone in politics. He was sure you were someone famous." She laughed.

"It was a very arresting photograph," said Matthew. "This Bennett fellow must be very good to get a picture like that of Alice."

I said, "He didn't tell anyone that he had a show downtown or that I was in it. I didn't even know he had taken my picture."

"What are you all mumbling about?" Gram said. "I can't hear a word you're saying."

"We've really got to go," Peter said loudly.

Gram said, "You just got here."

"We're going to try to beat the traffic back into the city," Olivia said. "It was wonderful to see you, Gram. And Alice."

When they were gone, Gram said, "Aren't they lovely? You should find someone like Matthew or Peter. Maybe Candace and Olivia could have a party for you. You'd have to do something about that hair, though."

"I don't like Matthew or Peter," I said.

Gram said, "There's your problem."

She started giving me suggestions about my hair, but I wasn't listening. I cleared the tea things.

Gram said, "You're not putting that tea set in the dishwasher, are you? I hope you know that has to be washed by hand."

Monday morning, when I came up the escalator at Penn Station, there he was again, Dan, just sort of standing there in his baggy overcoat, dark sunglasses (freezing rain was the forecast), and headphones, his hands in his pockets. I took off my headphones. Now was the time to ask him about the photograph, I thought. "Dan," I said. "I forgot to wash your handkerchief."

He put his headphones in his coat pocket and said, "What'd you do, spend the weekend down there?"

"Yes," I said. "I ate hot dogs and read magazines all weekend."

"Where you going?"

"Work," I said. "I'm going to work."

"I'll walk you."

Six

"I'M PREGNANT"

$\mathscr{T}$HERE WERE THREE doctors in the practice I chose; one of them would be on call when my baby was born. At my first appointment, the nurse weighed me. I already felt fat, but I had gained only four pounds. The nurse showed me the bathroom and gave me a cup to pee into for another pregnancy test. I left it in a special cupboard in the bathroom and went back to the examining room to wait for the doctor. The magazines they had there were giveaways for pregnant women, with lots of ads for diapers and formula. I read an article about how to reduce morning sickness and one about the value of childbirth classes. These were not the sort of article I was looking for. I wanted to know what I was supposed to do to train myself to become a mother. I had never had any special feeling toward children that I could remember. In high school, I didn't baby-sit, the way other girls had; I had been a part-time file clerk for a dentist instead. I was worried that I had no maternal aptitude, that I would be lousy at it and have no idea how to improve, that I would make countless mistakes right from the start and ruin a child's life. Every time I thought about this, a feeling of hot panic nearly overwhelmed me. On the examining table, in a paper gown, I looked through another magazine for an article about prenatal anxiety attacks, but I couldn't find anything.

I was starting to wonder if they had forgotten all about me, when the doctor finally walked in. "Howdy," she said. "I'm Jennifer Carver." She looked younger than me. I was thirty-three and had not had this experience before. She was small, with fine features, curly red hair, freckles, and dark-rimmed round glasses. She looked like a doll version of a doctor, a toy for little girls, to let them know that women could achieve high-status positions. She washed her hands while looking down at my chart, open on the counter. "Hm. You're pregnant," she said. She dried her hands and smiled at me over her shoulder. She turned around to face me, picked up my chart. "How have you been feeling?"

"Nauseous and tired," I said.

"Perfect. Is the nausea starting to taper off now? Let's see, you're about thirteen weeks."

"No, it's not tapering off at all. I throw up every day."

"I'm sorry," she said. "Try to eat small, frequent meals. It helps some women to eat a couple of saltines before getting out of bed in the morning. And some women swear by ginger ale. Try to notice what makes you nauseous, and avoid those things if possible. Other problems?"

"I'm single," I said.

"Yes?" said Dr. Carver.

"And I don't feel, you know, one hundred percent sure all the time that I'm doing the right thing, that I know what I'm doing."

"I see," she said. She folded her arms. "You've considered an abortion, you mean?" I nodded. "And decided against it." I nodded again. "Well," she said, "believe me, there are very few people who can just get pregnant and have a baby and not feel sometimes that they're making a big mistake. It's a big scary deal to have a tiny person dependent on you for absolutely everything." She twisted a ring around her finger. "I'm pregnant myself," she said, "and I'm probably worried about the same things you are. My husband's a doctor too, and we have these horrible schedules. We never see each other." She bit her lip. "Sometimes I wonder if we're going to stay together." She laughed unconvincingly. "Anyway. What else?"

"Nothing," I said. "That's about it."

"Are you interested in childbirth classes?"

"Yes."

"Try to sign up early. They fill up fast. And if you can, find someone who is willing to be with you during the classes and right through the delivery. That support really helps a lot."

"I'll try," I said, though this seemed unlikely. I went over the same cast of characters I had reviewed when I was waiting my turn at the abortion clinic: Gram, Nick, Laura, Eric, Dan. "But I don't have to have anyone there, do I?"

"Oh, no. It just makes it easier for you." She put on a glove to examine me. She pressed down hard on my stomach, with her other hand inside me. "Good. OK, fine," she said, frowning at the wall and feeling around. When she was finished she said, "Your last period was when?" I made up a date that was approximately two weeks before Nick left. I never wrote down when I had my period, but I didn't want to admit this to a doctor. She consulted a little cardboard wheel. "OK. You're due on August seventh. Now, think of that date as a guess. You could be two weeks away from it in either direction and still be considered on time."

A technician took out three tubes of my blood. I tried not to look, because I knew the sight of it would make me gag. I left with a big envelope full of literature about pregnancy, along with coupons and ads for maternity products and baby equipment and services.

A few weeks went by, and I still hadn't told anybody. It was easier than I thought. No one seemed to notice how poorly my clothes fit now or that I was throwing up all the time. Keeping my pregnancy a secret was going so well that I decided I wouldn't tell anybody until I had to wear maternity clothes. But then, one day at lunch, my sister asked me if I wanted to go to her health club after work and use the steam room. "I'm pregnant," I said. "And I'm going to have the baby. Steam baths are out."

Laura said, "What? You're kidding."

"No, really. I am. Nick's the father, in case you were wondering."

"Of course I wasn't wondering. Don't be so stupid. When are you due?"

"August seventh."

"My God, Alice," Laura said. "Jesus. And you're going to have the baby? Are you sure this is . . . What are you thinking? Why didn't you tell me before?"

"At first I didn't tell you because I was going to get an abortion. Then I changed my mind, and I just kept putting it off."

"That wasn't fair," she said. "I should have been the first to know."

"You are," I said. "I haven't told anyone else. I mean,

I went to a doctor, but she doesn't count. I don't even know her."

"Oh, God. What are you going to do? Call Nick and tell him? You know you don't have to do this. How many weeks are you? Maybe we could still—"

"No," I said. "I'm sixteen weeks. Besides, I've decided."

"Did you even talk to Nick about it? Did you talk to anyone? You better call him right away."

"I wasn't going to call him. I was going to wait until he calls me, then tell him."

"Oh, my God. This is crazy. What if he doesn't call?" Laura said.

"I'm sure he'll call. I mean, sometime. And if he doesn't, then I'll send him a birth announcement."

Laura pushed her plate away. "I'm wondering if you've thought this through. You don't make enough money. You're worried about coming up with a deposit for an apartment. You can't count on Nick for anything, of course. Do you have any idea how much it costs to raise a child? On one income, and a pretty small one at that, it's going to be really hard. And it's also going to be almost impossible to have no support from anyone at home. A baby is a lot of work. I don't think you realize how much. It's exhausting, and how are you going to handle that all by yourself?"

"I haven't quite figured it all out yet," I said.

"Oh, really?" Laura said, leaning back in her chair and crossing her arms. "Frankly, that sounds a little naive. Worse than that—reckless. I don't think you're acting responsibly at all. You need to think about this child first, Alice. What kind of a life are you going to be able to give him in some tiny apartment in Manhattan on not enough money? And who is going to take care of him while you're at work? Have you got that organized? Because all the good day-care centers have waiting lists. We've been thinking of having a child, and I've researched this. I know what I'm talking about."

"I expected you to be more positive," I said. "Are you saying you think I should have gotten an abortion?"

"Personally, I think that would have been the mature thing to do, under the circumstances."

"Well, I didn't," I said. "I made up my mind that this was what I wanted to do, and I'm doing it." I ate my lunch.

Dan and Eric and I went out after work on Friday. Eric didn't have a girlfriend at the moment, so he was always organizing things to do with other people. Dan wasn't involved with anyone either, as far as I knew, and was frequently available to go along on the outings Eric suggested. I was not looking forward to the weekend ahead with my grandmother. Eric was meeting a friend at The Meaning of Food and asked if we wanted to come. I ordered potato skins right away and then a salad because I felt guilty about the greasy potato skins. I finished both pretty fast and ordered some scrambled eggs and toast. Eric and Dan each had a beer and drank slowly, watching me eat.

"I saw that commercial Nick made," Eric said. "The one where he's roller-skating with his children and falls and has to take a non-aspirin pain reliever for his minor aches and pains?"

I looked at him. "You're kidding. I haven't seen that one. All of a sudden he's making all these commercials."

"What?" Eric said. "Are you saying you didn't know about it?"

"We split up," I said.

"Oh, geez," Eric said, shaking his head. "I didn't know. I had no idea. What happened?"

Dan said, "Eric, it's none of your business."

"No, I want to know," Eric said. "She can tell me herself if it's none of my business. What happened, Alice?"

"He fell in love with someone else."

"Ah," said Eric. He covered his face with his hands and sat still a few seconds. Then he put both hands over his heart and looked at me sadly. "I'm sorry. That's awful. How many years were you guys together?"

"Five."

Eric made clucking sounds and shook his head. "Can you believe people?" he said to Dan. "Five years with this woman, and he throws it away." Dan took a sip of water. I finished my eggs.

Dan said, "I'm sorry, Alice."

"Thank you," I said. "I'm OK."

Eric's friend arrived. "OK, guys," Eric said, "we're going to the movies. We'd like to hang out, but it starts in ten minutes."

"Have a good time," I said.

Eric said, "Alice, I'm really sorry." He squeezed my shoulder.

"See you Monday," I said.

They started out. I heard his friend say, "What happened to her?"

"Boyfriend dumped her," Eric said. "Son-of-a-bitch actor."

Alone with Dan, I tried to think of something to say. Stupid, I thought. The more I try, the harder it's going to be. Then Dan started to talk. "Alice," he said. "It's really too bad about Nick."

"Yeah, thanks. I'll get over it, I guess."

"But I'm glad too, because I've always been attracted to you." My face felt hot. "I think you're a wonderful person, and if you hadn't been living with Nick, I would have asked you out a long time ago." He reached across the table and put his hand over mine. I didn't want to pull my hand away, because I didn't want to hurt his feelings. I couldn't think of anything to say. My hand grew uncomfortably warm under his. I had to pull it away and put it around my glass of ice water.

I said, "Dan, I'm pregnant."

"You're—oh, no. God. How did that happen? I mean, that's too bad. I mean, how awful. What are you going to do?"

"No, it's fine. I'm happy about it. I'm going to have the baby."

"What? You're going to have the baby? That's crazy, Alice. Why would you do that? You don't have to do that. You're not religious or anything, are you? Do you need to borrow some money or something?"

"No, thank you." I picked up my glass of milk.

"I'm serious. I can easily lend you some money. You don't even have to pay me back right away. I'm a single guy, living in a rent-controlled apartment. I'd be glad to lend you whatever you need."

I said, "I want to have the baby."

"Oh," Dan said. "Why?"

I got my coat off the back of my chair and put it on. Pulling some money out of my wallet, I said, "I have to go. I don't want my grandmother to worry."

"OK," he said. "See you Monday."

"See you Monday."

"Now, who's going to drink that?" my grandmother was saying. I had just picked up a gallon of milk. It was Saturday. We had finished getting Gram's hair done and were buying groceries in the Shopping Basket.

"I am," I said. "I'll drink it."

"It's fattening, you know," she said.

"I guess it is." One of these days I was going to tell her that I was pregnant. I was hoping she would just figure it out on her own. The longer I waited, the more likely this was. She had already started making comments about my weight.

"We need some of these," she said. She was waving a wrinkled coupon in front of my face. "With the double coupons, that's a dollar off." The coupon was for diet frozen dinners.

"The freezer section is next," I said.

"Well, let's get going." She was leaning on the grocery cart, starting for the next aisle. Leaning on the cart made it easier for her to walk. If she had one of these at home, I was sure that it would not be so difficult to get her out for her walk every day.

I found the dinners she was looking for. "How many should I get?" I said.

"Don't you want some? I got an extra coupon from Mary Lou."

"No, thank you," I said.

"Three hundred and fifty calories, including dessert, and practically no fat."

"Those things are full of salt and chemicals," I said. "And I'm not on a diet."

"Well, you should be. What do you care what's in them?"

"I just don't want to eat that stuff," I said.

"I think you should be a little more concerned about your weight."

"I'm going to buy some tuna. Where is that? Do you like tuna?"

"Look at you. Your clothes don't even fit you. I'm saying this for your own good."

"Thanks. I really appreciate it. Oh, here it is. Tuna. It's on sale. Want some?"

"A young girl like you—well, really you're not that young anymore—but a young woman like you should watch her figure. *I* always did. Men don't like women who don't take care of themselves."

"Do you want tuna or not?"

"I hate tuna," she said.

"Fine. That's all you had to say."

"Peanut butter. Let's get that. It disappears awfully fast these days."

"I'll get my own jar," I said. "You won't have to worry about how much I'm going to eat."

"Eat as much as you want. Who says you can't eat? What did I say? You're so sensitive."

"What else do you want?"

"Bread, butter, chicken broth. Where is that?"

Slowly, we made our way around the store. We had to backtrack a few times. It took well over an hour to reach the checkout counter. By the time we started putting our things on the conveyor belt, I was desperate to get out of the store. "Put the tuna on this side with the milk," my grandmother said. "It's yours. I want to keep things separated. What's *this*?" She held up a bottle with two fingers, as if it might hurt her.

"It's shampoo," I said.

"Oh, my God. I didn't know what that was." She put it next to the milk.

"Let me unload it, would you?" I said. "I'm fast. Just back up. Here. Read this magazine."

"Is Fergie in this one? I want one with Fergie in it."

"Give me some room here, would you?" I was snapping at her. The checker, a teenager with a lot of eye makeup and unbelievably long fingernails, gave me a sideways glance. I finished unloading. The checker totaled the groceries. "Seventy-eight ninety-six."

"Now, don't you do anything, Alice. I'll get this. You can pay me back later for your things." I handed her her purse. She had forgotten it was in the grocery cart. "All right now. Let's see." She opened it. It was full of wrinkled pink tissues with lipstick on them and old coupons that she kept stuffing in there and not using. Most of them had probably expired. She rummaged around until she found her checkbook. I heard the man behind us groan. "Now," Gram said. "I want to make this out for fifty dollars over the total. How much would that be, dear heart?" She smiled warmly at the girl at the cash register.

"Oh. One twenty-eight ninety-six," the checker said and smiled back. My grandmother started to write. It seemed to take a long time. But we were almost finished, I kept reminding myself. She tore off the check and handed it to the checker. "Your Shopping Basket check card?" said the girl.

"Pardon me?" said Gram.

"Your Shopping Basket card. You need it to pay by check."

"Oh, well, I did have one of those, but what did I do with it? What color is it?"

"It's white, ma'am. With black and red letters on it."

"Well, I don't know where that is. I have my license, though. That will be enough, won't it?"

"I'll get a manager, ma'am," said the girl. She picked up a telephone and dialed. We heard her voice over a loud-speaker: "Check approval on eight. Check approval." The groceries were bagged now, and a boy put the bags into the shopping cart. "Ma'am," said the checker. "Would you mind waiting over here so I can ring up the next person? Thank you."

We walked to the front of the store. My grandmother sat down on a stack of dog food bags. "Gram, don't you usually bring your check-cashing card? Do you know where it is? Or you could get all the cash you want from the ATM right outside. Where's your ATM card?"

"Oh, I don't have to do all that. They know me here." She surveyed the store. "I think this is an excellent market," she said. She looked me over. Her face was about level with my stomach. "Alice," she said, "you're fat. There are some excellent diets. I've got some at home, I'll show you. And there are all sorts of things you can buy these days. They have powdered drink mixes, the frozen dinners that I buy, meal bars—they taste just like candy. But you're going to have to do something about that stomach of yours. It makes me sick when I think of how young you are and already letting yourself go like this."

"I'm pregnant," I said. "That's why I'm fat. I'm going to have a baby."

"Oh, here comes our little man," said my grandmother.

The store manager approached. He looked about twenty. He had a name tag that read Jeremy, Store Manager. He looked around, then saw my grandmother. "Mrs. Williams? Are you sure you don't have your Super Shopper Loyal Customer Card with you, ma'am? Your driver's license has expired, and I can't approve your check without some valid form of ID."

"I've been coming to this store for years," said my grandmother.

"I'm sure you have, ma'am. I remember you from a couple of months ago. But then your license was still good. I reminded you then about the card. You said you'd try to find it. Would you like to apply for a new card today, ma'am? We could have one in the mail for you before next Saturday."

"This is the silliest thing I ever heard. Is this the way you treat the customers who have stuck with you all these years?"

"That's what the card is for, ma'am. Loyal customers like yourself earn points on selected items that turn into savings at the checkout counter. But you need to bring the card and swipe it through the machine. We can't do it on facial recognition. There has to be a number on the check."

"It just makes me sick," my grandmother said.

The two of them looked at me. "I'll go to the cash machine outside," I said.

All the way home, Gram complained about the store and how rude the staff were. I was relieved that she didn't talk about my being pregnant. I hadn't meant to tell her anyway, so it was a break that she hadn't heard me. I put the groceries away. When I came out to the living room, Gram was still in her coat. She was watching television, an old movie. "Why didn't you tell me?" she said. "I would have given you the money."

"What money?"

"You know what I mean."

"You mean for an abortion? I decided not to. It wasn't the money. I decided I wanted to have a baby."

"You don't know what you're saying. You don't know what a baby is. You won't be able to go out and have fun. You're giving up your freedom, Alice."

"I understand all that. I've taken that into account, and I've decided I want to have a baby. Freedom hasn't been all that much fun for me anyway. I realize that my circumstances are not ideal for starting a family. But they're all I have to work with."

"Listen to you. You sound like a television show. You sound like someone on Oprah." She started to take her coat off.

"Don't do that. We're going for a walk now."

"Oh, no. I'm tired. I wish you'd talked to me before. I could have helped. Now it's too late."

"Let's go."

"Not now, Alice."

"I'll give you a cookie when we get back. Two cookies."

"Oh, all right." I pulled her to her feet and steered her outside and down the front steps.

My grandmother held my arm so tight that I had to struggle to keep my balance. On average it took me half an hour to get her outside for her walk. She said she would do it tomorrow. She said it was too cold. She said she was coming down with something. She was too tired. I would have to remember to use bribes again. The fact that she still had her coat on was a big help too. Usually I had to go and get her coat and coax her into it.

"Slow down," Gram said when we got outside. "You're dragging me."

"Sorry. Look at these little flowers down by your fence. Did you plant those?"

"Oh, a million years ago." We went down her cement walk. Gram's head was bent in concentration on her feet. She had on her brown walking shoes with the leather tassel laces that always came untied. This morning I had tied them in double bows. The grass was brown on both sides of the walk, but crocuses were coming up around the fence posts at the edge of her yard. We crept our way past the mailbox, the gravel at the side of the road crunching under our feet. The house next door to Gram's, like all the others on the street but hers, had been built in the sixties. The people who lived there had expanded and modified it several times over the years, so that it no longer resembled the ranch style it had once been. There was a second story now, with two or three added bedrooms and a three-car garage. Last year, the family had installed a Jacuzzi, inviting Gram to use it anytime she wanted. "All right, I will," she had said. "Now, if anyone sees an old lady sneaking naked through the bushes, don't you dare call the police." But of course she'd had no intention of using it. "Don't be crazy," she said, when the neighbors kept urging her. "I have a heart condition."

The next house had two Corvettes in the driveway. "Silly-looking cars," Gram commented as we got closer. "I remember when those boys were born—twins. You've met them. Now they're in their thirties, with their own handbag business on Seventh Avenue. Doing very well. I don't know why they spend so much time out here with their parents." She stopped to catch her breath.

I knew what she was going to say next, and she said it. "Ours was just a farmhouse when we bought it." She waved her hand in front of her. "This was all fields. Potatoes as far as the eye could see." She stood there a minute, resting. "Do you think they can tell?"

"Who can tell what?"

"The neighbors. That you're pregnant."

"Oh. I don't know."

"They can. I'm sure they can. How much weight have you put on anyway?" I didn't answer. "What does the doctor say about your weight? Did you tell them at work yet? You're going to have to, you know. And what about Aunt Louise? She's going to have a fit."

"You can tell Aunt Louise, Gram."

"That makes it easy for you. She's going to call anytime now, you can bet your life on it. She's going to want to know how things are going."

"So tell her I'm pregnant. She's going to know eventually. But I don't want to tell her."

"Why not?"

"I don't want her to criticize my decision. I don't want her to say that I'm making the wrong choice. I've already heard that enough, and I can say it just as well to myself."

"Doesn't that tell you something? You should hear yourself. Let's go back. I'm tired."

"We'll walk to that mailbox today," I said. "You see the one with a picture of a cardinal on it? We're walking to that."

"I can't walk that far."

"Yes you can. Stop talking, and you won't get winded."

Aunt Louise called from London to check on us. "Fine," Gram said. "Just perfect." She looked at me meaningfully. "Yes, I'm walking every single day. . . . No, I just stick to the diet. I gave Alice the low-salt cookbook. She said she wanted to learn how to cook, so it worked out wonderfully. . . . A few disasters, yes. She's just learning, of course, but I think she's enjoying it. . . . Neat as a pin. Immaculate. . . . Well, all right, I am exaggerating, but the house looks fine. Have you been to the theater? . . . Yes, it is. There's just no comparison. . . . I know. Well, I wish I could go to Europe one more time, but I think I'm past it now. Listen, I won't keep you, because I know this is costing you a bundle. But Alice has some very important news. Have a lovely trip." She handed me the phone. "You're on. Break a leg."

I covered the mouthpiece with my hand. "I want you to know that I think that was really mean and uncalled for. You're nicer to the people in the grocery store than you are to me. I hope you realize that." I put the phone to my ear. "Hi, Aunt Louise. Sounds like you're having a wonderful trip."

There was a slight pause while my voice traveled to my aunt in London. She said, "I wish we'd done this years ago. I really do. So how are you? What important news do you have for me? I hope it's something nice for you. I know you've just been through a hard time with Nick and everything. Is it a new beau?"

"Bow?" I said. For a second, I thought she meant for my hair. "Oh, *beau*. No, sorry. It's not that."

"Well, what then? It's nothing bad, I hope. Tell me, would you? I'm on pins and needles."

"I'm pregnant. I'm due in August."

There was a rushing empty sound. I pictured the miles and miles of gray ocean between us. "How did that happen?"

"The usual way," I said.

"Nick?"

"Yes."

"Does he know? What are you going to do about it? Is there still time?"

"No, he doesn't know, and I'm going to have the baby."

"Oh, Alice." There was a long sigh of defeat, which traveled from Aunt Louise in a London hotel room to a satellite out in space and back down to me in a remodeled farmhouse on Long Island and still sounded exactly like the defeated sigh I had heard from Aunt Louise a thousand times before. If it hadn't been the kind of sound that could make you feel lonely and worthless for days, it would have made a nice commercial for the long distance company. "Why do you do these things?" she said. "Why do you make things so hard for yourself?"

"Thank you," I said. "I'm very happy about it too. So enjoy your trip, and we'll see you when you get back. Love to Uncle Richard." I hung up. Gram looked at me. "Aunt Louise said congratulations," I told Gram. "She said she thought I'd make a wonderful mother. She said she was happy for me."

"Well," she said. "Will wonders never cease." She picked up the remote control and turned on the television.

———

I went to my sister's apartment for dinner on Monday night. "Alice," said my brother-in-law, Mark, as he opened the door. "I heard your news. Very exciting."

"Thank you," I said.

Laura said, "Come in. We've made a really nutritious dinner for you. Very healthy. Go on into the living room, and I'll get us something to munch on."

Their place was so small that instead of a regular couch they had bought a love seat. I walked over to sit on this, feeling as if I was going to occupy more than half of it. As I sat down, the button popped off my skirt and flew halfway across the room. Mark picked it up and handed it to me. "Oh my gosh," Laura said. "Let me get some sewing things." She went to the bedroom and came back with a tiny box. It contained needles of various sizes, tiny spools of thread in different colors, a thimble, and a little pair of scissors.

"Forget it, Laura," I said. "Just give me a safety pin."

"No," she said. "I know you. You'll never get around to this. You'll throw the skirt into a corner somewhere and just never wear it again because it's missing a button."

"That's right," I said. "I probably will. But you have dinner to worry about. Give that to me. I'll take care of it." I was hungry, unbelievably hungry, as if I hadn't eaten all day, and it was making me edgy.

"This will only take a second," she said. She sat beside me and sewed the button on. Like everything Laura did, it seemed to take a long time. She was far too careful. No one would ever see the button, and before long, I would be too big to wear the skirt at all. By the time I was the right size for it again, I might not even like it anymore.

Finally, she snipped off the thread and said, "There. Good as new."

"Thanks," I said. "Great. Perfect." But she must have put the button back in a slightly different place; and now I couldn't close it. I pretended to button it so that she wouldn't notice and start all over again. I pulled my sweater down over my skirt.

"I'll go get us those munchies," she said. I could see her pulling something from the refrigerator. She brought out a platter and set it on the coffee table. I was hoping for something like tortilla chips dripping with melted cheese. Instead, it was raw broccoli, celery, and carrots, with some kind of dip. "There's absolutely no oil in this," she said. "So it's not fattening at all. I got the recipe out of a diet magazine."

"Oh," I said. "Wow." It was awful.

"Nonfat yogurt and herbs. Can you believe it?"

"Wow," I said again, chewing some broccoli. Then I ate all the carrots. Mark didn't have any of this.

By the time dinner was finally served, I could have eaten anything. It was a vegetable lasagna. "This has spinach for iron—pregnant women often get anemic," she explained to Mark, assuming that I knew this. "It has two kinds of low-fat cheese, for calcium and protein, and I used whole-wheat noodles."

"That was very thoughtful of you," I said.

"And we have spinach salad for fiber and, again, iron. Go ahead and start, Alice. I'm just going to toss the salad here, and I'll be there in a second."

I took very small bites. I tried to chew them a long time. Still, I was almost finished by the time Mark started to serve the salad. "Oh, gosh, Alice," Laura said. "You're starved. You poor thing. Mark, give her some salad." Mark dished some leaves onto my plate. "Get her some more of that lasagna from the kitchen. That wasn't enough."

Mark said, "There isn't any more. That was it. But you can have some of mine, Alice. Here, I haven't touched it."

"Oh, no, Mark," I said. "You have that. I'm fine here. It's just that I ate too fast. No, you go ahead and eat that. It's excellent, Laura. You're going to love it."

"Have some of mine," Laura said. "Please. I can't eat all this. I've got way too much here."

"Please, you guys, stop. I don't want your food. I ate too fast, that's all."

"Alice, you're *pregnant*. We can't let you go hungry." She cut her portion of lasagna in half with her fork and started to scrape it onto my plate.

"Stop," I said a little too loudly. "Don't do this. I don't need any more. Really."

"OK, OK, Alice." Laura patted the air. "Have some water. No one's going to make you eat anything you don't want to. All right. That's better. Now, Mark, go to the kitchen and get Alice some of that bread that's on top of the microwave. You're hungry, that's all."

I didn't say anything else for a while. Mark handed me half a loaf of French bread. I broke off a piece and ate it. We talked about Mark's job and about all the people who were getting fired because of the recession. Dessert was an apple crisp made without sugar. It was sour. I ate my portion slowly. Laura asked me three times if I wanted more. Then Mark offered me an after-dinner mint. I ate four. We drank decaffeinated coffee, and I put sugar in mine, though I didn't usually take sugar. It was more filling that way.

After dinner, Laura said, "I got you something. Oh, don't get all excited. It's not much." She handed me a present wrapped in yellow paper with little storks on it.

"You didn't have to do this," I said.

"I know," Laura said. "But I felt bad about the way I acted the other day. I was mean. I'm sorry." I opened the present. It was a book about pregnancy, broken down into three sections, one for each trimester, and further broken down into chapters for each month. There were personal narratives throughout the book, as well as suggested recipes for proper nutrition and lists of equipment to buy for after the baby was born. There were sketches of women in every stage of pregnancy; drawings of fetal development, week by week; and color photographs of three different deliveries. Laura said, "Since I'm older, it bothered me that you were going to have the first baby. Stupid. I don't think I'm ready. I might never be. So I didn't want you to think that I wasn't going to support you, that I wasn't happy about it."

I said, "You just needed some time to get used to it. Thanks, Laura. It was nice of you to buy the book. I really need it, because I don't know what I'm doing at all."

"You do," she said. "Of course you do." We hugged.

Mark picked up the book and started leafing through it. "Oh, my God," he said, staring at one of the pictures. "Jesus. I can't believe so many people are willing to do this. Look at that!"

I took the book from him.

"Thanks for everything, you guys," I said as I left.

"And call us," Laura said, "if there's anything you want us to do. Anything." Mark put his arm around her.

"OK. Thanks," I said. "See you."

"See you."

Before I got on my train in Penn Station, I bought a bagel and a hot chocolate. The bagel was fresh—made right there—and they put a lot of butter on it, which melted because the bagel was still warm. The hot chocolate was the powdered kind that you pour boiling water into. It was so hot it scalded my tongue. By the time the train pulled out of the station, I had finished both. They were excellent. I read my new book all the way home.

Seven

A LITTLE CHEST COLD

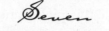 WORE MATERNITY CLOTHES NOW. I had told just about everyone I knew, and everyone else could tell by looking that I was pregnant. Strangers in stores asked me when I was due and compared notes on pregnancy.

Gram caught a cold. On the second day, a Saturday, she came downstairs in her nightgown, the Dior one with the ripped lace. She asked for a blanket to put over her lap. She made a big deal about it. "I'm chilled," she said. "Right to the bone."

"Well, I'm not surprised, Gram. It's pretty cold in here for just a nightie."

"All right, Miss Smartie. Just get me that blue afghan from my bed."

I went upstairs. At the end of her bed was a large pile of junk: library books opened halfway through and lying facedown on the blanket, old copies of *US* magazine, an empty Oreo bag, a hot-water bottle full of cold water. The afghan was there, all right—electric blue with an orange border. Something was spilled on it—pea soup or a milk shake, dried up and flaky. I brought it downstairs. "This is dirty, Gram," I said. "I'll just throw it in the washer. For now, use this pink blanket I found in the linen closet. Here, nice and clean."

"No. I want the blue one."

"As soon as I wash it."

"You can't wash that. You'll ruin it. Elaine across the street crocheted that for me."

"It's washable. It's synthetic. Look—acrylic."

She snapped at me. "You don't know that for a fact. Let me have it."

"Gram, it's dirty."

"What does it matter to you that it's dirty? Give me the blanket, Alice!"

"Oh, take it!" I threw it at her. It landed in a heap in her lap. This was the way it was with us these days. We had a lot of petty squabbles over nothing. We got on each other's nerves. She thought I was dismissible because I wasn't pretty, theatrical, rich, or married. On top of this, my being pregnant seemed an embarrassment to her, a badge I wore telling everyone how clumsy and stupid I was, how alone and unwanted.

What irritated me about Gram was the way she insisted on doing everything in the most awkward manner, the way she continually pointed out what she perceived as my faults, and the way she barked orders at me, then criticized the way I did things for her. And I was tired of hearing her stilted, practiced stories, over and over again.

Now Gram made a big production of spreading the blanket carefully across her lap. "Thank you very much," she said with a fake smile. "You're so gracious." I planned to wash it the next time she fell asleep, just to spite her.

She didn't ask me for anything for a while. Up in my room, I worked on a glossary. I had gotten as far as the *g*'s when she bellowed for me. "Alice! Alice! Come down, please." I went down. "I'm sorry I was short earlier."

"Oh, that's—"

"No, it's not all right. I was unkind, and I'm sorry."

I stood there for a second and felt guilty for throwing the blanket at her, for being so impatient. She was old; I should try to be more understanding and tolerant. She almost never apologized. "That's nice of you to say."

"I'd like some chicken soup."

"Oh, I see," I said. "OK. I'll go to the deli, then. They probably have it. Let me just finish what I'm working on."

"Oh, no," she said. "Don't go there. Their soup is awful." She flapped her hand. "I want homemade. It doesn't have to be fancy. You can just dump the chicken into some broth is all."

"I don't know how to make chicken soup."

"Well, it's about time you learned, then, don't you think?"

"Have you ever made it?"

"Oh, Lord, no. I don't cook. Never did. Here's your recipe." She handed me a little rectangle snipped jaggedly out of a magazine. She had been holding it as she told me how sorry she was. It was called Old-Fashioned Chicken Soup. It had lots of ingredients and looked difficult.

"I don't cook, either. You know that," I said.

She pretended she hadn't heard me. "You can just zip down to the Shopping Basket and get what you need. It will be done by dinnertime. Nothing to it. Get chicken breasts. I don't like dark meat. I know the recipe doesn't say breasts, but that's what I want. And don't do the peas.

I can't stand peas. As a little girl, I used to hide them in my napkin, then shake it out the window when the meal was over. Did I ever tell you that?"

"Yes," I said, giving up. "Breasts, no peas. I'll get my jacket."

"What is that you're wearing? Not very flattering."

"It's a shirt," I said. "A maternity shirt. What's wrong with it?"

"It's just that it looks like one of those things cleaning women used to wear over their clothes when they were working." She chuckled to herself. I got my coat from the hall closet.

"And I need some more tissues. Pink, but don't get Kleenex. It's too expensive. Get the no-brand kind."

"Yeah, OK. Cheap pink tissues."

When I came back from the store, I went through the back door so she wouldn't be as likely to shout any more orders at me. It took an hour to get all the ingredients for the soup cut up and sautéed and organized. Then the chicken was supposed to simmer in broth for an hour. I tried to get upstairs and back to my glossary without her seeing me, but I didn't make it. When I was halfway up, she called, "Alice!"

"Yes?"

"Come here, please." I went. "Are you going out?"

"No. Why? Do you need something?"

"Oh, just some cough drops and a movie. But I'll be fine. I'll just read this magazine." She picked it up. "Darn it," she said and put it down. "I've already read that one." She started coughing.

I waited for her to stop so that I could ask her why she didn't tell me about the video and the cough drops when I went out before. I had to wait a long time. She coughed so hard that her eyes watered. I wondered if there was some kind of Hollywood trick behind this, like biting the inside of her cheek or something. "OK," I said when she finally stopped. "I'll go. But if there's anything else you want me to get, tell me now, because I have work to do."

"Oh, no. Just this, and then I won't trouble you again, I promise."

When I came back, she was dozing in her chair. I put the cough drops and the movie next to her and went upstairs. In her bathroom, I gathered a bunch of her clothes from the floor. I wiped off the counter and scrubbed the bathtub and toilet. The mirror had toothpaste spatters on it, so I squirted on some Windex. I threw away a lot of old tissues with lipstick on them. I straightened all the little bottles on her counter. Some of them were empty. I threw these away. I took all the books off her bed and made a neat pile of them on her bedside table. I changed her sheets and cleared away some old water glasses to take downstairs. I hung up several dresses and sweaters that were draped over chairs. When I was finished, I stood in the doorway to admire my work. It was clean, it was neat, it was uncluttered. I was proud.

Downstairs, I checked the chicken. I pulled it off the bone, cut it up, put it back in the broth, and added the carrots, celery, and rice. To my surprise, it looked like real chicken soup. I could hear the television clucking away in the living room. I cleaned the kitchen. When my child was old enough to eat chicken soup, I would remember this recipe. I would have it on an index card in a little box with flowers on it. I would try to, anyway. After wiping the counter, I folded my cloth neatly over the faucet. Gram coughed.

I was so happy about the soup and getting the house in shape that I wasn't irritated at her anymore. I brought her a new box of tissues. She didn't say thank you. She opened her eyes and closed them again. "Gram?" She didn't answer. "Where's your thermometer, Gram?" She coughed and didn't open her eyes. All of a sudden, I remembered something my mother told me once about when Laura and I were babies. She said she always knew when we were dangerously ill because we would leave her alone long enough for her to get the house cleaned up and dinner made. A wave of fear swept over me.

I found the thermometer in the medicine cabinet and took Gram's temperature: 103.8. I gave her two extra-strength Tylenol, which she swallowed easily without water. I said, "Gram, I'm calling Dr. Rikkers now." She didn't answer; she was falling asleep again.

On Saturdays, Gram's doctor always tried to fit in his patients in the morning, but he was running very late today. When we walked in, the woman behind the desk said, "Mrs. Williams, long time no see. I love your coat."

"Oh, thank you, Deborah. I got it at Saks years ago. It's probably older than you are." The Tylenol was working.

"What are we seeing you for today, Mrs. Williams?"

"Just a little chest cold," she said.

I said, "High fever, coughing, no appetite. I gave her some Tylenol."

My grandmother laughed, as if I were a three-year-old who had just said something cute. "Alice," she said, shaking her head. "Deborah, I hope we're not taking time away from anyone who's really sick. Just put down that I've got a little chest cold."

Deborah wrote something. "The doctor's always glad to see you, Mrs. Williams," she said.

"She had a temperature of a hundred and three point eight," I said.

"You may have a seat, Mrs. Williams," Deborah said. "We'll try to get you in as soon as possible." She smiled at Gram.

We had to wait a long time. I went to the desk. "Can you tell me how much longer it will be? I'm really worried about my grandmother."

"I'm sorry," said Deborah. "Saturday is always crazy. If you can come during the week next time, the wait will be considerably shorter."

"I'll remind her to get sick at a more convenient time for you. Thank you for your concern," I said. Deborah answered a ringing telephone and did not look at me.

We had to wait twenty more minutes. Finally, Deborah came and stood in front of my grandmother. "The doctor will see you now, honey." Deborah offered her hands to Gram to pull her up. They started walking toward the examining rooms. I followed.

"You've cut your hair," my grandmother said to Deborah. "Now, is that a perm or natural curl?"

"Natural," Deborah said. "Drives me nuts."

"Oh, if I had your hair, I'd be on my knees with gratitude every day."

"You wouldn't." Deborah steered Gram toward one of the rooms. She helped her up onto the examining table. "You'd hate it."

"And how was your little girl's visit with her father?"

"It turned out better than we thought, actually." Deborah got a cloth gown out of a drawer and unzipped Gram's dress in back. Gram took her arms out of the sleeves of her dress and slip while holding the dress to her chest. She put her arms into the sleeves of the gown and let the dress and slip drop to her waist. Deborah fastened the Velcro closures in back. "Your granddaughter had me a little worried, but I see you're as sharp as ever."

"Her temperature was almost a hundred and four," I said. "Then the Tylenol started to work, and she seemed much better."

"The doctor will see you next, Mrs. Williams," Deborah said.

"Why do you do that?" I said to my grandmother when she was gone.

"Do what?" she said.

"Act like you're at a party or something and pretend you're not sick?" She seemed so healthy that now I was starting to feel foolish for bringing her to the doctor.

"You have to be nice to people, Alice. I just try to be a little interested in the people I meet. It wouldn't hurt you to do the same."

"You're sick. You're supposed to tell them what's wrong. That's why we're here."

The doctor came in. He was about my age. "How's my girlfriend?" he said.

My grandmother twinkled at him. "I have a little chest cold," she said. She blinked at him a few times, smiling.

"She's had a high fever," I snapped, "and a terrible cough. I'm her granddaughter."

"Oh, for heaven's sake," she said. "To hear you tell it, I'm at death's door." She smiled at the doctor, as if they shared a joke.

"Let's take a look." The doctor listened to her chest for

a long time. He timed her breathing, looked at her throat, and checked her ears. He felt the lymph nodes in her neck. "OK," he said, writing in her chart. "I'm glad you came in when you did. You've got bronchitis that's dangerously close to turning into pneumonia. Is your granddaughter staying with you?"

"Temporarily."

"Fine." He turned to me. "If you think you can look after her for the next few days, I won't have to hospitalize her."

"*What?* I've got a little chest cold," my grandmother said.

The doctor ignored her and spoke quickly to me. "I'm going to write a prescription for an antibiotic and something for the cough. I'll need you to keep careful track of her symptoms for the next forty-eight hours. If she seems to get worse, I'm going to have to hospitalize her. I want you to give her plenty of fluids and have her stay in bed. If she stops eating or seems disoriented, I want to know about it right away. Here's my pager number." He wrote on his prescription pad: a page for the phone number, one for the antibiotic, another for the cough syrup. "The cough suppressant has codeine in it, which will make her constipated. Do you have some Metamucil at home, Mrs. Williams?"

"Yes, of course, but I don't see why you're—"

He kept talking to me. "Give her the Metamucil for the constipation. I'll need to see her on Monday again. Make an appointment with Deborah on your way out. Questions?"

"No," I said. "We're all set."

"You caught this early, which is really helpful. I wish more of my elderly patients had family members to look after them," he said. "Good luck with her. Feel free to page me. See you Monday."

"Thank you," I said.

"So long, Mrs. Williams," the doctor said. "You behave yourself now and do what your granddaughter tells you."

"Goodbye," she said shortly. She was mad at him, probably because he had come up with his own diagnosis and hadn't accepted hers, because he hadn't told her how sharp she was or that she was in great shape or that he couldn't believe she was eighty-nine years old. I helped her get dressed and get down from the table. "It's a chest cold," she said one more time, softly now and without much conviction.

We drove to the pharmacy near Gram's. I left her in the car, with the motor running so that she could have heat; she kept complaining about being chilled. I handed over the prescription and asked how long the wait would be. "About ten minutes," said the woman behind the counter. But this was hard to believe. A sick little boy slumped against his father in a chair. A mother paced with a baby in pink in a Snugli. A man and a woman who did not seem to be together stood reading magazines near a Kleenex display. "Do you want to wait or come back?" said the woman at the register.

"I'll wait," I said. I went outside and checked Gram.

"What's taking so long?" Gram said.

"There are already a lot of people waiting," I said. "It will be a little while."

"Did you tell them it was for me?" she said. "Frank, the pharmacist, is very fond of me."

"Your name is on the prescription."

"Go back in there and tell them it's for me. They'll do it right away."

"I can't do that. There are sick children in there."

"All right, then. Tell them to put it on my charge account. They like you to say that before they start to ring it up."

I went back to the woman at the register. "That prescription I gave you? My grandmother, Mrs. Williams, wants it on her charge account."

The pharmacist peered out from the window. "Mrs. Williams not feeling well today?" he said. "You a member of the family?"

"I'm her granddaughter," I said. "She's got bronchitis," I said.

"Oh, geez. So sorry to hear that. That can turn into pneumonia like that in an older person." He snapped his fingers. "You got a beauty of a grandma. Excellent gal. She waiting in the car?" I nodded. "Let me get right on this, then."

In a couple of minutes, he came through a half-door, down two steps, and out into the store with a bottle of pills and a bottle of liquid. "Here you go." I took the medicines from him. "Wait. Hang on." I followed him up an aisle, where he took down a box of chocolate turtles. "She loves these. Say 'Get well soon. From Frank.' "

I looked back at the people waiting for prescriptions. The father of the little boy said, "Excuse me. I believe we were—"

"I'll have yours in one minute, sir. Got an eighty-nine-year-old woman outside with bronchitis. Can't let that wait, can we? So long," he said to me. "You take good care of that grandma of yours, now."

"Thank you," I said. "I'll try."

In the car, I handed Gram the turtles. " 'Get well soon from Frank,' " I said.

"Well, isn't he the dearest man?" she said. "Now you see? I'm nice to people, and they're good to me in return." She looked into the bag that contained her medicines. "Damn it, Alice. You didn't get me anything to read. What's the matter with you?"

Gram was asleep. The chicken soup was untouched on the stove. Everything was neat. It was quiet in the house. The phone rang, and I jumped.

"Hello?" I said.

"What in heaven's name is going on? I called and called all afternoon, and there was no answer. We're in Paris." It was Aunt Louise.

I said, "Gram is sick. She has bronchitis. I had to take her to the doctor and get a prescription filled."

"Bronchitis! Oh, my God. Now, how did she get that? What did Dr. Rikkers say?"

"He said to make her stay in bed. He gave me his pager number in case she gets any worse. I guess it can turn into pneumonia pretty easily."

"Oh, Alice, I'm very worried about this," said my aunt. "How long did you wait before you took her in to the doctor? I mean, you can't let things go. It's not like when *you* get sick. She's old. She has a heart condition. You have to be very careful with any little illness she comes down with."

"I didn't wait. I took her in as soon as the cough got bad, as soon as her temperature went up. It happened really fast."

"Well, I'm sure you're doing your best," she said doubtfully. "It's my fault. I should have hired someone before I left. She needs someone who is used to caring for an old person. I see that now." I didn't say anything. There was a long pause. "I'd feel more comfortable if she were in the hospital," she said.

"She wouldn't rest in a hospital," I said. "She would be too busy being charming."

"Just make sure you call that doctor if anything happens. I don't want you to wait too long. She could deteriorate very rapidly."

"I didn't wait, Aunt Louise. Even Dr. Rikkers said I came in very promptly. He said he wished more of his elderly patients had family members to take care of them."

"Of course. I'm sure you're a very good little nurse. I'll give you our number here." She gave me a number, and I wrote it down. "Maybe we should come home."

"That's not necessary, Aunt Louise," I said.

"But if anything should happen when we're all the way over here . . ."

"Don't decide now. Call me back on, let's see, Tuesday. I have to take her to see Dr. Rikkers again on Monday, and I can let you know what he says."

"Oh," she said. "Good idea. All right. I'll do that."

"Fine. Talk to you Tuesday, then," I said.

We hung up. I put the phone down, and it rang again. "Hello?" I said.

"Hi, Alice." This was a familiar voice, but I couldn't place it. "It's Dan."

"Oh, hi," I said. "How did you get this number?"

"You told me your grandmother's name once, and I just called information. Anyway, I wanted to say I'm sorry about the way I acted the other night."

It took me several seconds to figure out that he was talking about his reaction to my telling him that I was pregnant. "Oh," I said. "That's all right. I understand. It probably took you by surprise. Don't even think about it."

"No, I've been thinking about it a lot, and I wanted to let you know that. I acted like a jerk and made you feel uncomfortable. I'm sorry."

"Well, it was a little awkward. But this isn't the best time for me to talk, Dan, because my grandmother is sick. She has bronchitis, and I've got to go and check on her. I appreciate your concern, though. Thank you very much for calling."

"Oh, I'm sorry. Bronchitis? That's awful. And you're taking care of her by yourself? Anything I can do to help?"

"No, thanks."

"You're still mad, aren't you?"

"Mad? I was never mad. I just have to go, that's all. Thanks for calling, though. I appreciate it."

I mixed up some frozen orange juice and poured out a glass. Gram didn't want it. Her temperature was up again, and it was too soon to give her more Tylenol. I had to feed her some juice with a spoon. It took thirty minutes to get her to drink half the glass. I took her to the bathroom. I got her back to bed. "I am so tired" was all she said. She kept coughing, but it wasn't time to give her the cough medicine again, either.

"You'll feel better tomorrow, Gram," I said. But she looked bad. I paged the doctor.

Dr. Rikkers called right back and explained that the way she was feeling was to be expected. Illnesses tend to look worse at night, he told me. And the antibiotic might take forty-eight hours to work. He asked if I had anyone to help me with Gram. I said no. He said, "She's not an easy patient. You're doing very well. Call me tomorrow and let me know how it's going."

I went upstairs and looked into her room again. It looked wrong because I had straightened it so thoroughly. The only mess left was all the photographs Gram had stuck into her mirror; some of them were so curled in on themselves that you had to press them flat with your hand to see who was smiling out. Most were pictures of my cousins: Olivia in her wedding gown; Candace in a bathing suit, smiling, her wet hair slicked down. There were some old people I didn't know, cousins of Gram's from back home in Iowa. And there was an elderly gay couple, Charles and Tom, costume designers, who had been friends of hers since her Hollywood days.

For about an hour, I sat in a chaise longue with a faded chintz slipcover, reading old copies of *Us* and *People*, until it was time to give Gram her Tylenol and another dose of the antibiotic. I spooned more juice into her and a little of the chicken soup. "Good," she said about the soup. "But not enough salt."

"You're not supposed to have too much salt," I said.

"I'm eighty-nine years old," she said. "How much longer do you want me to last?" She fell asleep.

I got a comforter and a pillow from my room and made myself a bed on the chair. At eleven-thirty, she woke up. The Tylenol was working again. I got her some water, and she held the glass herself and drank half of it. I took her to the bathroom. Then she started talking about her life. She was wide awake. As usual, the stories sounded practiced, as if she had written them down and memorized them. "The year I was born, my parents moved to a new house in town, and it's there to this day. There were four bedrooms and one bathroom. My parents each had a bedroom, and there was a door between them. I had a room, of course, and the fourth was a guest room." She paused. "Alice, you should be getting this down. If not for you, then for your daughter. It will mean a lot to her one day to hear the story of her great-grandmother's life. Get that little recorder of yours. Hurry up now. We don't want to stay up all night. I'm sick."

In my room, I dug around a pile of clothes on a chair until I found my tape recorder. Back in my grandmother's room, I put it beside her on the bed and pressed Play and Record. Gram glanced sideways at the machine. "What we really need is a video camera." I sat down in the chair again and pulled up the comforter.

She began. "When I first got to Hollywood, I kept running out of money. I was so stupid about what things cost. I had been teaching school in Iowa and saving all the money I could. For the first year after I left home—ran away, my parents would have said, though I was twenty-six years old, for God's sake—I had to keep asking my father for more. They wrote to me every day and begged me to come home. After a while, I opened the envelopes only to see if there was money in them and threw the letters away. They had tried to control me since I was a little girl, practically suffocating me. Going to the movies was always my escape. When I was a teenager, I read movie magazines all the time. As soon as I started working, I saved my money and got the hell out of Drinkwater, Iowa.

"Before too long, I met Walker Kincaid, the movie actor. Now I always wonder what would have happened if I hadn't met Walker. Things would have been a lot different, I can tell you. Or maybe I would have met somebody else just like him. But I did meet him, and I thought he hung the moon. I guess he liked me pretty well too, because we started sleeping together right away. I was a virgin, of course. Walker had quite a sex drive, and to hear him tell it, his wife didn't have any." Here Gram departed from the script I had heard so many times before. I became more alert, curious about what she was getting to. "They thought she couldn't have children," Gram went on. "Or at least that's what he told me.

"Before too long, I was making quite a bit of money. No starring roles, mind you, but I had an agent who liked me, and directors started to think of me for a certain kind of part—secretaries, small-town girl in the big city, the heroine's younger sister, that kind of thing. Small parts, all of them, but I was doing just fine, thank you very much. I saw Walker whenever I could. I was in love with him. I would have done anything for him.

"When I thought I was pregnant, I went to a doctor. I bought a wedding ring just to go to the appointment, can you imagine? Real gold, as if he cared. Well, he said, 'Yes, indeed, Mrs. Whatever Name I Gave, you're going to have a baby.' I smiled. 'How wonderful!' I said." Gram beamed broadly, clasping her hands together at her chest. "I was an actress. Then I ran out of that office just as fast as I could and cried. It was Walker's birthday. I bought him a beautiful jacket at a fancy men's store. I had it wrapped. The package had a big red bow. I'll never forget that. I went to this little apartment where I used to see him. His wife didn't know about this place, or at least she acted as though she didn't and never went there. I remember holding this big blue box with the red bow and waiting for him to open the door. Instead of Walker, this gal opened the door in his dressing gown with nothing under it. I guess she knew it was going to be me at the door.

"I had actually believed that he would divorce his wife and marry me. I thought he would be thrilled to find out that I was going to have a baby. I was that stupid. Well, after I saw this woman he was with—Teresa Something was her name, a dancer with big bosoms—I went straight back to the store to return the jacket. I put the money back in the bank and never spoke to Walker Kincaid again." Gram gently pulled at her hair, fluffing it out on the sides, then patting it.

"You could get such wonderful corsets in those days. You could hide anything. In this corset I bought, I didn't show at all. I kept working and saving my money. I'm not sure what I had in mind for that baby, but I thought the key to my survival would be to have my own money, as much as possible. Finally, I went home when I was seven months along and that damn corset was squeezing the life out of me.

"I don't know what I was thinking, going home like that. My mother was so ashamed that she insisted I stay in the house until after the baby was born. They told everyone that I was ill. I did not see a living soul. I had a baby and named her Rosemary. In my mind, of course. They took her right away from me. My parents arranged for an adoption. After the baby was born, I cried for almost a year. I did get sick. I had rheumatic fever, a child's disease that did permanent damage to my heart. My heart did not recover, which didn't surprise me one little bit.

"Mother and Dad wouldn't let me go back to Hollywood. I gave my baby away, and they still wouldn't let me go. You know how they did it? They took my money. They could do that in those days in a small town. Took over my bank account. And of course they made me feel so cheap and low that after a while I was willing to give up and marry your grandfather. He was a salesman my father had working for him down at the store. His first wife had died. No children. The things you'll do when you're alone and desperate. Now, I don't want to make it sound as though I hated him or anything. He was nice enough. But I was not in love with him, I'll tell you that. He was nice and dull. People trusted him.

"I thought if I married him, I could get my baby back. I went to the doctor and begged him to tell me where the child was. He called me selfish. 'How can you ask for that child back when she has made two people so happy? How can you take her away from her mother and father? Have another baby,' he said, as if they were all the same and one could take the place of another.

"It still makes me ache all over to think about that baby. She would be sixty-one now. Her birthday is December twelfth. She had a lot of blond hair. Like Walker. Lots of blond hair. And she was so pink. I only saw her for a minute before they bundled her up and whisked her off somewhere. Rosemary is a pretty name, don't you think? The doctor told me she went to a loving home, but you never know, do you?"

She stopped and pulled at her blanket for a minute or two, took a drink of water. "Every time I had a little money, I hired a detective. Most of them were thieves. And I couldn't tell anybody, you know, because I didn't want your grandfather knowing what I was spending money on. We never mentioned Rosemary between us. We moved here, away from my parents. He did that for me. He started selling life insurance, did very well at it. We had a baby, your mother. Then we had another, your aunt Louise. I always kept my distance from them, and I'm sorry. I didn't mean to, but I was afraid of losing them. I was afraid they would die or be stolen. If they were late coming home from school, I just about keeled over from heart failure. Then your mother did die, of course. But that was much later; she was grown, with her own children.

"I had these fantasies about Rosemary. I looked for her when I went to the movies. If I saw an actress about the right age, with a certain kind of mouth or a nose that could have come from Walker's side, I would be convinced for a while that I had found her. She was an actress, I would tell myself; she had followed in her parents' footsteps. Then in a couple of weeks, I would start to worry again. She was an unhappy housewife in the Midwest. She was sick, she was dying, and she had never known her real mother. I don't know what became of her, of course. I have no idea."

"You never told Mom or Aunt Louise about your first baby?" I said.

"Certainly not," she said. "Now switch that thing off and let me get some rest."

"Wait. What happened to Walker? Did you tell him about the baby?"

"No; I kept my big mouth shut, for once. He got back together with his wife. They had a baby too. Also a girl. Later, when he couldn't get any work, he ran off with some chippy and lived with her in Mexico for a while. He died at fifty of lung cancer. He smoked. All right. That's it. That's my story. Now you know my dark secret." I stood up and went to get the tape player. "I'm going to sleep," Gram said. She closed her eyes, dismissing me for the night.

Eight

DINNER DATE

*M*Y GRANDMOTHER started to feel better
by the third day, just as the doctor said she would. On
Monday, I stayed home from work and took her back to
the doctor. He said she was much better. He told her she
was lucky to have me. Tuesday, Aunt Louise called again
from Paris, and Gram talked to her. "I didn't even know I
was that sick. Alice did. She just whisked me down there
in no time flat. You should have seen her take charge, barking orders at the nurse there. Dr. Rikkers was impressed
with her. I was too." This was the way Gram showed her
gratitude, by telling Aunt Louise that I had done a good
job when she knew I was listening.

On Wednesday, I went back to work. The woman across
the street, Elaine, said she would check on Gram around
lunchtime. I called to get a progress report. "She's fine,"
Elaine said. "When I left she was watching a talk show and
yakking on the phone. I heated up some frozen pizza for
lunch, and she ate almost all of it. Then I opened a can of
peaches in light syrup for her, and she had one of those

too. I gave her the pill and stood there while she took it, just to make sure she didn't slip it under a cushion or something. We had my mother with us for six years before she passed away, God rest her soul, and I know how tricky these old gals can be. They're as sneaky as five-year-olds."

"Oh, thanks so much," I said. "That's really a big help." I called Gram around four.

"Well, how do you do?" she said. "I'm watching Geraldo."

"I just wanted to see if you were all right."

"Me? Fine."

By the end of the week, she was almost her old self again, except for a little cough.

I arrived at work Friday morning and immediately started longing for the end of the day. I was looking forward to being away from what appeared to be hundreds of yellow Post-its that stuck out from nearly every sheet of paper in my office, demanding that I look up tiny, petty details that no one but me could be bothered with but that no one above me would let go. I sat down at my desk, and the day seemed to stretch out infinitely before me like a vast unmarked prairie. I got to work filling in missing bibliographical information for a psychology text in its eleventh edition. Many of the sources the author referred to were missing volume numbers, the second author's first initial, the month of publication. I was busy with a big stack of these, which I had been putting off for more than a week, when the phone rang.

"Alice Hammond," I said.

"Hello, Alice Hammond." It was Nick. "How's it going, Alice Hammond?"

"Fine," I said. "Fine."

"How's your grandmother?" Nick said.

"She had bronchitis, but she's better now. What's up?"

"You mean, why am I calling?"

"Yes."

"No real reason. I'm sorry. You want me to hang up?"

"Not necessarily."

"I miss you. That's why I'm calling. Because I miss you."

My grandmother would have had some snappy, mean remark to make now. I said, "Oh. Really? How's it working out with—I don't know your girlfriend's name."

"It's not. I don't have a girlfriend." He exhaled. "I made a mistake, Alice. Why didn't you just tell me I was doing the wrong thing?"

"I tried. I feel I made a genuine effort there, Nick."

"Yeah, you did. You were great."

"Listen, I've got a ton of work to get through here."

"Oh, sorry. I was just wondering if maybe you'd—oh, never mind. I'll let you get back to work."

"If maybe I'd what?"

"Pardon?"

I said, "You said you were wondering if maybe I'd—and then you stopped. You didn't finish what you were going to say."

"Oh, just get together," Nick said. "I was wondering if maybe you'd want to get together with me. Maybe for dinner. But I understand. You're busy."

"Dinner?" My palms were wet; my heart raced. "I don't know."

"Listen, I understand. You don't have to explain. I was an idiot. I did something really terrible. And I am paying for that mistake every single day, every minute. I shouldn't have called. It was wrong. I'm sorry. You're right; you shouldn't see me. I'm not good for you."

"No, I didn't say that. I'll see you."

"You will? You really will? That's great. I was so afraid you'd never speak to me again."

"But there's something I need to tell you, to prepare you for."

"Oh, no," Nick said. "No. You're in love with someone else. I knew it. I knew this would happen. I deserve this. Shit."

"That's not it," I said.

"Oh. It's not? What, then?"

"Listen," I said. "I'm pregnant. I'm going to have a baby. Now wait. Just don't say anything, because yes, I have thought this through. I do know how difficult and expensive it will be to do on my own. But I still want to do it. I mean, I'm going to do it. Sometimes I don't exactly want to at all. Honestly, I'm afraid I might be just a terrible mother. But I'll do my best. I'm twenty-four weeks. There's no turning back now, so don't even bother to suggest it. I've made my decision. This is it."

There was a long pause. When he spoke again, Nick was whispering. "Alice, this is great. This is fantastic. I wasn't expecting this at all. You mean, the time we . . . in the living room? That time? Everything has a reason, Alice. Now I believe that. I have to see you. I have to see you right away. I bet you look beautiful. A baby. I'm so excited."

"You are? Everyone else has been kind of horrified."

"Who cares about them? Fools. Imbeciles! Your family, you mean? They make me so angry. They don't know anything. How many times have I told you they always want to hold you back? When is the baby coming? Baby! My God, this is so great! When will it be?"

"August."

"Wow." He inhaled deeply, then laughed out the breath. "I'm happy, Alice. How could you keep this a secret? From *me*? Me, *Nick*. Why didn't you call me as soon as you found out?"

"Call you? *Call* you? Are you kidding? The last time we talked—"

"Yes, yes, you're right. I'm so sorry. You'll never know how sorry. Can we get together? Please? Right away?"

"I guess so. Maybe Monday? I won't be in the city over the weekend. I'll be out at Gram's."

"Oh," he said, disappointed. "You couldn't make it tonight?"

"Well, no. I mean, my grandmother is expecting me."

"OK, call her."

"I can't just—I mean, we always get a movie on Friday nights, and she'd be disappointed. I get her a movie on the way home from the train, and ice cream and chocolate sauce. It doesn't sound like much, but she looks forward to it. She expects it. I don't like to let her down."

"Oh, God, Alice, that's so like you. It's great just to hear you talk. Call her. You can get a movie another night. Come on, this is important. I'll meet you at six at that place with the candles in paper bags. OK? Please?"

"All right."

"Alice, I'm happy about the baby. This is the best surprise I've ever had. Say hi to Gram for me."

I didn't. I lied. I said I had to work late on the bibliography. She said, "See you later, then. Or tomorrow."

"I'm sorry about the movie."

"What movie?" she said.

"You know. We always watch a movie together on Friday, and now I'll be getting home too late to bring you one."

She said, "Every Friday night? No kidding. I hadn't noticed. Don't forget to bring home some ice cream and chocolate sauce. They're open until ten."

"OK," I said.

All morning I was fast and cheerful. I answered other people's phones when they were away from their desks, which wasn't my job. Jane, our managing editor, smiled at me and invited me out to lunch the following Tuesday. Dan, Eric, and I had lunch in Dan's office, where the lights were out, as usual, except for two little reading lamps. "Dark in here," I said.

"Jesus," Eric said. "How do you see?" He shook his head. Dan didn't say anything. "Dan, you're strange."

"Everyone is a little strange," I said. "At *least* a little."

"Oh, yeah?" said Eric. "And you? How are you strange?"

"I'm a slob, completely disorganized. I never pick up after myself. I have terrible hair, and I live with my grandmother. I always choose the wrong clothes."

"That's not strange," Eric said. "That's idiosyncratic. You have a personality, that's all. Nothing to worry about."

"Hm. A personality?" I bit into my sandwich. I opened my 7-Up. I was staying away from diet drinks and caffeine because of the baby. "You're being kind."

"Now, look at me, for instance," Eric said. "I'm overweight, balding. I look like somebody's uncle from out of town. And I'm only twenty-six. I go to a club to hear a band, and the other people there think I'm doing research on their use of slang or dance styles or something. But I don't consider myself strange. I'm a dork, yes, but not a pathological one. Now, Dan here is a sick individual. Look at this man. He doesn't turn on the *lights*. He works *in the dark*."

"Leave him alone," I said. "We're all equally odd. Can't we just let it go at that?"

"Alice?" Eric said.

"Yes?"

"What's going on with you? Did something happen? You seem happy."

"Jane invited me out to lunch on Tuesday."

"Congratulations," said Eric. "You're getting promoted."

"What makes you think so?" I said.

Eric said, "Has she ever asked you out to lunch before?"

"No."

"See," Eric said. "There you go. She likes you. She wants to make sure you stay."

"She likes me?" I said. "What does she like about me?"

"Your hair." Eric picked up his sandwich, a salami sub.

I moved closer to the door and turned on the fan. Eric looked at me. "No offense, but the smell of that makes me nauseous."

"Oh. Sorry." He took a big bite and chewed for a while. "You watch. Jane is going to promote you. You'll get a raise, and you won't have to do photocopying or express mail anymore."

"You're good," Dan said. "That's what she likes. You work hard and you do everything well. You're wasted in your job. They're finally recognizing what they have, and it's about time. What you ought to do is leave the company, get a job in some other industry. They're never going to pay you what you're worth. They don't do that here."

"Thanks," I said, "but I'm sure I'm not getting promoted. Really, you guys are wrong. Nobody gets promoted from this job. The last editorial assistant in this department worked here for three years, if you remember, at which point she took a waitress job, where she made more money. She trained me. She told me that the woman before her had put in two years when Jane asked her to go down to the deli one day to buy a visiting author's lunch. She never came back."

Eric said, "Oh, you can't let these stories intimidate you. Those people probably weren't any good. They probably didn't deserve a promotion. She asked you to *lunch*, Alice. That can only mean one thing."

I said, "It's nice of her anyway."

"OK, there's the lunch thing," Eric said. "But that's not it. You're not bouncing around here smiling at everyone, answering phones all over the place, just because Jane asked you to lunch."

I didn't say anything; I ate my sandwich.

Eric said, "It's Nick, right?" Dan looked up. They both peered at me, trying to read what I wasn't saying from the expression on my face. "Oh, man. He called." Eric put his face in his hands. "No, no, no, no," he said.

"Yeah," I said. "He called. We're having dinner tonight." Dan put down the pizza he was eating.

"Don't go," Eric said.

"But I want to," I said. "I told him I was pregnant, and he was really happy about it."

Eric and Dan looked at each other. "Alice, Alice, Alice.

Don't go," Eric said again. "Listen. We're crazy about you. We'll do anything to make you happy. You're getting a promotion. You'll have more money. You don't need Nick at all."

"But I love Nick."

"Shit," Eric said. "Oh, shit."

Dan sighed quietly and said, "Shit."

"What can I tell you guys?" I shrugged. "Shit." We all finished our lunches.

During the afternoon, I wrote two chapter summaries for the psychology book and made research phone calls for the marketing book. I did a lot of little things fast that I had been avoiding for a long time. At five-thirty, it was finally time to go and meet Nick. My desk was already cleared off, because I had been fidgety for the last hour.

I was putting my jacket on when Jim appeared in my door. "Oh, thank God you're still here," he said. "I'm in big trouble, and you're the only one who can save me. I'd do this myself, except that I'm supposed to call my author in"—he looked at his watch—"oh, Jesus, five minutes ago." He had a stack of paper in his hand, three chapters.

I said, "Sorry, Jim. I'm on my way out."

"This will only take a second. I need you to make two copies of this and just drop it in the Federal Express box on your way home. Here's the address. Oh, and I've written the letter that goes with it; it's here. Just type that up, and that's it. No big deal, right?"

"Right. If you'd given it to me an hour or two ago, it would've been no big deal. But I'm meeting someone for dinner. I can't be late. I'm really sorry. I could do it for you first thing Monday, if you want."

"Forget it," he said through clenched teeth. "I'll do it myself." He stomped off to the copy machine.

I got my purse out of my bottom desk drawer. Eric was in the door now. "I heard all that," he whispered. He raised a fist in the air. "Yes!" he said. "Good luck with Nick."

"Thanks," I said. "See you Monday, Eric."

"See you."

When I met Nick I was a graduate student in American literature at NYU, teaching two freshman courses a semester for tuition and a small salary. Nick had just moved to New York. I didn't know any actors then. He had a way of looking into my eyes and touching my face with his fingers just before he kissed me, as if I were some exceptional object he had unexpectedly received, something enormously expensive, hard to obtain, endlessly useful and interesting. We used to go out to dinner a lot. I never had an appetite. I was too distracted by the way his fingers curled around a water glass; the unique and perfect way his lips moved as they formed words; the way his dark eyes with their short, straight lashes narrowed as he considered my questions or replies. We sat on the same side of the table in the restaurant. I ordered, but when the food came, I couldn't eat more than a few bites. "You're finished?" he would say. "Really? You know, you don't eat very much." And he would touch my face and kiss me. "I could watch you not eat dinner all night long," he would whisper. "How did I get so lucky?" I was in love. I lost weight.

We saw each other every day for several months. Our relationship was simple. "I love you," he would say. "Of course I want to be with you all the time." Nick found us a dilapidated apartment in the East Village, which we were going to fix up. We would replaster the bathroom, remove all the terrible wallpaper and linoleum, reputty the windows, sand the paint off the wood floors.

The apartment turned out to be a larger project than we anticipated. We got all the plaster off the walls in the bathroom within a month of moving in. It was a mess, white dust all over everything—our hair, our clothes, our books, our bed. Then Nick went on tour for the first time. The show was a revival of an old musical I had never heard of. He couldn't sing, but he was excited about his first paying job. While he was gone, I cleaned up the dust. It took me days. Then I went to a hardware store and got some information on how to put up drywall and decided to wait until Nick came back before I tackled it.

I left the bathroom alone and moved on to the kitchen, where I pulled up linoleum so old and worn that the pattern was completely gone in front of the sink and stove. In the corners, where no one had walked, the pattern was light orange and dark orange bricks. Underneath, I found folded-up newspaper from the fifties, in which decades of cockroaches had hidden, lived, bred, died. Under the newspaper was more old linoleum, big overblown pink roses on a dirty yellow background. Under that was the floor, painted rotten planks, patched in three places with flattened Maxwell House cans. When Nick got home we tried to figure out what to do about the kitchen floor. More linoleum? Get a book on how to put down a whole new floor? Wait until we had money and hire somebody? We couldn't decide, so we moved on to another part of the house.

In the bedroom, we took off the wallpaper. Our scraping made the plaster underneath crack and crumble into bits in some places. The walls ended up clear of most of the layers of dark flowered wallpaper, but now there were huge white craters.

When people came over, Nick would give them tours of the improvements we were going to make. "This is going to be all white," he would say. "We're taking all this out and starting over with this stuff. It's going to look great. Do you know anything about windows? Because look at this."

These were still our good times, when we went to the movies sometimes a few times a week and snuggled up together in the dark, eating candy for dinner. We had secret names for each other and characters, voices, and stories that went with them. I was Annabelle Melissa Megan Courtney Tiffany Smith, heiress to a fortune made from diet cheese-flavored popcorn, who spoke eight languages and had never seen a piece of garbage. Nick was Vincent Zappone, the brilliant but misunderstood family gardener who had a speech impediment and a lame right leg. (Nick, being an actor, liked to go to extremes.) As Annabelle and Vincent, we loved each other passionately and understood each other as no one else did. But Annabelle's parents would murder us both if they found out that we were seeing each other secretly. Sometimes when we made love, we pretended that we were Annabelle and Vincent meeting in the garden-ing shed, the linen closet, or the pantry of Annabelle's enormous home in central New Jersey, adjacent to the cheese-flavored-popcorn factory. I got messages at work from Vincent, saying to tell Annabelle to meet him at such and such a restaurant after work.

At some point, Nick and I stopped working on our apartment and saying that we were going to finish it. In the living room, we left the floor and walls alone and put down a light gray carpet remnant that got dirty too fast. We never even started on the windows. Some of the panes had no putty around them at all anymore; they were just pieces of glass held in place by slots in the splintering wood sash, rattling dangerously in high winds. In winter, we taped up sheets of plastic to keep out the weather. We admitted that we didn't have the personalities for home repair, after all, but as soon as we got some money, we said, we would hire people who did. Nick always knew a lot of actors who were desperate for money, and some of them could put up drywall, paint, put down floors, and maybe even reputty windows. But we never seemed to have any extra money. By now our rent, under rent control, was a lot lower than anything on the market. I finished the graduate program I was in and got my job at Stringer and Russland, where I didn't make much more than I had made teaching. Nick was out of work a lot. We couldn't even consider moving to a place that was already fixed up.

By the time Nick started working regularly, our relationship had entered an uncomfortable phase, and we had stopped noticing that our place was missing paint, walls, and a solid floor. Annabelle and Vincent had all but disappeared. I tried to figure out where we went wrong, to pinpoint an event that had triggered the transition, but I never could remember exactly when things had started to change.

I annoyed him. He was irritated with me for being so messy; I had always been messy, but now it bothered him. He kept cleaning the apartment. I tried to be neat, the way he was, hoping this would ease the tension. I bought closet organizers and tried to force myself to put things away every time I used them. But before I knew it, the closet organizers were chaos, with so much junk crammed into them that you could hardly tell where one stopped and another began. I bought books on how to be neat, how to manage your time, how to clean a house quickly and efficiently. But I could not stick with these systems for more than a week.

It wasn't only that Nick was neater than I was; that was just the small, visible portion of the problem. Even I understood this. Before I knew it, he had friends who weren't my friends. When he was doing a show in the city, he would go out with people I didn't know after his performances and come home late. When I got out of bed to get ready for work, he had only been there an hour or two. And he was away a lot. He would come back changed by people, events, conversations I knew nothing about. He gave up watching TV and eating dairy products. He listened to jazz. He became so neat that he would throw away my grocery lists before I had even shopped. When we went out to dinner, we sat on opposite sides of the table. He paid for his meal and I paid for mine. We had lived together four years, and he wanted to make sure he paid only for his own entrée, drink, tax, and tip. For this purpose, he had a tiny calculator that fit into his wallet. It seemed as though he didn't love me anymore.

I would come home from work and ask what he had done all day, hoping to prod him into communicating again.

He said, "Not much."

"You must have done something," I said.

"Hey. What is this?" he said.

"Did you read? Did you talk on the phone? Did you see anyone? You used to tell me all kinds of stories—about your dreams and people you ran into on the street and weird food you'd tried. You don't do that anymore. I want it to be the way it was." I tried to make him talk the way, years before, my mother had tried to coax information out of me.

Nick shrugged. "Everything changes, Alice."

He started an exercise routine that included running up and down all the steps in our building—sixty-five from the first floor to the sixth—for forty minutes every day. His thighs and calves developed thick muscles. He drank a lot of expensive French water right out of the bottle. He was turning into someone else, even physically transforming into someone other than the Nick who had been my boyfriend. The night we made love on the living room floor was almost the last time we had seen each other.

Nick was waiting out front when I got to the restaurant. I saw him looking up and down the street for me, not sure which way I was coming. He didn't recognize me right away. I was wearing black maternity leggings and a purple knit top. My hair was pulled back in a big barrette. I had on my old denim jacket, left open because it didn't button comfortably over my stomach anymore.

By the time he saw me, I was only a few yards away. "Alice," he breathed. "You're beautiful." He held me for a long time. I closed my eyes and leaned against him, inhaling: Nick. He smelled good and felt good, like cool clean sheets on a hot night. "My best friend," he said. "I don't know how I survived these last couple of months."

We went inside. "Where do you want to sit?" he said, asking this for the first time in several years and looking deeply into my eyes, waiting for my answer.

"Anywhere," I said. "How about over there by the window?"

"Perfect." His hand lightly touched my back as we

crossed the room. We sat down. "How are you feeling? Is everything going OK? What does the doctor say?"

"She says it's going fine. I'm feeling sick to my stomach a lot, but she says that just happens with some people. I usually throw up about once a day, but I'm getting used to it. There's a lot of heartburn. I gobble Tums by the handful."

Nick said, "Alice, poor you."

I shrugged. "It's not so bad."

We ordered. Waiting for the food, he stared at me. It was hard to think of anything to say. He said, "You're going to have a baby." He closed his eyes for a second, as if visualizing this, then opened them. "Why didn't you tell me? I still can't believe you would keep this a secret. From me!"

"I didn't keep it a secret, exactly. It's just that we weren't speaking."

"Still, it isn't like you. You always told me everything. That's one of the things I've always loved about you, your openness, your trust. Not everyone has it, you know."

"Nick, you were sleeping with someone else. And you lied to me about it." My face burned. "I wasn't going to tell you anything ever again, if I could help it. You called me long distance and broke up with me over the phone. You gave me six weeks to find a place to live. Remember? I had to move in with my grandmother, who still doesn't like me. I had no place else to go."

"God," he said. "I was an idiot." Now his eyes filled with tears. "I don't know why I did it. How could I have done that to my best friend? I guess our relationship had reached such a point of intimacy that I got scared. I had to pull away for a while. But I'm over that now, Alice. It's like I woke up from this terrible nightmare all of a sudden. That's why I had to call you."

Our food came. We didn't say anything while the waiter put things down on the table. When he was gone, I said, "What happened to what's-her-name? Did you tell her that we were getting together tonight?"

"Jacqueline? I told you, it's over. And anyway, I never had to tell her anything. It was never that kind of relationship." He reached for the salsa on the table and spooned it over his enchiladas. "I don't see her anymore."

"What do you mean, it's over?" I said. "What do you mean, you don't see her anymore?" I wanted to be sure. I wanted to be careful.

"Just that. It's finished. We've split up." He took a bite of food, chewed it, swallowed. "Anyway, no one is like you. No one knows me as well. No one. I would always be lonely without you. We go way back, Alice. And if I have anything to say about it, we're going way forward too."

"Wait just a second. Who ended the affair? You or Jackie?"

"It was a relationship. And her name is Jacqueline. What difference does it make who ended it? It's over. Forever."

"I want to know. Who ended it?"

"We both did."

I pressed on. "But whose idea was it?"

"Oh, hers, I guess."

"You guess, or you're sure?"

He looked out the window for a second, watching a young guy with long hair lock his bicycle to a No Parking sign. Nick shifted his eyes back to me. "I really didn't expect this from you, Alice. I'm disappointed. What do you want from me? A blow-by-blow description of our last hours together?"

"I want to know how it ended."

"All right. She met someone else, someone she liked better, someone who has a good-sized role in a movie that starts shooting next week in Milan. She dumped me. OK? Are you happy now?"

"How long ago?"

"Why do you want to know all this?" He touched my arm, lightly stroking. "Isn't it enough for you that I'm here now, that I love you and want to be with you?"

"Wait. Just a second. When did this happen?"

"All right, all right." He threw up his hands. "Monday."

"Monday? You mean four days ago? Just this past Monday?"

"OK, it was pretty recent, but it had been over for a while." He shook his head. "We weren't good together. It was never right."

"In the beginning of the week you break up with Jackie, and now you want to get back together with me?"

"It's not like that. I've been thinking about you since we split up."

"I have to go," I said. "I have to go right now." I grabbed my coat off the back of my chair. Squeezing between two tables, I knocked over a wineglass with my stomach. I still wasn't used to my new shape and size. There was a crash of breaking glass and some swearing behind me. But I didn't turn around.

I had to wait twenty minutes for a train. I bought myself a hot chocolate and a buttered bagel. I ate quickly on the platform, in case Nick came running up, breathless, looking for me. I didn't want to be standing there working on a big mouthful of bagel when he found me, butter smeared on my chin. I scalded my tongue on the hot chocolate and got heartburn from eating too fast. He didn't come. The train pulled in, and I got a seat by the window.

The trip home seemed to take forever. I walked fast from the station to Gram's house so my tears would not start to overflow too early. She was still downstairs when I got there, something I had not counted on. She seemed to be waiting for me. But I was not sure of this, as I was only a little over an hour later than usual.

"Look who the cat dragged in," said Gram.

"Hi. I finished earlier than I thought."

"So I see."

"I think I'll just go to bed. I'm really tired."

"It's eight-thirty."

"All right then, I'll go read. Anyway, I'm going up-stairs."

"Where's my ice cream?"

"Oh. I forgot all about it. I'm sorry."

"I knew you would," Gram said.

"Why do you say that? I almost never forget any of the stuff you make me do. What about your mascara and those shoes you had me get resoled and the library books I've reserved and picked up, and what about taking care of you when you were sick?" I was crying. Tears were pouring out. I always tried to avoid letting her see that she had gotten to me, and this felt like a big defeat. "You probably drank Hershey's chocolate syrup out of the bottle all day anyway. You don't need any ice cream," I sobbed.

Gram took a sip of water. She seemed to be smirking, but it might have been the lopsided way she had put on her lipstick. Setting her glass down on the cluttered table beside her, she said, "How was the dinner date? Is he working?"

My face burned. "Pardon?"

"Nick. Any more commercials? I just saw a new one. It's a Mitsubishi voice-over. He's pretty convincing when you can't see him. Is he training his voice or just lucky?"

"I wouldn't know," I said. "I don't see Nick anymore, don't even talk to him on the phone. I don't know what he's doing."

She laughed. "Now, Alice. Don't forget who you're talking to. Don't forget what I told you. I wasn't delirious, you know. It was all true, every word. I know how it feels to be in your shoes right now. I was a terrible mess. Did I tell you I cried every day for a year? And look at you. You're working, you have your baby on the way. You're way ahead."

"Ahead?" I said. "Ahead of what?"

"I mean it will work out—certainly not the way you want it to, but I guarantee you, you will not feel like this forever."

I turned to go upstairs. "Good night," I said. "Don't forget to take your pill."

"It takes time, Alice," she called after me.

Nine

POSITION AND PLACE

ICK DIDN'T CALL ME. My grandmother had said he wouldn't. I grew. Some of my maternity shirts were too short now, and some of the pants were too tight.

One Tuesday before work, I went to the doctor. Her own stomach had grown so big that she could no longer button the lab coat she wore over her dress. "Do you feel the baby moving?" she asked me, scribbling something in my chart.

"Yes," I said. "But not all the time. Sometimes I don't feel anything for the longest time. I mean, how much is enough?"

Dr. Carver smeared blue gel on me and listened to my stomach with her special stethoscope, then let me listen. The heartbeat sounded fast to me and electronic, but there was definitely someone in there. If I used my electric pencil sharpener at work or the blender at Gram's, the baby jumped inside me, starting at the loud sound. "Nice, healthy heart rate," said Dr. Carver. She measured me from the top of my pubic bone to the top of the big lump in my stomach. "You're big for the number of weeks along you are, but this has always been the case, so we won't get too concerned." I nodded. "The baby seems to be growing just fine, Alice. Any questions?"

"I have heartburn. And I still vomit almost every day." Being out of breath and certain smells always made me throw up. An empty stomach after too little sleep would make me dry heave while I was toasting a bagel. Smelling someone else's food in the office, I frequently had to fumble for my women's room key and run, praying for an empty stall so that I wouldn't have to throw up into the sink. I always had to put my hands in cold water afterward, and I wished I could do this to my feet too.

"For the heartburn, carry Tums with you. I've got it too. It's supposed to mean a baby with a lot of hair." She shrugged. "Another wives' tale. For the vomiting, there's not too much you can do, except frequent small meals. Don't get too hungry. See you in a few weeks."

Later that day, I was to have lunch with Jane. I wore my one maternity dress. Luckily, it still fit me. I pulled my hair back into a ponytail and tied a scarf around it. "What are you all dressed up for?" Eric wanted to know. "Oh, it's Promotion Day."

"Come on," I said. "You don't know that for sure."

"Maybe she'll move you out of this office and give you a window. Jim has a window, and he's only been here a year. But he whines. Hey." Eric tilted his head to one side, thinking. "I may have just hit on something. Maybe that's the secret to getting somewhere in this company—whining. Or wait—in the world. You know, this could be big. I may even have an idea here for a trade paperback—*Perfecting the Art of Whining* or *Whining to Win*. I'm going to write a proposal and an outline. Don't you think that's good? The potential market is huge!"

"Enormous," I said.

"Good luck at lunch," he said.

Laura called; she had heard about an apartment in the East Village. She gave me a number to call. "Get right down there, because tons of people are interested. Your old neighborhood. I think you should take it. I would."

The rent was twice what Nick and I had been paying, but maybe with the extra money I would be making in my new position, I could just about do it.

Five minutes after I hung up with Laura, Katharine stopped by. "My brother owns a building on the Upper East Side," she said, "and there's a vacancy. Are you still looking? OK, here's his number. Try to get there as soon as you can. These apartments go really fast."

"This is great!" I said. "Thanks so much." Maybe I would get a promotion and a place in the same day. Maybe things were going to work out better than I thought. I made appointments to see the two apartments. Then I called the library to check some information on cookie companies for the marketing book. I wrote a chapter summary on personality theory for the psychology text and photocopied eight chapters of the book, planning as I copied to show the new editorial assistant Jane hired how to clear paper jams, something that had saved me a lot of time.

Jane stopped by my office at one. "Shall we?" she said, smiling.

We went to a place nearby that I had been to only once before, on my first day of work at Stringer and Russland. Jane took each new employee in our department to lunch here, and it was also the place where she celebrated good news about promotions and raises or strong sales on books. She had made a reservation. "Your table will be ready in just a few minutes," said the hostess. While we stood there I saw a waiter I knew. He had directed a showcase Nick was in two years before. I hoped we wouldn't have to sit in his section. I didn't want him to ask me about Nick in front of Jane. But he probably wouldn't remember me.

Our table was ready. It was in the director's section, as it turned out. He walked over with menus. I picked up mine and looked down at it. "May I tell you the specials for today, ladies?" I didn't look up while he listed appetizers, soups, salads, fish.

I ordered lasagna, a green salad, garlic bread, and a glass of milk. Jane ordered the Caesar salad and a Perrier with lime.

The waiter took our menus. "You know," he said to me, "you look familiar. Are you an actress?"

"Me?" I said. "No. I work for a publishing company." I smiled at Jane.

"Oh," he said. "But I think I know you."

Jane looked up, interested. "I don't think so," I said, looking down at my napkin.

"Really? I don't look familiar to you? Well, it'll come to me. I'll get your drinks," he said. He left the table.

When he was gone, Jane said, "Alice, I want you to know that everyone in the office likes your work very much."

"Thank you," I said. I smiled at her again.

"And I appreciate that you've waited a long time for a promotion, longer than most people in your position and longer than you should have."

"Two and a half years," I reminded her.

"Exactly," Jane said. The waiter returned with our drinks on a small tray. He put down Jane's Perrier. "Thank you," she said.

He put down my milk. "Thank you," I said.

The waiter said, "Do you ride the uptown R train around four-thirty in the afternoons?"

"No," I said.

"I'll get it," he said. "I know I'll get it." He left the table.

Jane wiped off her lipstick with her napkin and took a sip of Perrier. I drank half of my milk. Jane went on. "Under different circumstances, it would be my great pleasure to promote you." I waited, my throat starting to feel squeezed. "It's just that right now, with the budget so tight, we can't promote anybody. It's unfortunate, and I'm extremely sorry about it, but honestly, there's not a thing I can do."

"Oh," I said. "There isn't?"

"No. Sorry." She affected a sad, apologetic smile.

"Oh."

"I wanted to talk to you about it because I know you've expected a promotion. But I can't even say when we would be able to move you up." I drank some more milk. I wanted to run out of the restaurant, but we had a whole lunch to get through. I wished I hadn't ordered so much food. Jane went on. "I know this must be a big disappointment for you. You've worked hard, and you should be rewarded. I would understand completely if you started looking for another job."

"Pardon?" I said.

"If you'd like to send out your résumé, I'll do everything I can to help you get a new position."

"A new position? But I'm going to have a baby in three months. Who would hire me?"

Jane picked up her glass and considered. "Oh, right, I see what you mean. That's a problem."

"Are you saying that I should look for a new job? I mean, are you telling me to move on or something?"

"No, of course not. We'd love to have you forever. It's just that you're very capable and bright, and I can see that you're not, well, satisfied with the work you're doing. It's not enough for you, and that's understandable."

"Satisfied?" I said. "Enough? Well, sure I'd like more money and, you know, a little more of a challenge, and maybe the sense that I was getting somewhere. But I'm satisfied; I mean, it's plenty. It is."

"Some of the editors have mentioned, oh, I don't want to call it an attitude problem, but let's say a little irritability. Now, we all understand that you're going through a difficult time now, but I expect you to behave professionally at all times."

I said, "The editors have complained about me? But what have I done? I thought I was doing a good job for them. I've even answered their phones and done their photocopying and mailing. I take work home every weekend. Who complained? What did they say? Jim, you mean? Because I couldn't do his copies and Fed Ex something for him at five-thirty Friday evening? Was he the one who complained? I was meeting someone. I had to go."

Jane said, "No one complained. That's putting it too strongly. But there were some comments in our meeting yesterday—oh, thank you." Our food had arrived. Jane leaned back in her chair to watch the waiter serve us. He put her enormous wooden salad bowl on the table and a plate in front of her. He set down my lasagna in an oval dish, my salad beside it, and a basket of steaming garlic bread between us. "Would you like fresh pepper?" he asked.

"Yes, please," we said in unison. He stepped away for a moment and returned with a pepper grinder designed for a giant in a fairy tale. He had to step back from the table to aim it at our plates. He gave us each three grinds. "Thank you," we said.

"You're welcome," he said. "You didn't go to high school in Appleton, Wisconsin, did you?"

"No," I said, "I didn't." I made a halfhearted attempt at smiling, but my face wouldn't budge.

He wrinkled his brow, shook his head, and left the table. Jane said, "They always make such a big deal about the pepper. I mean, it's just pepper." She picked up her fork.

"What did the editors say about me?" I said. "I'd like to know."

"Oh, only that you were a little short with them, a little snappish, I guess. I just wanted to say that I'm sorry we can't pay you better and that if you wanted to quit I would understand. But that's entirely up to you. Your decision."

"Short? Snappish?" I said. "But I stay late and do a lot of things for them that are not even my job."

"And I'm sure they appreciate that. I just wanted you to be aware that sometimes it's better for everyone if you don't let all of your true feelings be known."

We started eating and didn't say very much more. I wasn't hungry anymore, so I plowed my way through the food, as if eating it were some required chore. While I was still working on the lasagna, Jane finished her salad and asked the waiter for a telephone. "Sure thing," he said. He brought her a cordless. Jane called someone and started talking—as if she were already back in her office with this lunch behind her—about color separations that didn't look right. The waiter came back and picked up her plate. "I used to have a girlfriend named Jacqueline," he said. "Did I meet you through her?"

"Jacqueline?" I said. My face became hot. I shook my head. I wanted to get out of there. "I'm finished too. You can take all this."

He cleared the table. In a minute he was back with the dessert menu. Jane was still on the phone. "Not for me," I said. Jane shook her head at him and pantomimed writing. He went away to get the check. When he came back she put down her credit card and gave back the phone.

"I just wish we could make you happier," she said, shaking her head.

"I'll be better," I said. "I'll be happier. I promise."

The waiter handed Jane the credit card slip and a pen. She signed. While she was putting her card back in her wallet, he said to me, "This is going to drive me nuts until I get it."

"Let's go," Jane said. Outside, she said, "That guy was very irritating."

"She took you out to lunch to tell you that you're *not* getting a promotion?" I was in Eric's office, with the door shut. He shook his head. "This company smells," he said, shaking his head. "Bad. So bad." He picked up his phone, pushed thirty-one for Dan on the other side of the building. He said into the phone, "Jane took her out to lunch and told her that the editors had complained about her and there wasn't enough money to promote her. . . . I know. Can you believe people? Seriously, I know. . . . No, she's doing

OK." He glanced at me. "Standing right here. Yeah," he said.

"I'm going to leave early," I said. "I have two apartments to look at. Now that I know I'm never getting promoted, it doesn't matter what I do."

"She says she's going to leave early to go look at apartments," Eric said into the phone. "I don't blame her. What were the exact words she used about you?"

"Short and snappish," I said.

"Short and snappish," Eric repeated into the phone, laughing bitterly, shaking his head. "I feel like leaving with her. We should all go. Maybe we can get ourselves fired." I started waving my arms to stop him from inviting Dan. Since Dan had confided his feelings for me and called me at my grandmother's, we both felt awkward when we were together. Sometimes when we were all eating lunch I would look up from my pizza or sandwich to find him staring at me, only to look quickly away. He avoided speaking to me directly, unless he absolutely had to. Once, he left a single pink rose on my desk when I was out of the office. I knew it was from him because I had seen him sneaking out my door. As I waved at Eric on the phone, trying to keep him from encouraging Dan to come, he looked at me questioningly. He didn't get it. "Want to go look at apartments with Alice, Dan? We'll meet you in front of the building." He hung up. "What?" he said. "Why not? Something wrong? Hey, what happened with you guys that night I went to the movies? You can't turn your back for five minutes in this place without something happening that no one is going to tell you about."

"Nothing happened. I just mean it's a lot of people to go look at apartments."

"No it isn't. Just three people. Three is not a lot." Eric marked his place in the galleys he was working on. He looked up. "Really. What's going on?"

I looked him straight in the eye. "Nothing." Then I shifted my eyes to the papers on his desk. "It's just that you guys are very opinionated, and I want to decide about these places alone."

He stood up, opened the office door for me. "Would I try to interfere? Certainly not. I just want to give you my complete and absolute support. Let's go get the Ponytail."

First we took the subway to Astor Place to see the apartment on St. Mark's Place that my sister had told me about, a ground-floor one-bedroom. We waited at the front door for the super. He smelled of old sweat and cigar smoke. I pressed my finger against my top lip to keep from throwing up. I tried to think about something cold and clean to offset the smells: new snow. He unlocked the apartment door and stood back while I walked in, followed by Eric and Dan. "This is for the three of you?" the super said.

"No, just me," I said. "My friends are just keeping me company."

"Oh," he said. He glanced at my stomach. "Whatever." We followed him inside. It smelled of burned food. The current tenants were out but still living there. The place was at the back of the building, which made it dark. The bedroom window was on an air shaft, where the garbage cans were stored. The smell of garbage was thick and deep. "You got your closet over there," the super said. "You got your bathroom through there." He pointed and I went there. The toilet wasn't clean. I vomited several times, flushed, and stayed long enough to run cold water over my hands.

"Well, thank you very much," I said as I came out. I wiped sweat from my forehead with a piece of blue toilet paper I'd pulled off the roll.

Eric said, "Should I get you something?"

Dan said, "You want to sit down?"

"No. I'm fine now," I said.

The super looked nervous. "You sick?"

"Just pregnant," I said.

"OK," he said. "Listen, you want the place, you gotta do something today, miss. We got people lining up for it."

"No, thank you."

"Suit yourself," he said with a shrug.

I hurried out of there. Dan and Eric followed. "Alice, what are you doing? Are you sure?" Eric said. "That place wasn't bad. With someone else's stuff in it, it looked lousy, yeah, but you clear all that out, clean it up a little, and you could make it look nice. You don't want to lose it, Alice. It's *available.* Let's go back. Let's just take one more look around."

Dan said, "It made her throw up. It was dark and smelly in there. She didn't like it."

"But it was available," Eric said. "Don't forget that. We might get up to this other place and find that it's already taken. What do you think, Alice? Let's go back."

"I didn't like it," I said.

"You see," said Dan. "She didn't like it. Don't push her, Eric."

"All right, all right," Eric said.

We got back on the subway at Astor Place and changed at Fourteenth to an express train to Eighty-sixth Street. When we got there, I hurried up the street, with Dan and

Eric following. "This one is on the second floor," I said, pushing the bell when we reached the building.

"Yes?" said a woman's voice over the intercom.

"I'm here to see the apartment?" I said.

"Name?"

"Alice Hammond."

"Yeah, OK." She buzzed the door.

We went upstairs. The woman stood in the doorway. She was wearing a leotard and tights, a sweatband around her forehead, and wrist and ankle weights. She was sweaty and out of breath. "Come in," she said. "What? You're all moving in together?"

"No, it's just for me. These guys are just keeping me company."

"Oh," she said. "Right. OK, take a look around." She turned up some music on the stereo and started doing knee bends and flapping her arms up and down. There were burglar gates on the windows. She pointed to these. "I installed those myself. They're three hundred, if you want the place."

"Three hundred dollars, you mean? For the gates?" I said.

"Right. I paid more. But I never got ripped off, the whole time I was living here, not even once. So think what I saved. All my stuff, first of all. Then there's the stress of being robbed." She switched to running in place and shooting her arms overhead, then down again. "No, I'm serious; it costs a lot more than you think to have someone break into your place."

"I guess so," I said. A dog barked. Even over the music, it sounded like a very big dog, very close by. "What's that?"

"A dog," she said.

"But does it live here in the building?" I said.

"Yeah, right next door. A Doberman. The guy's never here, which is why he has the dog, so it barks all day. It keeps a certain element away, if you know what I mean."

"Like the gates," I said.

"Right," she said. "And see this closet here? One fifty for that. My ex-boyfriend built it. It would cost you a lot more than that to buy one. And the shelf organizers for the kitchen and bathroom are seventy-five. Pretty good deal, if you ask me."

Eric opened the closet. Some scarves and gloves fell out on his head. "Sorry," he said. He picked them up and started folding them, peering into the closet.

Dan went to the kitchen, opened a drawer, a cupboard, the refrigerator.

"Bathroom?" Eric said to the woman. She pointed. Eric and Dan went to look at the bathroom. They stood in the doorway. The dog was still barking.

"No tub," Dan said to Eric. "Just a shower."

"Do you take baths, Alice?" Eric said. "Or just showers?"

"Well, wait a minute," Dan said. "She's going to have a baby. You need a bathtub for a baby."

Eric said, "But don't they have those little plastic tubs for babies?" He gestured with his hands. "I think I've seen those somewhere."

"Maybe you're right," Dan said, nodding. They both poked their heads into the bathroom one more time.

"Excuse me," I said. "May I see the bathroom?"

"Oh, right," Eric said, backing out.

"Sure," said Dan. "You might be able to put some shelves over the toilet there. I could help you, if you want."

I backed out of the bathroom. "Thank you for showing it to me," I said to the woman as we left.

We walked back to the subway. There were no seats. We all stood, holding on to a pole. This was another express train, going very fast. It was hard to keep my balance, hard even to fit my big stomach in between all the people. Someone tapped on my shoulder. "Would you like a seat?"

"Thank you," I said, "yes." I sat down before I realized who had given up his seat: the waiter from my lunch with Jane.

"Hi," he said. He stood in front of me, holding a bar overhead. Dan and Eric moved over to the bar too. "You again. Who are you anyway?"

"Alice," I said.

"Joe," he said.

Eric and Dan looked at him sideways. I had to yell in the noisy train. I said, "You directed my boyfriend—my ex-boyfriend—in a play a couple of years ago. His name is Nick."

Joe's eyes widened. "Nick. *Nick.*" He put a hand over his face. "Nick and my girlfriend Jacqueline were having an affair for a year before I found out about it. *A year.*" He pursed his lips and shook his head. Eric looked at Dan, then back at Joe, waiting to hear more. "For a while, I wanted to rip his face off, but I think I'm getting better." He looked around wildly for a few seconds, as if Nick might be lurking in the crowd somewhere.

"I'm sorry," I said. "I didn't know about it, either." The train stopped and some people got out. The waiter sat down next to me. "It takes a long time to get going again," I said. "Nick and I split up a few months ago, and I'm still looking for a place."

"And you're pregnant. The man is low. *Low.*"

"We didn't know I was pregnant when we split up."

"So that makes it OK, I guess?" Joe shook his head. "And here you are, out looking for an apartment? All alone?"

"No," I said. "These guys went with me." I gestured to Eric and Dan. Eric gave a little wave. Joe nodded at him. I told him about the apartment with the gates, the closet, the shelf organizers, and the dog next door.

"You don't have to pay for that stuff," Joe said. "If you want the apartment, take it, and just don't speak to this woman again."

"Yeah," Eric said. "That's not legal, what she's trying to do there."

"I'm not going to take the apartment. There's a big, barking dog in the next apartment. I'm going to have a baby, who will need to sleep. I might want to sleep occasionally myself. This dog sounded huge and ferocious. It was a Doberman, all cooped up in a tiny apartment. No wonder it was barking. I'm not living there."

"Listen, Alice. This is New York," Eric said.

"Yeah," said Joe. "You live here, you have to put up with a lot of shit."

"I realize that," I said. "I know, but—"

"But she can choose which shit she's willing to put up with," Dan said. I looked at him. "Right, Alice? Isn't that what you were going to say?"

I said, "I guess so."

The train stopped at Grand Central. Eric, Dan, and Joe stayed on. I got off. "See you," Joe called. "Good luck with everything."

"You too."

Dan waved.

"So long, Alice," said Eric. "See you tomorrow."

"See you." I fast-walked to the Times Square shuttle, then had to wait fifteen minutes until it came. I waited again for the train to Penn Station, which arrived full of people. I squeezed on. I was afraid I was going to miss the train I usually took to Long Island. My grandmother would be annoyed. She would be sitting in the dark in front of the TV. She would say something like "Well, it's about time" or "I'd just about given you up for dead." I got off at Thirty-fourth and hurried up the stairs, then past Macy's, which seemed to go on and on. I tried to run down the escalator in Penn Station, but I was afraid to. Given my size, this might be dangerous. I did run from the escalator, past the ticket windows and onto the platform. I got there just as my train was about to pull out. The conductor saw me running and waited before closing the doors, which had never happened before. I must look big and pathetic, I thought.

There was one seat, in the back near the bathroom, where it smelled awful. I was out of breath, which on top of the bathroom smell made me nauseous. I could stand the smell of old urine, I thought, if I could just catch my breath and not smell anything else disgusting before I recovered. I sat down between a woman reading a newspaper and a man eating a sausage sub. In the close quarters of the train, I was getting sweaty and had to take my coat off. The sandwich smelled strong, and I thought I might vomit. The woman next to me had her paper spread out all over, which would make it impossible to get out of my seat fast. I took Dan's handkerchief out of my coat pocket. I kept forgetting to give it back to him. I pressed it against my nose and mouth and closed my eyes. My hair felt wet with sweat. My hands and feet were hot. If I could just throw up and get some cold water on my hands, I would feel a lot better.

The woman next to me nudged my elbow. "Deep breaths in through your nose and out through your mouth. Here," she said. She handed me a package of saltines, the kind that came with soup. "I'm a labor and delivery nurse."

"Feeling sick?" said the man with the sandwich. "Let me get out of here." He stepped over us, holding his sandwich high above his head. "My wife was the same way with both our kids. You're going to have a girl," he said, and I chose to believe him. "I'll just get this stinker out of your range." He went to the other end of the train. I couldn't say thank you; opening my mouth would have been risky.

I ate the crackers and started to feel better. "Thanks," I said to the woman next to me. "That really helped."

"Here." She pulled a can of 7-Up out of her bag. "Would you like this?"

"Thank you so much." I pulled the tab.

"The sugar helps. You were hungry, right? A couple of months, and this will all be over."

"Three," I said. "Three more months."

She looked at my stomach. "Three? Are you sure?" She picked up her paper again.

"Where are you going to live is what I want to know," Gram said.

"Something will turn up," I said, but I doubted it myself.

"It's going to have to," said Gram. "The child is not going to wait, and you are not going to stay with me. I'm too old to put up with a screaming, miserable infant."

"So you've mentioned. I'm not going to stay here. It's too far from work, for one thing." I didn't go into the other things. There were too many, and I was hungry. I walked past her to the kitchen.

"I talked to someone else I'm not going to hire today," Gram shouted after me. She was interviewing women to take care of her and not doing much better than I was with apartments. One wanted to go home at three every day and not work Fridays or weekends. Some had never had this kind of job before and had no references. Several didn't drive.

"What was wrong with this one?"

"She didn't want to do anything upstairs. It seems she has a heart condition too. That's all I need is to worry about somebody dropping dead on me."

Later, I called my sister to tell her about my lunch with Jane and to say that the apartment she told me about wasn't going to work out. I got her answering machine. I said, "It's me. I'll call back." For the briefest moment, I thought about calling Nick. But even I could see that this was out of the question now.

I went upstairs to my room and sat on the bed. My hands and feet were swollen. When I took my shoes off, they left deep indentations on my feet. There was a watch-shaped impression on my wrist. My face was puffy.

If I weren't pregnant, I would have quit my job right away, even before looking for another one. The fact was that disappointment was not all I was feeling. I was sorry I wasn't getting a raise, but I was also relieved about not getting a promotion. I didn't want to do more advanced work with textbooks. I wanted to do something else, but I didn't know what.

When I was little, my mother had had this same problem. In high school and college, she had wanted to be an actress. But my grandmother had teased her, damaging her self-confidence beyond repair. "Gram can be very unkind," my mother told me more than once. "There are some things that you can never let her know about you. You have to protect yourself."

My father didn't understand the way my grandmother could cut into my mother's very heart, depressing her for days with a single offhand comment. "Ignore her," he would say. "Just don't pay any attention."

For several years, my mother tried to find some kind of work that she liked. She helped my father in his dry-cleaning store while she took classes at the community college in French and gourmet cooking, came close to opening a travel agency that specialized in trips for college students, and got a license to sell real estate. When a group of local people started a theater company, my mother got involved. She was helping one of the actresses with a quick change from a hobo costume in one number into an evening dress for the next, when she realized what she wanted to do. "It was just clothes and makeup and fake jewelry," she told me, "but this woman seemed to transform completely from one person into someone else. In a flash." She snapped her fingers. "Like that. At the end of the evening, we hung up those costumes, and she was Terry Reed again, the girls' gym teacher at the junior high. To me, it was magic the way a person could change that way on the outside while staying whole and unaffected inside."

When I was ten, my mother opened a costume shop. She designed and constructed many of the costumes herself. Her first big custom job was to make four doughnut costumes for the employees of a local bakery to wear in a parade. She continued to outfit the theater group and its productions of *The Skin of Our Teeth* and *A Midsummer Night's Dream*. She designed and custom-made costumes for people to wear to parties. When she was working at the sewing machine or behind the counter in the shop, she always wore a costume herself. You would see her at the 7-Eleven nearby, buying a Coke, all dressed up as a penguin or a belly dancer or a football player. Once, I fell at school and had to get stitches in my knee. My mother came screeching down to the junior high dressed as a court jester. I made her take the hat with the bells off before she walked me into the emergency room. "Oh," she said, "sorry, peaches. Did I embarrass you? God, I'll have to watch that."

The costume shop was in walking distance of my school. Every day, I had to go there and stay with my mother until it was time to close. She gave me little sewing and finishing jobs to do. And I put on a lot of costumes, so that my mother could see what they looked like. I modeled a giant foam hot dog, and she squinted at it, saying, "Do you think it needs more relish?" A small tuxedo fit me just right. It had a magician's top hat with a cloth rabbit that could be turned inside out to make a dove. There was a Cinderella ball gown that snapped apart to reveal a rag dress underneath. "Not fast enough," my mother said, timing me, and she replaced the snaps with fewer, bigger ones. I sewed in a special pocket for one of the plastic shoes that looked just like the glass slippers I had imagined in the story.

I thought my mother was brilliant, the way she could turn a piece of flat cloth into a glittering gown or the head of a beast. But her triumph came during the time when I was mad at her. I never got to tell her that I thought she was a genius, that I was proud she was my mother.

Laura didn't hang around the shop the way I did. She was old enough to take the bus home and stay by herself until dinnertime. Besides, she got claustrophobic sitting amid the costumes squashed on crowded racks. And she didn't like our mother working dressed up. "Can't you just put on a skirt and blouse and a pair of nylons? Do you have to get dressed up and act like a clown all the time?"

"Yes, I do, dear heart," our mother said. "People need to see that whoever you are inside, putting on a costume can make you look like anything at all. Why, you can scare people to death, get people to believe in a product, make them laugh or cry, anything you want, and still protect that special *you* inside and keep all your secrets." She laughed with delight. "A costume is really a wonderful thing. Now, some people worry about looking silly. They'll go to a costume party in their old graduation cap and gown. They need a little help. And this is why I dress up every day—to show that it's just the *costume* that is silly. The costume will be silly *for* you—or scary or glamorous. What people may see is a walking, dancing hot dog. But underneath is you, unchanged and giving away nothing."

By the time the shop had been open three years, my mother was a big success, organizing theme parties, costuming trade show productions, and doing a successful rental business. The home ec teacher invited her to talk to our class about other uses for sewing skills beyond making and mending your own clothes. She was on a local TV talk show about successful women in business.

At Thanksgiving dinner at Gram's one year, my father mentioned that two of the costumes had won prizes in a masquerade ball in New Orleans. My grandmother, who had given my mother two thousand dollars to open the shop, said, "Now that you're such a hot ticket, maybe I can get my money back. I need new carpeting downstairs."

My mother had looked down at the food on her plate. My father said, "Lydia, you got your money back two years ago. Don't you remember?"

"Oh, right. I forgot," Gram said, putting another big glob of cranberry sauce on her plate.

All the way home on the plane, my mother cried. Gram never said anything kind or congratulatory about her original ideas or her ability to make a profit. My grandfather was dead by then. He would have toasted my mother at dinner that night and told her that he always knew she was going to be a big deal. He would have visited her shop and let her show him the costumes she had made herself and the ones she had bought for practically nothing, then fixed up until they were outstanding. He would have hugged her and said, "Wonderful job, angel, beautiful work."

Instead, my father did this. "Have you met my wife, proprietor of our city's most innovative new business? This woman has talent that is not to be believed." And he said to my mother privately, at home, "Did it ever occur to you that your mother is jealous of your success because her own career never quite panned out?"

"Oh, Jack," my mother said, blinking. "That's not— she never—she was a big success in Hollywood, beautiful and working. She got married, and then I was born and Louise, and she gave it all up for us."

"First of all, she was never beautiful. No." He shook his head. "Look at the pictures, Carrie. She was never attractive. She was downright homely. That's why she needed all the makeup and clothes and fooled around with her hair so much. You know, like a costume, to cover up.

Second, she only had a few small parts in a few mediocre movies in a period of just three years or so. From that little, short experience, she has told the same ten or twelve stories over and over again for forty years. She's gotten a lifetime of wear out of a few scraps of material. She couldn't cut it in the movies, so she got married and had some kids."

My mother sat with her mouth open. Then she said, "I just don't see how you can say that. You simply don't know what you're talking about."

This was the way I remembered their discussion anyway. They never agreed about my grandmother. Now I knew that they were both partly wrong, knowing just some of the story. They didn't know about her broken heart or her baby that was taken away from her or her parents stealing her money and keeping her from going back to Hollywood. And I wondered how much of what I thought I knew about *my* parents was actually true.

I wished I had a tape of my mother talking about her costume shop, to find out if what I thought she said was actually what she said or if I had changed it in some way. There may have been more to it than I remembered. Maybe she said something then that I had tuned out, something I needed to know now. My mother was always talking about the way costumes allowed people to keep their secrets. And I had become the kind of person people told secrets to. I wished for the millionth time that I could hear her talk again. I would like to have a tape of her speaking about herself, like the one I had made of Gram, something I could always refer to, to be sure that what I remembered her saying was what she actually said. Often I imagined the costumes my mother was so crazy about hanging in a dark storage warehouse—the chiffon and the burlap, the fake fur and the lace—the materials she worked with so intensely, which must be the only things left on earth that contained some truth about her.

I took off my clothes to change for bed. There was a mirror on the back of the door, where I studied my big body. Beneath my breasts was a red line, an upside-down U-shaped crease outlining the top of my uterus, where my skin had folded while I was sitting down. The rest of my torso was a smooth white lump of belly, right down to the triangle of my pubic hair. Now, as I watched, there was a sudden frenzy of movement. The lump shifted and shuddered of its own accord, small hard knobs near the top seeming to try to bang their way out through my skin, then it quieted and settled down again. In contrast to this expanse, my thighs looked thin, sticklike and insubstantial, hardly capable of supporting their tremendous load. I didn't see how I could grow much more without bursting open in the middle. I reached for a flowered flannel nightgown, too hot for tonight but gathered at the neck and billowing, tentlike, to the hem, the only thing I had left that covered everything. I lay down on the bed, exhausted and grateful for the arrival of night, thankful that at least for the next several hours I wouldn't have to carry around my huge, heavy stomach or try to solve any problems. I closed my eyes.

Ten

HORMONES

OURTH OF JULY," Gram was saying. "I arrived in Hollywood on the Fourth of July. I'll never forget it." She tipped her head back and gazed off into the distance as if she were an actress in a movie, setting up a flashback. "It was hot as all get-out. I had sat up on the train all the way from Iowa." She stopped and slid her eyes sideways to look at me without moving her head. "Where's your tape recorder? Go get it."

"You know, I'd like to, Gram, but I'm supposed to be proofreading a bibliography."

"If they're not going to promote you, why do the extra work?" she said, frowning at me.

"How did you know they weren't going to promote me?"

"I heard you talking to Laura." She held up her hand. "I know what you're going to say. You have no privacy here; it's terrible. Now get that tape recorder, please. One of these days you'll be glad you did it."

"You're amazing," I said and went upstairs.

When I got back, Gram said, "You know what would be better?"

"What?"

"A video camera. Much better. I could get dressed up, put on a little makeup. It would be wonderful."

"Gee, Gram, why don't you hire a camera crew, with lights and everything."

"Wouldn't that be expensive?" she said, narrowing her eyes. She shook her head. "Just a video camera and a tripod would be enough. Now, who has one?" She tapped a manicured finger against her chin. The fingernail, much longer than I ever managed to get mine, was painted with Raving Red polish, especially for the holiday. The color went perfectly with the red, white, and blue dress she was going to wear. Underneath the polish, her nails were thick and yellowed. "I can't think of a soul," she said. "Can you?"

"Maybe Aunt Louise and Uncle Richard have one," I said. They were coming later today for a Fourth of July dinner. My cousins and my sister and their husbands were coming too. Aunt Louise and Uncle Richard had returned from their long trip to Europe a few days before and were going to tell us about it, then, if it didn't rain, we would go to see the fireworks at the recreation center nearby. Talking about the holiday had triggered the reminiscence about Gram's arrival in Hollywood.

"Louise and Richard?" Gram said. "Are you kidding me? Changing the channel on the TV with the remote control is almost beyond them. They could never figure out a video camera."

"OK. We don't know anyone who has one, then. You want to tape this story or not? Because I have work to do."

"Sure. But it would really be better if we had a video camera. Maybe one of your friends has one."

"Not that I know of."

"Hm," Gram said. She paused, looking down at the buttons on her dress for a moment, as if getting into character. She lifted her head. "You can switch it on now." I pushed the Play and Record.

"I arrived in Hollywood on the Fourth of July, 1931. I got off the train, and my clothes were soaked with sweat. I had sat up all the way from Iowa, and I was exhausted. Everything was closed for the holiday, of course. I hadn't figured on that when I bought my ticket. I got a cab and asked the driver if he knew a place I could stay. Imagine how stupid that was, not to even have a place lined up ahead of time. Well, he did know one. It was a boardinghouse owned by a big fat woman named Esther, the cabdriver's sister. She didn't want to take me that day because she said with all the stores closed, she didn't think she would have enough food. I cried and told her I had nowhere to go, that I was tired. I put on the best innocent-bumpkin act I could muster. The cabdriver put in a word or two for my side. In the end, I agreed to pay an extra two dollars for the first week because I was moving in on a holiday. As it turned out, they were the better actors. I saw them do that same routine with seven or eight other girls: two dollars more because it was after four in the afternoon, two dollars because it was a weekend, because Esther would have to set another place at the table, do extra washing. They split the money. It was the Depression, and a dollar could make a difference.

"I stayed three years. Esther cooked big dinners for the

boarders: pork sausages, gravy, potatoes. Lots of cheap, fattening food, loaded with cholesterol. My mouth is watering just thinking about it.

"My friend at Esther's was Pauline. She was a secretary for a law firm. When she was a child she'd had scarlet fever and lost her eyelashes. As a substitute, she drew a brown line around her eyelids, top and bottom, every morning."

The phone rang. "Damn it, who is that?" Gram lifted the receiver. "Hello?" she said and smiled graciously as if welcoming an out-of-town guest. "Why, yes," she said. "One moment, please." She put a hand over the receiver. "A *man*," she said. My heart started to pound. "Not Nick," she said.

"Oh," I said, trying not to look disappointed. "Hello?"

"Hi, Alice. This is Dan."

"Oh, hi, Dan. How are you?"

"Fine, thanks." Lately Dan was everywhere. He always seemed to be behind me in line at the deli at lunch or the pizza shop or even the falafel place ten blocks away from our office. When I walked to the train after work, he was suddenly beside me, offering to carry my things. Now he had started calling every weekend, just to talk, to see how I was doing.

Gram hissed, "Isn't that the one who takes pictures all the time? Ask him if he has a video camera."

I didn't even look at her. "How's your holiday going?"

"It's deserted in the city," Dan said. "Everyone's gone for the weekend."

Gram said, "I certainly would like to borrow a video camera." She used her full voice this time, deep and loud.

Dan said, "What was that about a video camera?"

"Ignore that background noise," I said. "My grandmother wants to borrow a video camera for this little project we have. But she can't think of anybody who has one. Never mind. So what's up?" I was trying to hurry him along, get him off the phone.

"I do have a video camera. I never use it. You're welcome to borrow it. Do you want me to bring it out?"

"No. Certainly not," I said.

"I don't mind. No trouble. I could be out there in, let's see, an hour and a half?"

"No, please," I said. Then I worried that my voice had sounded a little too urgent. "I mean, I wouldn't know how to work it or anything."

Gram said, "He has one? I knew it."

Dan said, "I'll show you how. It's really simple."

I said, "Thanks for the offer. I appreciate it. But really, you don't want to come out here. It's such a long way."

Gram said, "What? Come out here? We'll give him lunch. Yes, tell him to come." She was practically yelling.

Dan said, "Just give me the address."

I gave it to him. After I hung up, I said, "Gram, don't do that again."

"Do what?" she said. "He offered. And he's obviously lonely and has nothing to do, or he wouldn't be calling you on the Fourth of July. Would he?"

"You have such a flattering way of putting things. I don't feel like spending my weekend with someone from work, and I think it was pushy of you to ask to borrow his camera."

She held up both hands. "Well, pardon my polished silver buttons," she said. "If I'd known this was one of your emotional days, I would never have mentioned it. Never in a thousand years. I was the same way when I was pregnant. Just flew off the handle at the slightest provocation. It's just hormones, Alice, that's all it is."

I went upstairs. I picked up the bibliography I had brought out to work on, but put it down immediately. What difference did it make now when I got my work done? Gram was right. I took one of Gram's books from the bookcase, the autobiography of a starlet I'd never heard of. I read a page and felt suddenly too sleepy to continue. I was tired and slow all the time now. And hungry. The baby seemed to grow bigger almost by the hour, her head like a hard round rock wedged into my pelvis; her arms and legs all over the place all day and night; her bottom up to the center of my rib cage, causing me to be short of breath even when sitting down and doing nothing; her shifts, twists, and shudders so large now that I truly felt my body was occupied by somebody with her own strong will.

I closed my eyes, just for a minute, and when I opened them again I heard voices downstairs, my grandmother talking to a man. I looked at my watch. I had slept over an hour in the middle of the morning. Dan was downstairs. I got up quickly, worried about what Gram was saying to him. He had that ponytail, and he would probably be wearing some Hawaiian shirt with big purple flowers all over it. She would comment on his appearance without any concern for his feelings. Or worse, she would be talking to him about me and my swollen feet, my unflattering wardrobe.

When I came into the living room, they both turned toward me, smiling. Gram was using the smile she saved for men. She craned her neck toward him and tilted her head to one side. Someone in Hollywood had once told her that she had a lovely long neck. Since then she had tried to stretch it upward to full extension whenever she remembered, but usually it drooped, causing her head to lean out from the rest of her body, like a long-stemmed flower wilting over the edge of a vase. "Here's Sleeping Beauty," Gram said.

"I wasn't asleep. Hi, Dan."

"Hi," Dan said.

"Alice, your hair's squashed on one side, and you have pillowcase wrinkles on your face," Gram said. "You were asleep."

"You look pretty," Dan said quietly.

"Thank you," I said. I felt myself turning red.

"What?" said Gram. Then, when he didn't answer, she said, "What did he say?"

"Is that the camera?" I said to Dan. There was a black case near the door.

"Yes," he said. "It's really easy to use." He picked up the case, sat on the couch next to Gram, and pulled out the camera and a collapsible tripod.

"Alice, what are you thinking? You haven't offered your guest a thing to eat or drink. Why don't you make us some of your delicious cookies?"

"My delicious cookies?" I said. "What are you talking about?"

My grandmother glared at me. "Oh, Alice, don't be so silly. Why, you have the dough all ready."

"Uh," I said. "Right. Oh, sure. Dan, do you want some cookies?"

"Don't go to any trouble," he said.

"It's no trouble. They're frozen," I said. My grandmother clicked her tongue. "I'll be right back." I could hear them talking from the kitchen.

"You have a nice house, Mrs. Williams," I heard Dan

say, as he pulled open Velcro and took things out of the case. "How old is it?"

"Over a hundred years. When we first came out here, it was nothing but fields. Nothing but fields. Now I've got neighbors who have been here almost forty years, and they still seem like newcomers to me. You know that gas station and the twenty-four-hour market you passed on the way in? There used to be a blacksmith who lived right there. Imagine. This was just a farmhouse. We added the bathrooms upstairs and the dining room. We built the garage. The house is completely changed. We bought it such a long time ago, and it was old then. Inside, I feel the same as when I was seventeen or seven. And here I am an old lady. Did Alice tell you about the tapes we've been making?"

"No, she didn't," Dan said.

"Well, then I will. She's gotten me to tell some of my recollections on tape for her to save. Of course, who's going to want to hear an old woman talk about her days in Hollywood about a thousand years ago? I keep asking her, but she's just convinced they'll have some merit. She insists we get everything down. She thinks they would mean an awful lot to her baby someday. Now she wants us to use a video camera. It will give a much deeper effect, she thinks." I looked out through the kitchen door. Gram was blinking and looking down at her hands, like a shy ingenue. "I might as well go along with it, if it's that important to her."

"You were in Hollywood? Were you an actress? Wow," Dan said.

"Oh, yes," said Gram. "I made twelve pictures in the thirties. Maybe you've seen them. Do you ever watch old films?"

"I majored in film at UCLA," Dan said. He was leaning toward her, hooked. "I'm really interested."

"Then maybe you'll enjoy our little taping today." She smiled. "I'm so glad you came."

"Would you like something to drink?" I said.

"Sure," Dan said. "Some water?"

"We have tea, coffee, soda, juice," my grandmother said.

"Just some water, thanks," Dan said.

"I'll have a glass of that apple juice," Gram yelled at me. "And not a great big glass. A juice glass. Why do you think they call them that? She's always giving me these enormous glasses of juice. It's just wasted." I came out with the water and a tiny glass of juice. "Are those cookies burning? I smell them."

"They have three more minutes."

"I don't like them too crunchy, you know. And how about putting them on a plate this time, instead of some old paper towel the way you usually do."

Dan smiled at me. He looked around for a coaster for his water glass and found one. It was a square piece of wood painted black, with a picture of grazing horses on it. The picture was peeling off, curling up. With a guest here, I was more aware of how run-down the place looked, how messy. The fabric on the armchairs and couch—a hunting scene in red on a white background—was gray with age and dirt, especially on the arms. The lampshade next to my grandmother's place on the couch had been ripped for a long time, a three-inch section of gold trim dangling. On the table next to her was an impossible mound of clutter— out-of-date *TV Guides*, candy wrappers, crumpled grocery coupons. Her cup of coffee, cold for hours now—instant

Taster's Choice with a splash of milk and three saccharin tablets—was still there from early morning. She liked to sip it all day long and refused to give it up until bedtime. A table in front of one window was covered with plants that were in a sorry state of thirst and malnutrition. And the carpet, a dull gray-green, was spotted from years of badly cleaned-up spills.

I brought out the cookies on a dinner plate. "Oh, Alice, we have nicer plates than that," Gram said, as I offered Dan a cookie and a napkin.

When it was her turn, she took three cookies. "Over-done," she said with her mouth full. "I told you."

"Delicious," Dan said. "You made these yourself?"

"God, no. The dough is frozen. You buy it already formed into the right-size globs and then just bake them. If you don't eat them right away, they turn into cardboard." I said. My grandmother gave me a disgusted look, as if I was such a hopeless case she didn't know why she wasted her time trying to help me. "I hardly know how to cook anything," I said.

"I don't cook much myself," Dan said.

"She may not cook, but she sure can eat. Look at her. What does the doctor say about all the weight you've gained, Alice?"

Dan said, "I think she looks great," and smiled at me again. My grandmother snorted.

I said, "Maybe we should get started with the video taping. I'm sure Dan has better things to do than sit around here all afternoon."

"No, I don't. I'm really enjoying this. Take your time."

Gram put on a lot more makeup while we got set up. In the drawer beside her, she had a cosmetic bag so jammed with bottles and tubes she couldn't snap it shut. Dan was right; the camera was easy to operate. I got it up on the tripod, and he showed me what to push to start recording and how to zoom in for a close-up. That was about all there was to it. It focused automatically and adjusted itself for available light. "Now, this is a two-hour tape," Dan said, "but the battery pack will last only about half an hour. I don't know how much you plan to say, Mrs. Williams, but if you're still going when the battery pack runs out, we can take a short break, put in this other pack, and keep going. I brought you some extra tapes, for later. You plug the battery pack into this thing to recharge it. I'll just leave the stuff out here for a while. I never use it."

"That's very nice of you," Gram said. "Let's get started."

Dan said, "Will I be distracting? Shall I go?"

Gram said, "Oh, I love an audience. You stay. That's fine by me." She repeated everything we had taped that morning and elaborated. She was good, looking straight into the camera, as if speaking to a dear, close friend she hadn't seen in years. For most of the time, I peered through the viewfinder at her, zooming in on her face when her expression intensified, backing up to get her hands when she gestured. She mentioned being on location in Nevada. "That's where I got my first diamond."

"Who gave it to you?" I said.

"A beau of mine," she said.

"What was his name?"

"Oh, all right. It was your grandfather."

"My grandfather? What was he doing in Reno in—what year did you say that was—1932?"

She sighed and looked out at the driveway. "He was

getting a divorce from his first wife." I went in for a close-up.

"I thought you said she died," I said.

"I did say that. She left him for someone else. I don't think he ever got over it. Anyhow, that was what he was doing in Reno. He decided to attach himself to me as an antidote. He kept coming out to California for the next year or so. Of course, I was stuck on Walker, then I was pregnant and then miserable after my baby was adopted. So it was two more years before we got married and moved here."

We used up the whole two-hour tape. When we finished, Dan said, "Ladies, you're quite a team." I started packing everything back into the case.

"How come you never told us Grandpa was divorced?" I said.

"I didn't want you to know," Gram said. She looked hard at my face. "I don't know how you do it, but you make me tell things. You're good at this. I'm not sure where it's going to get you. But you're good."

I straightened up, stunned that she had given me a compliment—and in front of a witness. I said, "Gram, that's so nice of you to say."

"Yes, well, let's not get all choked up about it," Gram said. Then she said to Dan, "She's very emotional lately. It's just the hormones, you know. They go crazy when a woman's expecting."

Dan said, "I think she's good at this too. I'm not surprised at all." The two of us put things away, while Gram got up and went to the bathroom. He said, "Alice, would you like to go somewhere—for a drive or something? We could get some lunch."

"A drive?" I said. "Lunch? Well, actually, I was working

on a bibliography. It has to be back to the author by Wednesday. He's really fussy, Jane says."

"I think you're taking these deadlines too literally. Maybe he'll be relieved if it comes back a little late. He might not be ready for it," Dan said. "And maybe if Jane had given you that promotion you were supposed to get about a year ago, it might make sense to keep working this way. We could go to the beach."

"Really, no, thanks," I said.

"The beach?" Gram said, returning. "Sounds nice. Go. Have fun."

"It's going to rain," I said. "And I'm really tired."

"You don't have to go bodysurfing," Gram said. "I'll be fine. Goodbye."

Dan said, "Just for a little while."

"I have to get my—"

"You don't need to take anything," Gram said. "Just go."

Dan's car was a flesh-colored Mercury Zephyr. It had already started to drizzle when we started off. There were tiny dots of water on the windshield. Dan drove slowly, as if in the style of his grandfather, who had left him the car five years before. On the expressway, people passed us on both sides. His driving made me nervous. I tried to look out the window and not notice what he was doing.

"Great house," he said.

"My grandmother's? I guess, but it's kind of a wreck now."

"Is it? I thought it was cozy."

"Well, it's a mess. And she never gets anything fixed. She doesn't like to spend money, so every year it gets a little worse. The roof was leaking, so her bedroom ceiling got a big brown stain on it. She should have had the whole roof replaced—God knows how old it is—but she didn't want to pay for it. She just had the cheapest asphalt shingle put on one section. So now the roof is old curling wood shake on about two-thirds of the house and green asphalt shingle on the part where the leak was. And of course, she never got the bedroom ceiling fixed or painted or anything. She has a certain amount of money, and she doesn't know how long she's going to have to make it last, of course. So she never wants to spend anything."

Dan said, "I didn't notice the roof. It must be scary to think you might run out of money before you die. My grandfather was the same way."

"Oh."

We drove to a beach with a playground. I had never been to it before. There were a couple of cars, but we didn't see any people. A snack stand looked open, though I couldn't see anyone inside. We got out and walked toward the swings, but the rain came down harder, so we went back to the car.

I thought Dan was going to turn on the engine and drive back, but he started talking instead. "When my sister and I were little, our parents left us with our grandparents for a week every year. We hated it. They brought us to this beach a lot, and we stuffed ourselves on hot dogs, because we didn't like our grandmother's cooking. We just missed our parents. Sometimes I still miss them, but they only live in Nyack, so I see them pretty often."

This was the most I had ever heard Dan say about himself. I said, "So you've always had a close relationship with your parents?"

"No," he said. "In high school, I hated them. They're

high school teachers. My mother teaches biology and my father teaches English. Lots of the kids I went to school with used to hang out at our house because they liked my parents. These kids would confide their secrets at our kitchen table, things I couldn't even begin to discuss. It made me feel lonely and cut off. Once, I ran away. I came out here and stayed with my grandparents. I think they were flattered that I picked them to run away to. They let my parents know where I was and told me I could stay as long as I wanted to. My grandfather made a big fuss over some pictures I had taken with my little Instamatic. He bought me a used twin-lens reflex for twenty dollars. You know what that is? The kind with two lenses. You look in the top to see what you're photographing. The negatives are big, so you get nice detail. Anyhow, he gave me the camera and told me I was a photographer. And I believed him. For a few days I took a lot of pictures of my grand-parents and came here to this beach and took what I thought were artsy pictures of that snack place closed up for the winter. It was over there then, and a lot smaller." He pointed. "I took pictures of the swings and the signs and the water. I stayed for a week. I came out here feeling lonely and cut off and like a loser, and I went home thinking I was a photographer. I still felt lonely and cut off, but having the camera made all the difference."

"So that's how you started taking pictures," I said.

Dan nodded, then looked embarrassed. "How did I get on that?" He looked at me, anxious to shift our attention to something else. "So," he said. "Are you excited about the baby coming? It's pretty soon now, isn't it?"

"Oh, let's not talk about that," I snapped without mean-ing to. "I'm sick of the whole subject." I looked out at the rain, and a big sadness, coming from several directions at once, dropped down over me. Sitting here with someone I didn't know very well made me miss Nick, whose life was almost as familiar to me as my own. I had no business having a baby when I knew nothing about it. I needed a place to live and a better-paying job that meant something.

Dan leaned toward me. He was going to kiss me or pat my shoulder or brush my hair off my face. I shifted away from him, pretending to look for something in my pocket. "I want to go home," I said before I could stop myself. "Would you mind going back, since it's raining and everything?"

"Back to your grandmother's? Sure. You OK?"

"Yes," I said. "Fine. A little sad, maybe. It's probably the rain or, I don't know, hormones. Could we just go now?"

"Certainly," he said quietly. He started the car.

We drove back, hardly speaking. It took forty minutes. The rain was coming down so hard that he had to drive even slower than he had before. Once, he said, "You sure you're OK?"

"Positive." What I felt was a kind of bottomless despair.

"That videotape was a great idea. I wish I had done that when my grandfather was alive."

I said, "It wasn't my idea. My grandmother made me do it. It wasn't her idea, either. She saw it on TV. I didn't know my grandfather was married before. She tells me secrets. Every time I do this, some big secret comes out. I don't know why."

"People trust you," he said. "I had a girlfriend, Nancy, who was a scientist. We lived together for a couple of years. We had been going out for three months before she told me she had once been married. Having people want to open up to you is a gift, Alice. Not everyone has it."

"That's one way of looking at it," I said. "Sometimes the people least likely to confide in you are those you want to hear from most." I was thinking of Nick before we broke up. "Where is she now?"

"Nancy?" he said. "She lives in Switzerland. She got offered a job there, and she took it."

"You didn't want to go?" I said.

"No," Dan said. "I wasn't invited, either." He shrugged. "I felt like I was going to die for three or four months after she left, but look—" He glanced down at his shirt. "I didn't. And I still have the TV she couldn't take with her."

"Consolation prize," I said.

"That's right."

I looked at him. He kept his eyes on the road. We pulled into my grandmother's driveway. Aunt Louise and Uncle Richard's car was there already. Dan turned off the engine, as if he was going to stay. "Alice," he said, "I think I'm in love with you."

I said, "No, you're not. You don't even know me. You see me at work. If you got to know me, you'd realize that I'm not what you think I am at all. I'm a slob, which would get on your nerves after a while. I'm not even very nice, and I have no clear sense of direction. In another month, I'll have a baby. You don't want to get mixed up in all this." I looked over my shoulder at my grandmother's windows. Gram would be watching me sitting out here with Dan, maybe speculating with Aunt Louise about what we were saying and doing.

Dan said, "I like babies. I do."

"I'm sorry. My aunt and uncle are here, and I really

should be inside, helping. Could we talk about this another time? Thanks for the drive. I'll see you soon. OK?"

Dan sighed. "See you Tuesday."

I sprang out the door and walked fast toward the house as he drove away. I said hello to my aunt and uncle and went upstairs to my room and closed the door. I put my hands over my face for a minute until I got my bearings again.

"In my day, twenty pounds was the limit. The absolute limit." Aunt Louise was getting dinner ready, chopping chives for her famous potato salad. "Dr. Grant would have hit the ceiling if I'd gained any more than that." She opened a drawer and closed it again. "There isn't a decent knife in this kitchen. Both times, after the baby, I went home from the hospital in my regular clothes." Aunt Louise and Uncle Richard were responsible for the Fourth of July dinner. My reputation as a noncook was well established in the family. Now Uncle Richard was on the back porch, trying to get the barbecue started in the rain. Aunt Louise opened the drawer again. "How do you cut anything?"

"This is pretty sharp," I said, offering a paring knife.

She glanced at it. "No, I'll use this one, thanks." Aunt Louise was known as an excellent cook and had taught her own daughters a lot. My mother hadn't been very interested in cooking, and there were still jokes about it. The cooking Aunt Louise was doing for tonight and my lack of ability were bound to trigger stories I had heard a thousand times about my mother's lousy cooking. Some of the jokes and stories in our family refused to die, even though everyone had heard them many times, even though the people they were about were long gone. Many about my mother still made me wince with pain, though no one seemed to notice.

Aunt Louise minced chives on a cutting board she had brought from home. She smiled, chuckled a little. "I'll never forget," she said, and I thought, Here we go. "Your mother was so excited about TV dinners. She thought they were great. I think you all ate them every night for about five years."

"No we didn't," I said defensively, exactly the way I'd said it countless times before. "Laura and I had them about once a month when our parents went out." But it didn't matter what I said; Aunt Louise was laughing to herself about her own version of things. We had had TV dinners the night our parents died, when two police officers came to tell us they were dead. I vomited mine on the grass in the backyard.

"Sometimes I think your mother started working just so she would have another excuse not to cook," Aunt Louise said, laughing again.

"She found something that she enjoyed that she could also make money doing," I said. "I don't see anything wrong with that."

Aunt Louise started chopping scallions. She frowned at the bowl. "There's nothing wrong with it, as long as she didn't sacrifice her family's well-being. This bowl is chipped and cracked. Don't you and Gram know that you're supposed to throw things away when they get broken?" She squatted and opened a cupboard, looking for a bowl.

"Is that what you think she did?"

"What?"

"Sacrificed our well-being?"

"You girls were alone a lot, I know that." Aunt Louise moved some stuff around the cupboard.

"But we were old enough to be alone. It's not like we were toddlers or something. And you were the one who told her that I was too attached to her and that she shouldn't let me be with her so much."

"Now, I don't remember that at all." She stood up and opened another cupboard, peering inside for what she needed.

"You did. Laura heard you."

"Oh, that was so long ago. Who remembers? Laura was a little girl. Is there any mayonnaise around here? Gram's not allowed to have it, but I thought maybe you would."

"Top shelf of the fridge. She eats it all the time. She doesn't follow her diet at all, as far as I can tell."

Aunt Louise got out the mayonnaise. "I don't think the costume shop would have lasted."

"Why not?" I said. "She was making a profit right from the beginning. Why do you keep saying these things, that she left us alone too much and that she started the shop because she couldn't cook and that it wouldn't have lasted? She was a success."

"All right, let's not get too excited." She took a big spoon out of a drawer. "I remember when I was pregnant, I was very emotional too."

"Why does everyone keep saying that? It's irritating. It's condescending. It's dismissive." I clenched my teeth and frowned.

"OK," she said. "Let's just have a nice evening. It will be a lot of fun with everyone together after such a long time. Don't you think?" She patted my shoulder. "I'll try very hard not to say anything to upset you."

Uncle Richard stepped inside the back door. He was wearing his raincoat. "Looks like it's finally going to go.

You can't leave the charcoal out there, though, Alice. It gets wet and takes forever to light."

"Put it wherever you want," I said. "I don't barbecue. I don't cook at all. Like my mother. Just like my mother."

"Oh, Alice," Aunt Louise said.

"Well," he said. "I better take more newspaper out with me, just in case." I handed him some newspaper off a stack in Gram's pantry.

"You want me to do something, Aunt Louise?" I said. She had made most of the food at home and brought it in plastic containers.

"No, no," she said. "I've done almost everything now. I just need a bowl for this potato salad." She crouched to look into a cupboard. "My God, how do you find anything?"

"Honestly, I haven't looked into this cupboard very much lately," I said. Slowly, I squatted beside her. "I haven't been down this low in a couple of months now. And Gram hasn't gotten down here in at least a decade." My stomach was so big that once I was down, it seemed I might not be able to get up. If I tried to reach into the cupboard for something, I might just tip over. I held on to the cupboard door for balance.

My aunt grabbed a bowl. "Here's something. No, this is chipped too. Look at that." She showed me and set it on the floor. Inside, my baby was starting to object to my position. She was thumping a leg against my rib cage, as if to let me know she was being squashed. I wanted to stand up. I looked for something to pull against. "I'll use this," Aunt Louise said. "Awful. It looks like she got it free at a gas station. Remember they used to give away dishes with tanks of gas? When was that?" She stood up and set the bowl on the counter. I held the edge of the counter and pulled. There was a loud crack of wood, but nothing collapsed. I was up. Blood rushed into my head, and I was dizzy for a second. "Good Lord, Alice," Aunt Louise said.

Gram came down. We could hear the steps creaking for a long time before we saw her. She was wearing her Fourth of July dress, silk with flowers in the colors of the flag all over it, a lot of perfume, and even more makeup than usual. One cheek had much more blush on it than the other. She had gotten blush on her hair on that side, coloring it dark pink. I took a napkin and rubbed a little of the color off. "What have I done this time?" she said, pushing her face toward me. "Did you get it?"

"Yes," I said. "Just a little extra blush. It's fine now."

"Well, thank you," Gram said. "I don't want to look like a clown. Is that what you're going to wear? Don't you have anything else?"

"This is it," I said. I was wearing a jumper I had bought at a recycled maternity clothes store. It was light blue and buttoned down the front. I had a white T-shirt underneath. The T-shirt no longer covered my whole stomach, so it only worked under something. I was wearing sandals; my swollen feet no longer fit into shoes.

"Mother, this kitchen is a disgrace," Aunt Louise said. "There isn't a single sharp knife."

"So you've told me," Gram said.

"And look at this god-awful bowl," Aunt Louise went on. "It's the only one left without a chip. Where on earth did you get it?"

"I love that bowl," Gram said. "I got it free at the Texaco right down here on whatchamacallit." She pointed out the window. "Where did you find it? I haven't seen it in years."

Laura and Mark arrived and came into the kitchen. Laura said, "There was traffic, even today. I mean, where is everybody going all the time?" She said this whenever she came out here.

"There's always traffic, Laura," I said. "In the middle of the night there's traffic." This was what I always said too. "You could take the train." At family gatherings we all repeated the same comments and questions over and over again, each person setting off the next, like people reciting lines they had memorized years before for a very long-running play and said so many times that the words had lost all meaning. Hearing these same stories, jokes, and opinions produced a kind of nausea in me that was as familiar as everything else about the holidays and celebrations that brought us all together in the first place.

My cousins arrived. They always drove out together in one car. As they walked into the kitchen, I knew one of them would say something I'd heard a million times too, and I braced myself for it. "Gram," Candace said. "What a nice dress. It's a good thing you're family, or I'd be worried about you stealing my man." She kissed Gram's cheek.

"Do you like it?" Gram said. "Ralph Lauren. I got it years ago."

"Gorgeous," Olivia said. "Wish I had one." She kissed Gram and her mother.

In a low voice, Matthew said to me, "Alice, would you make me some coffee, please?"

I reached across him and turned on the gas under the kettle. I got a mug and a spoon and put instant Taster's Choice into the cup. I leaned on the counter and waited for the water to boil.

"Alice! Look at you!" Candace said. "You're huge! I mean, I just found out you were expecting, and I didn't think you would be this big!"

"I was allowed to gain twenty pounds," said Aunt Louise. "No more."

"Amazing," Laura said. "I don't know how you did it."

"Carrot sticks and hard-boiled eggs," she said. "I lived on those. How much have you gained, Alice? Really. I want to know."

"Twenty-three pounds," I said.

"Oh, my Lord. And you've got over a month to go. Those last weeks are when you put on all the weight. The older you are, you know, the harder it is to lose. And this is all right with the doctor? What does your doctor say?"

"Actually, my regular doctor had some complications with her own pregnancy. She took a medical leave. Every time I go, I see someone new. So far none of them has said I've gained too much weight. I just saw someone yesterday."

Olivia said, "We're sorry things didn't work out between you and your, um, friend."

"Thank you," I said.

"Miserable little shit," Aunt Louise said. "Pardon my French."

"Rat," said Candace.

"We all wish him the worst of everything," said Olivia, smiling at me sympathetically.

"I never got along with him," said Laura. "He never liked me. He was unpleasant to me the first time I met him."

"Oh, Laura," I said. "Do you have to keep saying that? He didn't mean for things to turn out this way. I'm sure that if he knew how miserable I was going to feel, he would have behaved differently. Anyone would." There was silence. My relatives looked at me with concern. "Things will work out somehow," I said to reassure them. "I am very resilient, very resourceful."

"Sad," Matthew said, shaking his head. I poured boiling water into the mug, stirred, handed it to him. He took it, blew into it, sipped carefully, and said, "Is this instant?"

"What are your plans?" Olivia said.

"Um," I said. "Plans?"

"Are you moving soon?" said Candace.

I started to get hot all over. The subject of where I was going to live filled me with overwhelming anxiety, which was increasing as my due date approached. "I hope so." I managed a weak smile.

"Well, you'd better do something quick," said Candace. "It looks like as though that baby will be here any day now."

"Oh, no. I have four weeks. And first babies are usually late," I said.

"They are?" Olivia said.

"Yes."

"But not always," said Aunt Louise. "Both my girls were early."

"Anyway," Candace said, "I hope you're going someplace soon, because you can't stay here with Gram forever. She does have a heart condition, you know."

"Oh, for God's sake," Gram said. "She's not going to kill me."

"I realize that Gram would be better off with a more experienced person," I said. "She'll get somebody soon. I don't plan to stay. I didn't think I would be here this long. It's very hard to find a place in the city."

"Do you have any contact with . . . sorry, what was his name?" Candace said.

I didn't say anything.

"Rick, was it? The baby's father?"

"His name is Nick," Gram said. "Don't be rude, Candace. You've known him for years. And by the way, have you seen all the commercials he's been in lately? That boy is probably making more money than all of us put together."

Laura said, "I saw him on a cereal one last night. Have you guys seen it—the one with all the adults dressed like children? I didn't know Nick could do a cartwheel."

"Have you heard from him?" Olivia said. "Is he going to help you at all? I mean, financially?"

I said, "We are not in touch."

"Sad," Matthew said again.

"Sad?" Gram said. "What's so goddamn sad about it? What's the matter with you children? You're talking like old people from some small town like the one I came from. She's going to have a baby. She wants a family. You're not going to have to do anything about it, so what do you care?"

"I think what Matthew means," Peter said, "is that we all know how difficult it's going to be for Alice."

"You don't know anything of the kind. She might just be starting the happiest time of her life." I stared at her. "Well, you might." Gram looked out the window to the driveway. "Oh, look, here comes your boyfriend."

My heart jumped. We all looked out. But it wasn't Nick. Dan's Zephyr was creeping up the driveway, pebbles crunching under whitewall tires. "Oh, God, no," I said inadvertently. Dan got out of the car and walked slowly to the door. I hadn't noticed until today how slow he was about everything or how gangly-looking he was or how long his ponytail was getting. Seeing him out of context this way, with all my family looking at him, he seemed different to me, more peculiar than ever but at the same time almost heartbreakingly sweet, so that I wanted to protect him from possible danger or criticism.

The doorbell rang. I opened it. "Hi, Dan, honey," my grandmother called, as if she had raised him herself from boyhood. "I didn't know you kids had plans."

"What? I just—" Dan began.

Gram interrupted him. "Have fun! Enjoy the fireworks."

"Fireworks?" said my uncle, coming in from the barbecue. "It's raining. Hi, kids," he said to his daughters. "Oh, who's this now?"

"This is Dan, Uncle Richard. Good luck with the barbecue," I said. "You all have fun at the fireworks too."

"See you later," Gram said, "or tomorrow. Enjoy yourself."

"Tomorrow?" said my uncle. "Who is this fellow?"

I grabbed my purse off the hall table and stepped out onto the porch, slamming the door behind me. I exhaled. Dan looked at me, confused, alarmed. "Uh," he said. "I came back for my jacket. I forgot my jacket earlier, and my wallet was in it. Didn't realize it until I needed money for the tunnel. Had to come back."

"No problem," I said. "Where is it?"

"I think it's on a chair in the living room."

"I won't be a minute." I went back in. "Forgot something," I said. I found the jacket and put it over my arm. "See you later," I said, on my way through the kitchen again.

"Bye," they all called after me.

Handing the jacket to Dan, I said, "Can you get me out of here? Just for a couple of hours."

"Sure," he said. "What's going on?"

"They were picking on me, giving me a hard time about, well, I don't know, my whole life. Gram saw you coming, and she gave me an escape."

"That was nice of her," Dan said.

"Very," I said. "But don't worry. She'll find a way for me to pay her back later."

He stopped walking. "Or maybe not. Maybe she appreciates you now after all you've done for her. Maybe she thinks you deserve a break."

"Hm," I said, considering. "I suppose it's possible."

We got into the car. I waved to my family as we drove away. Only my grandmother waved back. The rest of them just looked, unable to comprehend or believe what they were seeing.

We went to a drive-through hamburger place. It was still raining. We ate cheeseburgers and french fries in the car, which got steamed up and smelled like onions. Dan turned on the radio. He had clammed up again. He wasn't talking at all, which made me feel especially lousy about what had happened when he dropped me off earlier. "Dan," I said. "I'm sorry if I haven't been very, um, responsive. It's just that I'm kind of—I'm so fat and it doesn't seem possible—it's not the right time for me to—"

"Forget it," Dan said. "Don't apologize. Don't explain. It's fine. I understand. I just like you, that's all. I like everything about you. I love you." He pushed buttons on the radio, searching for a station, stopping on a song, which then ended. "If you don't want to get involved, I can handle that. I'm not going to fall apart."

"Of course you're not going to fall apart," I said. "I knew you wouldn't fall apart. I just meant, you know, I didn't want you to feel—" I couldn't finish. I didn't know what I was trying to say, and Dan didn't help me out. We just sat there, not saying anything.

Another song started. Dan turned it up.

The music was loud and had a clarity that seemed incongruous in a car like this. It was X singing "Fourth of July," a sad song about two other people not coming together that I remembered hearing on some other radio, some other year. As I waited for Dan to speak again, I listened to the words, especially the last verses, where I knew things took a slightly more positive turn.

> *On the stairs I smoke a cigarette alone*
> *Mexican kids are shooting fireworks below*
> *Hey, baby, it's the Fourth of July.*
>
> *Whatever happened I apologize*
> *So dry your tears*
> *And baby walk outside.*
> *It's the Fourth of July.*

Guitar chords described a million-mile journey between despair and hope, traveled in a moment.

With one finger, Dan drew a heart in the steam on the window, looked at it for a second, then wiped it off with his hand. He smiled at me and shrugged. I leaned over and kissed him, just lightly at first. Then I opened my mouth, and a kind of electric shock ran through me, so hot that I was almost surprised not to see sparks flying around the car. He still tasted of his chocolate milk shake, cold and sweet. Maybe it was hormones making me behave this way so suddenly, so unexpectedly. Maybe it was the song. Once I started I didn't want to stop. We kissed for a long time before we decided to drive back to the city, to his apartment.

Eleven

DELIVERY

*G*RAM WAS SAYING, "She could be pretty if she'd lose some weight." We were watching *Roseanne*. It was the Tuesday after I'd gone home with Dan. I was too tired and uncomfortable to respond. A dull backache had kept me home from work that day. But as the pain came and went, nothing really incapacitating, I had felt guilty for not going in. Now I couldn't find a position on the couch that didn't feel wrong. I wondered how I was going to stand this for another four weeks, more if the baby was late.

Back when I bought my maternity clothes, they had looked enormous. Now everything pulled or rubbed or didn't quite cover what it was supposed to. The only thing I felt comfortable in these days was my nightgown. I decided to put it on now. I stood up, and as I did I felt something—liquid, a lot of it—soaking my pants. "Gram?" I said.

"What?" She didn't look away from the TV.

And then I didn't know what to say. "I'm going upstairs. Need anything?"

"No," she said, laughing as one of Roseanne's daughters, the younger one, Darlene, talked about sex.

I went to Gram's bedroom and looked up the number for the nearest hospital. I said, "My name is Alice Hammond. I'm thirty-six weeks' pregnant. My due date is August seventh, and I think my water just broke. My doctor is Jennifer Carver in Manhattan."

"Hold on, please. I'll page the doctor on call."

I waited. "This is Dr. Herold," a woman's voice said. "You're losing amniotic fluid? Is it a gush or a trickle?"

"A gush."

"Are you having contractions?"

"No. I just have a backache," I said. "I lugged a lot of books around a library yesterday. It's probably from that."

"Lower back pain that comes and goes?" she said.

"Yes."

"OK. Sounds like you're in the first stage of labor. You need to come in now and be admitted because your bag of waters has ruptured. Do you have insurance?"

"Yes," I said.

"Good. Grab your suitcase and have your husband drive you right down here."

"OK," I said. I did not have a suitcase ready. I did not have anyone to use as a husband.

I went to my room and took my nightgown off my bed, which was still unmade. Too late now. I got a bath towel to sit on in the car. I changed my pants. The clean ones got soaked immediately. I crammed the nightgown and towel into my bag. I went to the bathroom and got my shampoo, toothbrush, and toothpaste. I walked slowly downstairs and tried to appear calm. "Gram," I said, "I'm going to buy some popcorn." It was all I could think of.

"Popcorn? Did you eat all the popcorn again? You're going to be as big as the side of a barn."

"Right," I said. "I'll see you later." My heart was pounding.

"No you won't. I'm going to bed as soon as *Roseanne* is over."

"Good night, then."

As soon as I got out of the car in emergency parking, more liquid gushed out. Inside the hospital, a lot of people were sprawled in chairs, as if they had been there a long time and did not expect to be going anywhere soon. I stood in front of a desk, while two women filled out forms for other people. Fluid was dripping down my legs. "Excuse me," I said. "I need help. I'm going to have a baby."

"Can you walk?" said one of the women without looking up.

"Yes."

"Maternity is on seven," said the other woman. "Elevator's on your right."

"Thank you very much," I said.

I went to the elevator, leaving a trail of fluid along the floor. I hoped no one slipped on it. I got in the elevator and pushed the button for seven. A man got in and pushed four. He was carrying flowers. We waited. A woman got in. She was wearing a blue uniform and pushing a cart. She pushed three. We all waited, looking out at the lobby. My pants were sticking to me. The doors started to close, but another woman ran to catch them. She pushed six. We waited. The doors closed. We went up. More people got on, and we had to stop at every floor on the way to seven. By the time we got there, I was all the way at the back, behind seven or eight people. The doors opened and started to close; no one moved to get out of my way. "Hold the doors!" I said in a loud voice. "I don't feel like having this baby in an elevator." A wide path cleared, and I got out.

"Alice Hammond," I said to the woman behind the desk.

"Are you alone, Alice?" she said.

"Yes," I said. "Alone. So far."

"All right, have a seat here. Hold on now. Have you ruptured your bag of waters?" I nodded. She put a couple of disposable blue pads on the chair to absorb the fluid. "Now, unfortunately, we've got registration to do here, since you're not a patient of one of our doctors." She asked me questions, a lot of them, and typed my answers onto a computer.

"OK," she said. She picked up a phone and pressed some numbers. "Susie, your gal's ready."

A big woman in white was striding down the hall, pushing an empty wheelchair. "You look a little damp there, sweetie. We're kind of slow tonight, but everyone that's come in has been as wet as you are. Something about the barometric pressure. Everybody who's ready pops at the same time."

"I'm not ready. I'm early. I'm not even close to ready."

"OK, hon, we'll take care of everything. Is your husband parking?"

"No husband," I said. My voice cracked a little. I was afraid all of a sudden.

"Nothing to worry about. I'm a single mother too.

You're in great hands, if I do say so myself." She patted the wheelchair. "Let's go for a ride." She pushed me fast to a labor room. It looked sort of like the nurse's office in junior high: speckled linoleum, a green bedspread, no blankets. There was a TV, which Susie turned on. On the screen, Nick was stepping out of the shower again, smiling. The nurse helped me get up on the bed, and, changed into a hospital gown. She put my soaking clothes into a plastic bag and wrote my name on it with a black marker.

"All right now, Alice," she said. "We're going to take you down the hall here for an ultrasound to get a look at that baby of yours."

I got back into the wheelchair. In a dark room, I lay down on a table. A technician smeared blue gel on my stomach. It was cold. On a monitor, white shapes wiggled on a dark background. The technician clicked something, and the image froze. Another click, and there was more wiggling. A printer ground out the frozen image. I was sure that spending the night with Dan had gotten me here too early. I shouldn't have done it. I had behaved recklessly and irresponsibly.

The door opened. "I'm Dr. Herold," said a voice. I looked up at her. She was tall with short gray hair and glasses. For some reason, I trusted her right away. "We spoke earlier. How are you feeling, Alice?"

"Fine," I said.

The doctor laughed. "Let's take a look at this," she said. Susie stepped back so the doctor could see the monitor. "Good," she said. "Can you get the head?" There was a click. She looked awhile and then picked up the printout. "Fine. OK. That's enough, I think. Alice, this baby doesn't look early to us. Your dates must be off. The baby looks right on target."

I was so relieved that a couple of tears rolled out. "Thank you," I said in a choked voice.

"Now, now," said the doctor. "You're doing great. Susie's going to take you back to your room. If you don't start having strong contractions, we're going to give you an IV drip of Pitocin to get you started. Once your bag of waters has ruptured, the baby has to be born within twenty-four hours to avoid infection. Questions? OK, then. See you later."

Back in the labor room, Susie strapped a belt around my stomach to hook me up to a monitor. "We're going to keep an eye on your contractions." On a machine next to me, a pen made lines on a moving roll of paper like a seismograph. "Contractions are pretty weak," she said, looking at the monitor. "Be prepared that this might take a long time. We're going to watch some TV, drink some liquids, you can call your family. Here's the phone. Dial nine. I'll be right back. Press this if you need anything."

I woke Laura up. "Hi, it's me."

"Oh," she said. "I thought it was Mark. He's in California until tomorrow, and he always calls too late."

"Sorry to wake you. Listen, I'm in the hospital."

"Oh, no," she said. "Did she have a heart attack?"

"No, I—"

"She fell. Did she fall?"

"No, no. Not Gram. She's at home in bed. It's me. I'm going to have my baby."

"Oh, no. Now? Tonight? Isn't this really early? Is the baby going to be all right?"

"Yes. I thought it was early too. We were watching *Roseanne*, and my water broke. I had to come right in to the hospital. They gave me an ultrasound here, and it turns out I'm not early at all. The baby is ready. Listen. Go to Gram's. She shouldn't be alone, and she doesn't know where I am. I have her car."

"Where are you?"

I gave her the address and phone number. "And Laura," I said, "I don't have the stuff I need for the baby. I thought I had all this time. I thought I might still move, so I didn't buy anything yet. Do you think you could help me round up some baby things? I need a car seat. I was going to buy it this weekend. And clothes. You don't have to do a major shopping trip or anything, just the essentials."

"Here's what I'll do," Laura said. "I'll drive out there right now—there won't be any traffic, probably. What do you think?"

I said, "Midnight is about the best you're going to do on traffic, Laura, but there will be other cars."

"All right, all right. Then I'll stay at Gram's and come to the hospital first thing in the morning, as soon as I wake up. I'll see the baby, then go right out and buy all the stuff you need and have it ready for when we bring the baby home."

"Oh, thanks. Great. That will really help. I won't call Gram's before eight tomorrow, because I don't want to wake her. If she gets up early, just tell her where I am. The baby probably won't even be here before then. But they said you can call anytime for a progress report."

"OK. Don't even think about Gram. I'll take care of her. Good luck."

As I hung up, there was pain. It was big. I said, "Oh,

no," or I tried to, but no sound came out. When it was over, I looked out the window into the darkness and saw the lights of cars with people inside them who were going somewhere. I wanted to be in one of those cars. Deciding to have this baby was a mistake, I saw now. I wasn't equipped for it. I couldn't even remember the date of the last time I had had sex with Nick before he dumped me. And now the baby was coming before I could get organized.

There was more pain, searing, horrible pain, this time so severe that I couldn't catch my breath. I held the sheet and pressed down on the bed, as if trying to back up and away from the pain. Now I understood how so many women had died in childbirth. The process seemed brutal, violent: I could not possibly get out of this unharmed. I pushed the button to call the nurse, and it started again right away. "Yes?" said a voice over an intercom. "Alice?"

I got out, "I need Susie. Now."

"Hold on, Alice," the voice said. "She's coming. She's hurrying. From where I'm sitting at the desk, I can see her running. She's almost there now."

"Hey, what's going on in here?" Susie said, bursting in. "I leave the room for a minute and you go ahead without me? Let's take a look and see if you're starting to dilate. Oh my gosh, Alice. You're there." The pain started again. She put an arm around my back and held one hand. When it was over, Susie pushed the intercom button and said, "She's ten centimeters dilated. We need Dr. Herold."

The pain was there again. This time, I felt the baby trying to get out. "The head," I said. "I feel it."

Susie pushed the button again. "We're moving fast here. She's ready to push. OK, now, doll," she said to me. "The doctor is coming, and as soon as she gets here you're going

to push that baby right out. Super job. You're doing fine."
She smiled at me. How could she smile at me when I was
going to die? I was so hot. She handed me a cup of crushed
ice. I held some in each hand and rubbed my face.

"Where's the doctor?" I said. The head felt enormous
between my legs. It was moving, twisting downward, working its way out. Dr. Herold ran in.

"Here we go, Alice," Susie said. Then to the doctor she
said, "She's ready to push."

"Let's go, then. Could I have a stool, Susie?" She put
her hands on my knees, opened my legs, and peered at me.
She sat down on the stool Susie brought. "Wow, Alice,
your baby has a lot of hair. Is the father blond?" I shook
my head, grimacing with pain. I didn't want to talk about
Nick's hair right now. "Your little one here does. Good-
size head too. You're doing fine. Next contraction, I want
you to push. And the baby's going to try to slide back in,
so as much as you can, let's try to keep pushing. Here we
go now." I pushed. Susie and the doctor smiled. The doctor
said, "Yes!" grinned, and clenched her fists. "You're a pro.
Look how far she moved that baby with just one push,
Susie. You'd think she was the mother of five. Now.
Again."

About six pushes later, the baby was born: a girl. I held
her. She was warm and solid, not scrawny, the way I had
expected. "Cute," I said.

"What's her name?" Susie wanted to know.

"I don't know. I hadn't decided about that. I thought I
had more than a month to go."

"Ah, well. It will come to you."

Susie washed her and put a diaper and a cap on her,
wrapped her in a blanket with bunnies on it. I twisted

around to see what she was doing to her, while the doctor sewed me up and cleaned me off. Then Susie put her into a bassinet with wheels and pushed her off somewhere to be weighed and measured. I got pushed to another room. I missed my baby already and wanted her back.

"Eight pounds eleven ounces," a new nurse said a little while later, carrying her in. "Big kid."

"No wonder I felt like an elephant," I said.

"Are you kidding me? You already look like you were never pregnant. You look great."

"Everyone kept telling me how fat I was."

"Oh, please," she said. The nurse held the baby in the crook of her arm before handing her to me. "Now just look at this little rosebud. Isn't she something?"

I looked at her. She looked back, scrutinizing my features suspiciously. She *was* like a little rosebud, all pink and curled up tight in her receiving blanket. "Maybe I should call her Rose," I said. I thought of Gram's baby Rosemary.

"That's a pretty name you don't hear too often anymore," the nurse said.

I said, "I think I will call her Rose. Elizabeth Rose, maybe." But I didn't feel sure about it. Suddenly I wanted to tell Nick that the baby was born, that he had a daughter that I wanted to call Elizabeth Rose. I picked up the phone, realized it was still the middle of the night, and put it down again.

Laura called at five. "I'm still at home. I fell asleep after you called. Did anything happen yet?"

"You didn't go to Gram's? You left her alone? Laura!"

"What? So I'll go now. I fell asleep, that's all. She's all right. She woke up at four and saw her car was still gone and called me. She's mad at you because you didn't tell her where you were going. She made me call to find out what happened."

"It's a girl," I said. "I named her Elizabeth Rose Hammond. Do you think that's all right?"

"What! You had the baby!" Laura was choked up. She cried easily. "I can't believe it! Did it hurt?"

"Yes, of course it hurt," I said. "Listen, I need that stuff I mentioned. A car seat, diapers, and a few outfits. I don't have anything. I thought I had a lot more time, and I wasn't ready yet."

"Of course. I'll do it right after I visit you later. Congratulations. I can't wait to see Elizabeth."

As soon as it was light, I called Nick. "Answering service," said a raspy female voice.

"Tell Nick that Alice called," I said. "Tell him his daughter weighs eight pounds eleven ounces. Her name is Elizabeth Rose. She was born at one-nineteen this morning."

"Alice called. Then what?"

"Elizabeth Rose. She weighs eight pounds eleven ounces. We're at Greenwood Hospital."

"You got a number where he can reach you, hon?" I gave her the number.

"You got the baby's name, right?" I said.

"Elizabeth?"

"Elizabeth Rose," I said. "I want him to know the middle name too."

"Elizabeth Rose, then. Congratulations," she said flatly.

"Thank you."

I put the phone down and picked up the baby, who was asleep. Her eyelids had tiny veins in them. She had eyelashes the color of wet sand. I tucked her in next to me and fell asleep waiting for my sister to come and Nick to call me back. When I opened my eyes again, someone was pushing a food cart into the room. The phone was ringing. I answered.

"Hi, it's me. It's Nick."

"Hi."

"Congratulations," he said.

"Thank you. You too. Congratulations."

"Uh, well. Thanks," said Nick. "I haven't been very— I mean—"

"Are you going to come to the hospital to see her? I'm only going to be here today, and then you'll have my grandmother to face because I'm still living with her."

"Oh, Jesus. You know, I'll try to get out there. I really will. But I have two rehearsals. I didn't expect this. If I'd known, of course I could have—but I really—today is just—"

"No, no. I understand. No need to explain. You're too busy."

"Don't say it that way. Please, Alice."

Elizabeth started to cry. "I have to go," I said. "We can work out a time later." I put the phone down and picked up the baby. I offered her a breast. She wouldn't take it. I offered her the other breast, walked around. Then I called the nurse. "She won't stop," I said. "She just won't stop crying."

The nurse took off Elizabeth's blanket and quickly wrapped her up tight. The crying stopped. "Here you go," she said and handed her back. "They like to be wrapped up tight—like little burritos."

"Thank you," I said. I held Elizabeth. The phone rang.

"Is she gorgeous?" It was Laura.

"Yes, she's adorable. Are you coming now? Where are you? At Gram's? I thought you would have been here a long time ago."

"I can't. I think I have strep throat. I'm still in the city. I'm worried about passing germs along to the baby."

"You're not going to come? At all? I'm just going to be here by myself?"

"Maybe I'll be better tomorrow. I'll go to the doctor, and if it's strep, I should be a lot better soon. As soon as my appointment's over, I'll come out."

"Why don't you just come out here anyway and go to one of those walk-in clinics, then Gram won't be alone for so long."

"I'll be out there in a few hours."

"I was really counting on you for the car seat and stuff. And you know, I have this baby and no one's seen her."

"You don't want your newborn baby to get a sore throat, do you?"

"You could wear one of those surgical masks and not pick her up."

"I'd feel terrible if she caught something from me. Really, Alice, it wouldn't be smart."

"OK," I said. "Fine. See you when you feel better."

"Nick will come, won't he? He's her dad. He'll get there, and you can just hand him the list of stuff you need. He needs to get involved anyhow, right?"

"Right. I'll ask Nick," I said. "Sure."

"He'll figure it out. It will be good for him," Laura said.

As soon as we hung up, I called Gram.

"Hello?" she said.

"It's me, Alice."

"Congratulations."

"Thank you. I'm naming her Elizabeth Rose. Rose is for you-know-who."

"Ah," she said. "You did that for me? Alice, you're something. Damn it, I wanted to see that baby after waiting all this time. Now Laura's got her throat, and you've got my car. I could take a cab. Do you suppose a cabdriver would walk me to the front door? I know there are some steps."

"A cab is too much trouble and money, Gram. You'll see the baby tomorrow, anyway. They try to get you out of here as soon as possible. I was really counting on Laura, though."

Elizabeth started to cry again. "Oh, I hear her," Gram said.

"She cries a lot," I said.

"My God, she's got my temperament. You'd better go."

"I have to feed her," I said. "I'll talk to you later." I nursed Elizabeth. As soon as she was finished I would call Gram's neighbor Elaine and ask her to go and check on Gram. This was another one of those times when I wished I had a mother. I told myself that I wasn't going to be stuck here alone. I just had to wait, be patient. Nick and Laura weren't doing this on purpose; it had just turned out to be bad timing for them. I would try to be understanding about it. Somebody would come. Somebody would help me.

Twelve

POSTPARTUM

A DOCTOR I hadn't seen before came in to prod my stomach and ask if I needed anything for pain. "Pain?" I said.

"Some women need medication for the contractions they get the first couple of days postpartum," he said.

"Geez," I said, "this is nothing. Now, last night—that was pain."

"Let a nurse know if you need something," he said.

Elizabeth cried, and the nurse watched while I breast-fed her, said I was doing it right, and noted the time on my chart. When Elizabeth was finished, I held her on my shoulder while she slept. I didn't want to put her down. I rested my hand lightly on her back to feel it rise and fall with each little breath. The thought that I had someone else with me now, a brand-new actual person, kept coming to me, surprising me over and over. Someone filled the water pitcher next to my bed. A nurse set up a video about bathing your baby. A woman came in to ask her name for the birth certificate. An orderly checked the supply of sanitary napkins in the bathroom. There were all these people in my room all the time, but no one to talk to. The maternity floor wasn't very busy, so I didn't have a roommate. I thought about the birth again, going over it minute by minute. I fell asleep.

When I opened my eyes, Nick was there, crouching down to see Elizabeth's face on my shoulder. I pulled up the sheet over my fat stomach. I pushed hair off my face.

"I can't believe it," he said. "I just can't believe it. She looks like me."

"She does?"

"Oh, yeah. Look at that mouth."

"You want to hold her?"

"Me?" he said. He took a step backward. "She's sleeping. Let's let her rest. You need anything? Shall I get you something to drink?"

"No, thanks," I said. His hair was longer. He looked a little tired. "But I can ask for something for you. They'll bring you something to drink because you're the father."

He smiled, then looked embarrassed because he had smiled. "I'm the father," he said. "I can't believe it. Can you?"

"Not yet," I said. "Not really. Isn't she beautiful?"

"She's beautiful, Alice." He looked at me. "You did a great job. And all by yourself. You are so strong," he said.

"I thought you couldn't come today."

"I shifted a few things around," he said, making his palms parallel, moving them back and forth.

"While you're out here, I need stuff for Elizabeth. Could you go get a car seat, a package of diapers, and some clothes for her? You can take Gram's car."

"I don't know my way around out here. I wouldn't know

what to get. You'll have to go with me, when they let you go."

"I can't. That's just it. I can't take the baby out of here without a car seat. And she doesn't have any clothes. You can go to Toys 'Я' Us. It's right near here. I'll tell you exactly what to buy."

"What about your sister?" Nick said. "Isn't she going to do anything to help?"

"She's coming tomorrow, probably. She has a strep throat and doesn't want to give the baby any germs."

"Oh, right. Give me a break. She flaked out again."

"It's not as if you're the Rock of Gibraltar, either, you know."

"Alice, this is not the time to get into this." He ran his hand through his hair, pulling it back off his face. I could see why he was getting so much work these days. It was a face that could belong to a lot of different kinds of people. He looked at his watch. "I'm going to have to call my agent. She's working on something for me, and she said she'd have some information for me by three. I'll be right back." He started for the door.

"There's a phone right here," I said.

"That's your phone. People might be calling to congratulate you. This could take a few minutes." He was gone.

I prepared myself for his coming back to say he had to leave. He would have an important audition. A rehearsal he'd thought was canceled was back on. Another actor was sick, and he had to stand in at a tech run-through. It was the least he could do.

I put Elizabeth into the bassinet, got back in bed, and drank some more water. While I waited for Nick, Dan walked in. If I could have jumped into the closet before he

saw me, I would have done it. A lot had happened in the
last few days that made it easy not to think about the night
I slept with Dan. Now here he was. He was carrying
things—a car seat, a plastic bag from Toys 'Я' Us, a huge
package of diapers. He was sweaty from the effort. He put
the stuff on the floor next to the bed. "Hi," he said, smiling.
"You look pretty."

"Oh, I do not," I said. "My hair's dirty—I think there's
dried blood in it—and I was up all night. Look at this stuff.
You got everything. How did you know? My sister
wouldn't go, then I tried to get—"

He interrupted me. "Ah. What a little princess." He
looked at Elizabeth a long time, not saying anything. I
wanted to warn him that Nick was there, but I didn't want
it to seem as though I was trying to make him leave when
he was here to help me.

"When you didn't come to work again this morning, I
called your grandmother's. She told me the baby was already here. She couldn't find the envelope she had written
your hospital number on, but she gave me your sister's
number. Laura said she wasn't coming and that you needed
someone to buy a few things. So I called my sister in Col-
orado to see what a new baby needed, and I got a whole
rundown. She has four kids. She told me exactly what to
get. And here I am." He picked up the car seat to show
me. "Could you move your feet a little?" I pulled them over
to one side of the bed. He set the seat down. "This works
for newborns up to forty-pound kids. My sister says that
even if you want to get the kind for babies up to twenty
pounds that doubles as an infant carrier/rocker seat, you'd
have to get this one for later anyhow. This kind has the
five-point suspension seat belt, as opposed to the three-

point. A lot of people say the five-point is better. That's the current thinking anyway. And I got this thing." He rummaged in the big plastic bag and pulled out a horseshoe-shaped pillow with little ducks printed on it. "This is for head support. And the seat reclines so the baby won't just fold over in it when she's still small. I didn't know what you wanted to do about diapers, but my sister said you'd need at least some disposables, so that's what I got. And here are some clothes." He pulled out three tiny pink outfits. "All cotton. I just couldn't see putting polyester on anybody so tiny. And I got a little sweatshirt with a hood that my sister said would be really useful. She recommended this sling as a carrier." It was in a box. There was pink material with little flowers, showing through a cellophane window. "I guess her last kid really liked it. She said you'll have to practice with it awhile, but it's worth it. Here's a bathtub for her. It came with this boat and duck. And here are some pacifiers and a rattle I couldn't resist. See? When you hold it like this, the beads fall through the tube into here." He handed it to me. "That's about it."

"You did a great job, Dan. Thank you. You really thought of everything."

"Think so?" He smiled. He looked at the car seat. "The cover is washable, of course." He looked at me. "I love you, Alice."

Things I had said to him, things we had done together a few nights before, filled my head all at once. I remembered sitting in his kitchen, starting out to tell him that I had surprised myself when I decided to have the baby, how I had not expected to become a mother now. Then, before I knew it, I was talking about my own mother, all sorts of stories and details about her spilling out, as if I had been waiting years to tell someone all my secrets, and now I had to say everything right away. I had even told him about the sequined sweater. I remembered Dan patting me, stroking my hair, saying, "Sounds like she was really nice." I told him about the feeling I had for a long time after she died and then again when Nick left. "There was this torn, kind of biting ache," I said, locating the precise spot for him by pointing to the pocket on the front of my maternity jumper.

Dan had blinked for a second, then said, "A broken heart. Alice, your heart was broken."

"Yeah," I said. "It was. I never thought of it that way."

We had sat in his kitchen for a long time, kissing until we were both exhausted. After I told him that just coming here was farther than I should have gone, he had put sheets and a pillow on the futon in the living room. We said good night and kissed some more. Then he went to his bedroom and closed the door. I sat in the living room, frozen, for several minutes. Then I went to the door of his bedroom and knocked. When he opened it, I said, "Dan, I want to sleep with you."

And he said, "Please." He held me for a long time before he unbuttoned my dress.

Now, in the hospital, with Dan sitting a few feet away and Nick just down the hall on the phone, I had to fight an urge to pull the bedsheet over my face. I took a breath to tell him about Nick, but Dan spoke first. "May I hold the baby?"

"Sure," I said.

He went to the sink. "I'll just wash my hands," he said.

I stood up and took the baby out of the bassinet. I was achy, as if I had taken several exercise classes the day before that I wasn't in shape for. I hoped there wasn't any blood on the back of my nightgown. He sat down in the visitor's chair, and I put Elizabeth in his arms. Nick could stay on the phone a long time sometimes. If I was lucky, this would be one of those times.

"Ah," he said. He beamed at me. "She looks exactly like you. And she feels really good." He closed his eyes and leaned his face down to smell the top of her head.

From the doorway, Nick cleared his throat. I jumped. Dan looked up, startled. He looked at Nick, then at me. He looked down at Elizabeth and turned bright red. "Dan, this is Nick. Have you ever met Nick?"

Nick said, "No," but did not step forward to shake hands.

Dan said, "Once at a party, the year before last. Maybe you don't remember."

"I don't," Nick said. "Whose stuff is this?" He pointed to the car seat and diapers.

"Elizabeth's," I said. "Dan brought it for her. Wasn't that nice? Now you won't have to do it. Make sure you give me your receipt before you leave, Dan."

Nick glared at him, and Dan looked at me. I had never noticed until this moment that Dan's eyes were green; not hazel or light brown but really green. They were open wide, with a stunned look of alarm and grief, like the eyes of a boy watching a Christmas tree burning. I tried to think of something to do or say to help him. I opened my mouth and closed it again.

"Excuse me," Nick said, walking over to Dan. "Mind if I hold my daughter?"

"Oh, of course not," Dan said. He handed over Elizabeth.

Nick took her clumsily, so that her foot dropped out of the blanket. She twisted her face around and made a little noise, but she didn't wake up. Dan gave up the chair, and Nick sat down with Elizabeth. Dan shuffled awkwardly for a few seconds. "Well," he said. "Guess I'll go now."

"Don't," I said. "You came all this way." But I wanted him to go. I just wanted to be with Nick and didn't want to be reminded of how, in my most vulnerable moment during his absence, I had revealed myself completely to Dan.

Dan said, "I, uh, have things to do in the city. A whole bunch of work. I'm really just, oh, behind on everything."

"I see," I said. "Well, thanks for bringing the stuff. It's really a big help."

"Yeah, thanks," Nick said. "We really appreciate it."

Dan looked stung. It was the way Nick said "we" that did it. He looked at me, as if discovering that I had tricked him into giving up all he had, and then he backed out of the room. "Goodbye, Alice," he said.

"What was he doing here?" Nick said. "Was he trying to move in on you when you were pregnant? Jesus, that's creepy. You should have called me. I would have gotten rid of him for you."

Dan was at the door again. "I forgot something. I brought a camera. I put some film in it for you." He handed it to me. It was an old Olympus and felt heavy in my hands, substantial. "It's one I don't use anymore. You can have it as long as you want. Forever. It's yours." He left.

Nick waited a few seconds. Then he said, "That was weird." He shuddered, as if recalling a bug crawling out of a sandwich he had been eating.

As much as I had wanted to get rid of him a moment

before, now I wanted to defend Dan against attacks from Nick. I said, "He's my friend. That's what he was doing here. I think it was really nice of him to bring all this stuff. He made a big effort. You didn't want to do it. I hope I didn't hurt his feelings. I did. I know I did. Oh, God."

"I was going to go get the stuff," Nick said. "Even if I didn't want to. Of course I was." Elizabeth's blanket slipped off, and she started to scream. The sound was loud and piercing. Nick stiffened.

"You can give her to me," I said. He handed her over quickly. I rewrapped her blanket. She kept crying. I opened my gown to give her a breast. Immediately, she started sucking so hard she was hurting me, and the room was quiet again. I looked up. Nick was looking out the window. "You don't have to stay," I said. "Why don't you leave?"

"No, it's OK," he said. "I'll stay." He paced, being careful not to look at me.

A nurse came in. "Oh, you're feeding her. What time did you start?"

"Just a minute ago," I said. The nurse wrote down the time. Then she came over and pulled my gown open further. "Let's see how she's doing. Oh, great! You know, you have the perfect nipples for breast-feeding. Ideal. Some women have flat or inverted nipples, but look how easily she can latch onto yours. You don't know how lucky you are. Excellent nipples. Beautiful." Nick left the room. "The father?" she whispered. I nodded. "Some men are squeamish about nursing."

When they brought my dinner, Nick went out for something to eat. I had ordered vegetable lasagna, grilled chicken, rice pilaf, potatoes au gratin, peas, and string beans. I was hungry. Nick said he was hungry too. "I'm going over there," he said pointing out the window at the deli across the street. "I'll be right back."

"Have some of this," I said.

"No, thanks," said Nick. "That looks pretty bad. Want me to bring you back anything?"

"I don't think so," I said. "But thanks. Thanks very much for offering. That was nice of you."

He shrugged on his way out the door. "Not really," he said. "Be right back. Two minutes."

In the afternoon, I had been surprised to see him show up. Now I was surprised that he was staying. I kept expecting him to say, "I have to go. I'm going to be late for rehearsal." Before long, visiting hours would be over. Fathers could stay later, of course.

I finished all the food on the tray and still didn't feel full. When Nick came back with his food, he had some ice cream and cake for me. "For Elizabeth's birthday," he said. I cried. I was hungry and emotional. "Oh, Alice," Nick said. "Come on now." He walked over to the bed. "It's all right now. Really, kiddo. This is going to be fine."

"You think?" I said. "I'm not sure I can handle it."

"Alice, you are a very capable woman," Nick said. "You can handle just about anything." He sat on the bed and hugged me, twisting my hair around his finger. I had a fluttery feeling in my stomach, the way you do when, unexpectedly, the person you have a painful crush on says some little thing that suggests he likes you too.

Elizabeth started to cry again. Nick went to her bassinet. He looked at me. "Shall I pick her up?"

"Sure, I guess so," I said.

He lifted her carefully and then walked slowly back to me. "Here," he said, handing her over. "She's so small," he said.

"Thanks." I opened my gown to let her nurse.

"What time do you want me to pick you up tomorrow to drive you back to Gram's?"

"You're coming back? But Laura can do that, you know," I said. "Eleven, the doctor said. And I've still got Gram's car here. Oh, God, I forgot. It's still in emergency parking, and you're only allowed to leave it for twenty-four hours."

"Alice, face reality, Laura won't come through. I'll go move the car now to the parking garage. Tomorrow I'll take the train and walk from the station. We'll use Gram's car."

"The keys are in my bag, over there in the closet."

Nick got the keys. He was so agreeable, as if some unseen alien had landed and taken over his body. "I'm going to go now and let you girls get some rest." He kissed me on the forehead, then walked to the door. He stopped and came back, leaned down to kiss Elizabeth on the head. Not understanding the significance of this, she went on sucking. "Bye," Nick said, and he was gone.

Soon after Nick left, Elizabeth began to cry. She put her whole body into it, tensing every muscle. She turned dark red with effort. Her blanket fell off and her clenched fists and arms looked pathetically tiny coming out of the little undershirt. The diaper she was wearing looked way too big. She was screaming so loud that I worried that people in the hall and in other rooms would think I had dropped her. I tried feeding her again. She sucked a couple of times and then resumed screaming, as if the breast had been empty or the contents sour or too hot. I picked her up and walked around. She was a hard ball, her arms and legs like wiry, wiggling spokes. I couldn't keep the blanket on her, she was flailing so much. Then I remembered the nurse telling me they like to be wrapped up tight. I held Elizabeth in one hand and spread the blanket on the bed with the other. Small as she was, she was not easy to hold in one hand, particularly when she was writhing in misery. I put her down on the blanket and tried to remember the way the nurse had shown me to wrap her up. One corner over one shoulder, tuck something under an arm. She was screaming so hard now that in between wails she didn't breathe for a long second. I tried to hurry with the blanket. I got it arranged the way I thought it was supposed to be, but as soon as I picked her up, the whole thing fell apart. Maybe the blanket wasn't the problem at all; maybe it was her diaper.

I put her down and opened the diaper. It was full of dark meconium, the stuff I had read about that filled her intestines while she was inside me, which was all to come out in the first day or so after birth. Without the diaper to contain it, meconium immediately spilled on the receiving blanket. "Hold still," I said to Elizabeth. "Please." It was on her thighs, her stomach. Her kicking heel got dirty. I got a baby wipe and started to clean her off. A new kind of cry came out of her, piercing and sharp: the wipe was too cold. I continued. "OK, Elizabeth," I said. "I'm going as quickly as I can. You're going to be all clean in a minute." I knew you were supposed to talk to babies to calm them, but it didn't seem to help at all. I reached for another wipe and got a whole pile by mistake. I had to put them all down on the bed, grab a corner, and shake one free of the others, while keeping my other hand on Elizabeth. I wiped her again. She was a mess. After three more wipes, she was clean enough for me to put on a new diaper, which was not as easy as it looked when the nurses did it. I got soap from the baby wipes on one of the tapes. It wouldn't stick. I had to use another diaper. When I closed it, the whole thing looked incredibly lopsided. I found a clean blanket in the bassinet, wrapped her again—badly—and picked her up. She was still crying. I opened my gown and gave her a breast, realizing only after she got started that it was the one she had been on most recently and for a long time. You were supposed to start on alternate sides. But she took it and the screaming stopped, so I didn't switch her to the other breast. She sucked so hard that I had to breathe in slowly through my nose and out through my mouth to tolerate the pain. But anything was better than the screaming. I leaned back on the pillows, exhausted.

My sister never made it to the hospital. She didn't have strep, as it turned out. It was just an ordinary sore throat, but she stayed home anyway. Elaine, Gram's neighbor, checked on Gram and made her dinner.

When Nick and I arrived at my grandmother's the next day, I held my breath, worried that she would say something mean to him, just when things were going so well. She said, "Hello, Nick, you're looking very fit." I exhaled. "That baby doesn't look anything like you."

"And what a relief that is," Nick said. "Want to hold her?" He put Elizabeth very carefully into Gram's arms.

"A great-grandchild," she said. "Imagine. I just can't realize I'm so old." Nick carried the diapers and a bag of my things upstairs. "Well," said my grandmother, as soon as Nick disappeared. "Who would have thought?"

"Isn't she beautiful?" I said, eager to change the subject.

"Yes, she is," Gram said. "Here, take her back, would you?"

I took her. She was sound asleep, thanks to the car ride. I was hoping that maybe the screaming fits she had had in the hospital were over.

"Where are you going to put her?" Gram said.

"In my room. I'll just set up the crib."

"I can do that," Nick said, returning from upstairs. "Where is it?"

"In the attic, under a whole load of junk," Gram said.

"Fine," he said. "I'll get it. What color is it?"

"Oh, I don't know. Can't remember," Gram said. "Isn't that awful? But it's the only one up there."

"Yellow," I said. "It has a little duck painted on one end."

"How do you know that?" Gram said.

"I remember from when we used to visit and Laura and I played up there."

"That was a hundred years ago," Gram said.

We heard Nick rummaging in the attic. It took a long time. There were several crashes. I was afraid that if it was too difficult or took too long, the good mood he was in might evaporate. Finally, Nick came down. His hands were dirty. There was a big gray smudge on his face. "I don't know," he said. "It looks like some parts are missing, major important parts. Also, the spaces between the bars are too big. They're supposed to be two inches or less apart. These are about five and a half. I'm going to buy a new one."

Gram's mouth opened. She looked at me.

"What?" Nick said. "They gave us a whole pile of safety handouts in the hospital. I read them. Is that so weird?"

"I didn't say a word," Gram said.

I said, "Are you sure you want to do this?"

Nick said, "Alice, I'm surprised at you. That crib is not safe. Gram, I'm taking your car."

"Good. Have it. Go," she said. After he was gone, she said nothing but just stared at me significantly, as if no words could describe what we had witnessed.

Elizabeth woke up and started crying. "Oh, my God," Gram said. She put her fingers in her ears. I hurried to open my shirt. Elizabeth sucked with fixed concentration.

A few nights later, Elizabeth woke up and screamed, as she had several times every night so far. It was dark, so dark that I couldn't see the new crib that Nick had bought, a crib that seemed oversized and looming in this room full of furniture. I jumped up as fast as I could and took one giant step, my arms outstretched to reach Elizabeth before her piercing wails woke Nick, asleep in the other twin bed, or Gram down the hall. Nick had a commercial to shoot the next day and might be upset if he looked tired for it. In my hurry to silence Elizabeth's cries, I stubbed my toe on the leg of the crib. Although it was painful enough to make me scream myself, all I said was "Mn." I scooped up Elizabeth, took another giant step back to the bed, and started to nurse her. I hoped she didn't need to be changed; that would only make her start screaming again. The bed squeaked as I wiggled into a better position. I heard Gram's light click on and Gram getting out of bed. Maybe it was a coincidence. Maybe she just happened to wake up at the same time as Elizabeth.

Nick said, "This is never going to work out."

I jumped. Then I felt as though the bottom had dropped out of my stomach. Only two days before, Nick had said to me, "Alice, I want to try again. I didn't know what I was doing, leaving like that. I made a mistake. I had to go through that to see how important you are to me. Now I just want to be with you and Elizabeth. You think about it. I love you, Alice. I want to try. Please." I didn't have to think about it. I said, "I'll try too." Nick had smiled the same way he had on the deodorant soap commercial: broadly and with his whole face, so that there were little creases like parentheses in his cheeks and a distinct happy twinkle in his eyes.

Now he was saying it wasn't going to work. "Why?" I said. "It's only been forty-eight hours. You mean you miss what's-her-name?"

"Oh, no. Is that what you thought? No, I just mean the three of us living here at Gram's. We need to be on our own. I think we should go back to the apartment in the city. God, I'm sorry. I wonder how long it's going to take before you trust me again."

"I don't know," I said.

"But listen, I was thinking we could use that small room that we always dumped our junk in as Elizabeth's room. We'll put the crib along the south wall. The changing table will go next to the door. I think it will fit."

"I don't know," I said again. "I had kind of given up on the idea of living in New York with a baby. And Gram has become pretty dependent on me."

"Alice, she needs to hire someone. You can't take care of a baby *and* an old lady. You need a life. Besides, we need some privacy. And our own bed."

He wanted to sleep with me again. My stomach flopped once more, but this time for joy. "OK," I said. "I'll tell Gram tomorrow."

"Good," he said. "It's really for the best. For everyone." He fell asleep before Elizabeth did. He started to snore.

I was moving again. This time it was a little easier, because most of the boxes had never been opened, but also more difficult, because I could pack only while Elizabeth was asleep. She seemed to require constant attention when she was awake. I had imagined a new baby sitting in an infant seat, looking around for short periods, then dropping off quietly to sleep for long stretches. Maybe there were babies like that, but I didn't have one. If I put her down in the little infant seat I had bought for her, she screamed. She screamed when I bathed her, changed her, put her in her crib awake. I had to hold her all the time. My shoulders ached. It was hard to believe that anything so small could make my muscles sore, but she had. To get her to sleep was a project. I had to take her for a ride in the car, walk her in the sling Dan had bought for me, or feed her. Sometimes I had to try all three before something worked. So even though there wasn't very much to pack this time, I was having trouble getting it done.

While I was out on one of my many shopping trips to get baby stuff, Gram interviewed somebody to work for her. "Her name is Barbara. She's about your age. You might like her. She doesn't have much experience in this kind of work, but she has excellent references. I can train anybody. Don't you worry about me. Thank God that's settled."

"As long as you're happy with her," I said.

"Oh, it will work out fine," she said.

Nick borrowed Gram's car to take all my stuff back to New York. Several trips were necessary because of the crib and all the baby stuff. I worried that he would be annoyed and start asking if I *really* needed a special bathtub for Elizabeth or couldn't I just leave some of the things here for now. In a very short time we had acquired a lot. Some of it we had bought ourselves, and some had come in the mail, gifts from friends and relatives. My office had sent a diaper bag; my aunt had sent a silver cup and rattle from Tiffany's with the baby's name and birthdate engraved on both; Nick's parents, surprised but happy about being grandparents, had ordered a rocking chair that would be delivered to our apartment in New York.

Nick didn't seem to mind all the baby stuff we suddenly had. He seemed cheerful, actually happy about the way things had worked out. When the last load was finally packed up, I put Elizabeth in her car seat in the back, facing backward, the way she would ride until she reached twenty pounds, kissed and hugged Gram, and got in the car next to Nick. We took off for the city. Gram waved from the driveway until we couldn't see her anymore. She looked so old. Barbara was due to arrive in just a few hours. Still, I felt guilty leaving Gram alone there. And surprisingly, I was a little sad about moving out. I would miss seeing her every day.

We took the expressway. Nick got into the middle lane, a comfortable distance behind a florist's van. "OK?" he said. "How are you doing?"

"Fine," I said. "Good."

"OK," Nick said. "Elizabeth, you?" Elizabeth started to scream. I turned around in my seat to try to figure out what was bothering her. I couldn't see her. I had to kneel backward and lean over the seat back to check her. As I was doing this, feeling to see if the seat belt was too tight or the label of her little outfit was scratching her neck, Nick said, "Let's get married."

I looked over at his face to see if he was kidding or serious. Serious. I said, "OK."

Thirteen

THE WEDDING

T WASN'T going to be anything fancy, just a city hall wedding. Laura and Mark would be the witnesses. There would be no other guests, and we weren't having a reception. Nick's parents lived in Seattle, which was too far to come on short notice. We weren't even going to tell them until afterward. Planning the wedding was mainly a matter of deciding what to wear. Nick had a suit that he liked and didn't get to wear often. He said, "And you can wear a nice dress." I said I didn't have one. He went to my closet and came back with a dress. "What about this?" he said.

I said, "That's a maternity dress. Besides, it's bad luck. It's the one I wore to lunch with Jane when I didn't get the promotion."

"We'll buy you something," he said. "Something special just for the wedding."

"Are you sure?" I said. I still wasn't used to Nick having money.

"Of course I'm sure," he said. "It will be a special day, and you need something special to wear."

We went to Lord & Taylor. Nick picked out a dress. I tried it on and it fit, even though I was still seven pounds overweight. Nick said he liked it. I stood in the dress and my socks, looking into the mirror, trying to decide. Then Elizabeth started crying, and I just wanted to get out of the store quickly. I changed, and Nick paid for the dress. It was cream-colored silk and it cost a lot. The money seemed like a waste when I was sure I would wear it only once, no matter what the saleswoman said. All the way home on the subway, with Elizabeth asleep again in the sling, Nick kept saying how much he liked the dress. "Really?" I said. "I just don't feel like myself in it."

Nick said, "That's because you've never been a bride before." He kissed me on the cheek and squeezed me around the shoulders. The change in Nick was so striking that I thought maybe he had needed to go off like that with someone else to get things in perspective. On the other hand, I worried that maybe this other, happy Nick was just an act. Then I was annoyed with myself for being so cynical and pessimistic.

The morning of the wedding, I couldn't figure out what to do with my hair. I wanted it to look special, so I French-braided it. That made me look like a schoolmarm, so I tried pulling out a few strands around the front. Then I thought it looked messy, so I had to start over. In the end, I took out the braid and brushed it again. I put on a headband. I didn't look the way I had wanted to, but I was out of time, so I gave up.

Just before we left, I sat down on the couch and fed

Elizabeth, hoping that she would last until we got home again. I spread cloth diapers all over myself while she nursed, in case she spit up. Elizabeth, now almost four weeks old, was wearing pink, as usual, a little suit with white cloud shapes on it, a zipper from one foot up to her neck, one of the outfits Dan had supplied. I had bought her special socks for the occasion, white with lace around the ankles.

Nick was wearing his suit, usually reserved for important auditions, and a purple tie that I once gave him for a birthday. His hair was slicked back, making him look like a lower-echelon criminal in a television movie. Every time he caught my eye, he smiled and said, "This is it, Alice. The big day" or "I'm a lucky guy." He was nervous; he wasn't himself. He never said things like this.

We took a taxi downtown. Laura and Mark were waiting outside the Municipal Building. Laura was wearing black pants and a white shirt. She had brought flowers for me to hold and a carnation for Nick's lapel. Mark had on a blue shirt and khaki pants, no tie or jacket. I could tell from Nick's face that he didn't like their clothes; he had wanted us all to dress up. "Don't say anything about what they're wearing," I said as we walked toward them. "Please don't fight with Laura about this. Or anything."

"What? I wasn't going to say a thing. Except you would think that when people come to a wedding, they'd at least—"

I cut him off as we got closer. "Hi, you guys," I said. "I hope you weren't waiting long. Thanks for the flowers." I smelled them. "Mmm."

We went upstairs, turned in our forms, and signed in. There were a lot of people waiting, and all the chairs were taken. Nick started pacing and looked a little sweaty. Elizabeth was asleep in Laura's arms. Laura was going to hold her during the ceremony. "Give her to me for a minute," Nick said to Laura.

"No, don't," I said. "We don't want to wake her up, Nick. Then I'll have to feed her again."

"OK, OK," Nick said. "Take it easy, sweetie." He squeezed my shoulder and kissed my cheek. He had never called me sweetie before.

When we had been waiting forty-five minutes, a man called our names. A feeling of panic shot through me: I didn't want to do this; it was wrong, a mistake. Nick would walk out on us as soon as I relaxed and started to believe he was going to stay. I would have to be on my guard all the time, watching for signs that he was growing weary of family life and preparing myself. I would save money, a cash reserve, in case he suddenly disappeared, leaving us with nothing. But Nick had taken my hand now and was walking with me through the open door. Mark, Laura, and Elizabeth followed. People got nervous before their weddings and had second thoughts that didn't necessarily mean anything; I knew that.

The room was dimly lit, with a podium at one end. Behind it was a large backlit piece of colored plastic designed to suggest a stained-glass window without being religious. There was no real window in the room. A sign said not to throw rice. I looked behind me. Elizabeth was still asleep. The clerk said, "Do you have rings?" and Elizabeth opened her eyes and started to scream.

"Yes," Nick yelled over the noise.

Laura shifted Elizabeth to her shoulder and gave me a desperate look. "Sway back and forth," I said. She did, but it didn't help. Nick started rummaging through the diaper bag that I had set down on the floor behind us. "What are you looking for?" I said.

"A pacifier."

"She doesn't like those," I said. "That never works."

He found one. He put it in Elizabeth's mouth. She closed her mouth for one second and then opened it again to scream. The pacifier dropped on the floor. Mark picked it up.

I said, "I should have brought the sling."

"May we begin, please?" said the clerk.

"But the baby's crying," Nick said.

"I'm sorry," said the clerk. "We can't wait. We have a roomful of people out there."

"Give her to me," I said.

"You can't hold her and get married at the same time," Laura said.

"Why not?" I handed my flowers to Mark and took Elizabeth. She didn't stop crying. "OK, go ahead," I said.

The clerk said some things. I wasn't listening. I was rocking back and forth. After a few seconds, Nick nudged me, and I realized that it was my turn to say something. "I do," I said, but as soon as I did, I knew that this was not the right response. The clerk paused a second and then went on. "I mean, I will," I said, interrupting him. He stopped and started his sentence again. Nick looked at me, annoyed by my mistake. I looked down at Elizabeth's open mouth and planned to feed her the minute, the second, this was over.

"I will," said Nick perfectly when his turn came.

The clerk said that if anyone knew any reason why these two should not be joined they should speak now or forever hold their peace. He paused. Elizabeth's cries escalated. Mark and Laura smiled at this, the idea that Elizabeth was protesting our union. The clerk went on, as if every possible joke about getting married had been made in this room and now the whole subject just made him tired. By the power vested in him by the state of New York, he pronounced us husband and wife. It had happened fast. It seemed there must be something more to it than that; I hadn't even been listening. Nick kissed me. Then he kissed Elizabeth, who was still wailing. Laura hugged me. Nick and Mark shook hands. Laura and Nick hugged; Mark and I hugged.

"It was so quick," I said, but no one heard me because Elizabeth was screaming so loud.

"We're married," said Nick, smiling at me. "Can you believe it? You're my wife. I'm your husband." He laughed crazily.

The clerk said, "I'll have to ask you to step outside now. Others are waiting."

We all went out. "Asshole," Nick said.

"Jerk," said Mark.

I said, "I have to feed Elizabeth." I put her on my shoulder, where she cried into my ear.

"What, here?" said Nick. "No way."

"Where can we go, then? There's nothing around here. I have to feed her right now. Come on, she's miserable."

"We'll find a place," Nick said.

We all went downstairs and outside, with Elizabeth yelling all the way. There was nowhere to go, just gray office buildings and newsstands, a lot of steps. I looked down at Elizabeth's red face and round open mouth. I wanted to cry myself. "I have to go back inside and feed her, then we can find somewhere to go when she's settled down again."

"No," Nick said. "I don't want you nursing our baby in some depressing plastic chair in a dirty city office on our wedding day."

"She's hungry," I said. "Who cares what the fucking chair is made of?"

"OK, let's not get upset now," Mark said. "We'll go back to your place, and Alice can feed the baby and change her clothes."

I looked down and saw that my milk had soaked through the nursing pads, my bra, and my dress, making two expanding round wet spots over my breasts. "Oh, God," I said and raised an arm. "Taxi!"

Fortunately, we got one of those fast drivers who didn't care about red lights or pedestrians or potholes. He just wanted to get there. As soon as we arrived, I jumped out of the cab and ran with Elizabeth, wailing, to unlock the door of the building. Mark came behind me, carrying the diaper bag and my bridal bouquet. Nick was behind him, saying, "Should I go and get food, or do you guys want to go out somewhere?" Laura was paying the cabdriver.

"Just come inside, and we'll figure it out," I said. "I need to feed Elizabeth, and I can't think about anything else right now."

On the way upstairs, one of our neighbors passed us, coming down fast in exercise clothes and running shoes. "Hi, George," Nick said. "We just got married."

"Congratulations and good luck," George said without stopping.

Inside, I took my shoes, dress, slip, and stockings off as fast as I could and got right into a pair of jeans and a T-shirt. I managed to do this without putting Elizabeth down. Then I sat in an armchair and pulled up my shirt. My bra was soggy and cold. Elizabeth sucked hard and fast, and I could hear the milk slosh in her throat as it went down. I exhaled and leaned back in the chair. "Phew," I said.

Laura was picking up the clothes I had dropped on the floor. She looked at the milk spots on my dress. "I don't know about this," she said. She took a hanger out of the closet. "I think it's ruined."

"Do you have to be so negative all the time?" Nick snapped. "We just got married. The dress will be fine. We'll wash it."

Laura said, "It's silk, OK? You can't wash silk."

"All right, we'll take it to the cleaners, then."

"I just think the milk stains are going to be hard to get out. That's all I'm saying. Do you have to take offense at *everything*? You're always jumping down my throat, whatever I say. And I'm sick of it."

"I'll tell you what I'm sick of," Nick said. "I'm sick of you having something negative to say whatever I do, whatever Alice does. I'm sick of your criticism, so cut it out, Laura."

"Criticism?" Laura said. She looked at Mark. "Did I criticize anyone?"

Mark said, "Laura, can't we just—"

"Hey, if I'm being accused of something, I'm going to defend myself. I said the stains were going to be hard to get out of the dress, Nick. I didn't say anything about you or Alice. You're just being self-righteous and defensive, as usual. It's really hard to do anything right around you."

"OK, so you don't like me," Nick said. "What else is new?"

"I didn't say that, either," said Laura. "Every time I—"

Nick cut her off. "Your feelings about me don't matter one bit, Laura. I'm in the family now, whether you like it or not."

Laura glared at him. "Until you change your mind again, right?"

"That's enough," I said. "You guys, cut it out."

"Fine with me," Nick said.

There was a thick silence. Then Elizabeth burped loudly.

Nick put on a David Byrne tape, a song about being naked now. We all listened without saying anything. I changed Elizabeth on a pad I spread out on the couch.

After the song was over, Nick pushed Stop on the tape player and said, "I'm going to get food. What does everybody want?"

"Oh, I'm not hungry," said Mark.

"Nothing for me, either," Laura said.

Nick looked crestfallen. "Come on, you must be a little hungry. It's after three and nobody's had lunch."

"Pizza," I said. "Get a pizza."

"Please. I'm not getting pizza," Nick said. "I just got married. I feel like having something a little nicer than pizza. I want to have a celebration here, with—I don't know—I thought something elegant. And cake. I want to have cake, don't you? It's our wedding day."

"Good. Why don't you go out and get some nice, elegant food and some cake? Then bring it back and surprise us. Whatever it is will be fine with us. Right, Laura? Right, Mark? See that? You go and get it, we'll eat it. I think a celebration is a very nice idea, don't you, Laura?" I bored a stare into her.

"Oh, yes," she said quietly. "I do. Nice idea. Very."

"OK," Nick said. "I'll do that, then. I'll get something great that everyone will like, something surprising that you don't eat all the time. You guys are going to love it."

"We can't wait," I said.

Nick started for the door. Halfway there, he turned around and said, "Alice, do you have any cash?"

Laura clicked her tongue.

"My purse is on the bed," I said.

After Laura and Mark were gone, Elizabeth fell asleep. I had nursed her almost all afternoon. I would have fallen asleep too, but I was lying on the couch, holding her across my stomach, and didn't want to move for fear of waking her up and starting her screaming again. I couldn't sleep on my back. Nick was still wearing most of his wedding clothes, but he had taken off his tie and tossed it over the back of the couch. His jacket hung from the bedroom doorknob. "So," Nick said. "How does it feel?"

"Fine," I said. I closed my eyes.

"Well, does it feel different or the same or what?"

I almost told him about the panic I had experienced just before the ceremony, but then I looked at him. His hair was all over the place, and the gel he had used to slick it down now made it stick out in stiff lumps. He looked young and sweet in a way I hadn't thought possible for a long time. He leaned forward slightly, eager for me to tell how it felt to be married to him. "Different," I said. "It feels different. Everything's changed. We have a baby, we're back together. And we're married. It's all different. It will take a while to get used to everything."

"I don't think it's different. It feels the same to me. It feels good. Marriage doesn't change anything." His feelings were hurt. I had said the wrong thing.

I looked at him. "So why did you do it?"

"For Elizabeth," he said. "So she'll have a family to grow up in. Wasn't that your reason?"

"No," I said. "I did it because I love you and I want us to stay together for the rest of our lives."

He looked at me for a few seconds. Then he said, "I think I'll change my clothes."

I called Gram. "What do you mean, you got married?" she said and then recovered. "How wonderful! Congratulations!"

"It was a simple ceremony at city hall. Laura and Mark were our witnesses." She didn't say anything. I decided to change the subject. "So how's it going?" I said. "How is Barbara working out?"

"Very well," she said. Then she held the phone away to say, "Don't put that there. It will leave a water mark."

I said, "She's right there with you?"

"Always. Yes," said Gram. "Always, always."

"She won't leave you alone? She's always hanging around, and you have no privacy?"

"Precisely," Gram said.

"You'll have to fill me in on the details later, then. Do you want to talk to Nick?"

"What for? Oh, yes, to congratulate him."

"Here he is." I handed him the phone.

Nick said, "Hi, Gram. . . . Thank you. . . . I'm sure we will. . . . Yes. . . . Thank you, I will. So long." He hung up.

"What did she say?"

"You know, congratulations and all that stuff. She hates me. Let's call my mother."

"She does not," I said. "She does not hate you."

Nick's father was still at work. But we got his mother. She was so happy she cried. She always liked me and had been disappointed when we split up. She said, "I want to see the baby. How is she?"

"She cries all the time," I said.

"Just like her father," she said. "Is she hard to get to sleep? Is she crabby when you've just fed her and changed her and done everything you can think of?"

"Yes," I said.

"That's Nick all over," she said. "Miserable from day one. Well, chin up. Maybe she won't be as bad as he was. I used to put him in a stroller next to the dishwasher and turn it on. The noise soothed him. Sometimes. Or you can hire a baby-sitter. Anyhow, good luck. Give me a call anytime."

"Thanks."

Elizabeth started crying again. "Oh, God, I hear her. That sound cuts through me just like a knife. You better go. Bye."

I fed her. It took half an hour. Nick changed her. He had done it before, and he was proud of the fact that he could do it. He put a clean outfit on her because she had thrown up on the other one. It took him a long time, and she screamed through it all. When he was finished, he gave her back to me. She was still crying. I walked around the apartment with her on my shoulder. She still cried. We didn't have a dishwasher.

"Let's go somewhere," I said. "Let's take her for a walk. Let's just get out of here."

"Sure," said Nick. "What should I bring?"

"Nothing. I'll stick her in the sling and we'll go. If she keeps crying, we'll come right back and try something else."

"OK." Nick followed me through the front door.

Elizabeth was screaming in the sling, writhing and wiggling as if I'd tied her up. "Hey, hey," I said. "It's supposed to feel cozy."

Outside, it was noisy, which either terrified her into silence or calmed her down; she was suddenly quiet and still. "What's her face doing?" I said to Nick.

He leaned down to look. "Eyes wide open. I think she's OK." We kept walking. She wasn't crying. We didn't talk because we didn't want to set her off again. We got to St. Mark's Place and then we turned left, passed all the hair-cutters and restaurants, passed Cooper Union and the subway and kept going. "When are we going to turn around?" Nick said.

"Are her eyes closed?"

"No."

"Let's keep walking until she closes them."

At Seventh Avenue, we turned uptown. She conked out around Thirteenth Street. We started walking back. It seemed like a long way. We were tired.

Back home, we stood next to the crib and Nick slipped the sling over my head while I held my arms under Elizabeth, hoping she wouldn't notice the transition. I leaned over the crib and slowly, gently, carefully laid her down on the clean, white, all-cotton sheet with a receiving blanket spread on top so that the cold sheet on her cheek would not startle her. Nick and I tiptoed out of the room without a sound. In the living room, we both sat down on the couch. We exhaled in unison. Then Elizabeth started to scream.

Nick put his hands over his face and rested his elbows on his knees.

I went back. I picked her up. I fed her. She was wide awake. We took another walk, which didn't work; we took turns standing near a noisy fan and swaying back and forth; we tried the pacifier again; I fed her some more; Nick changed her; then we took turns walking her around the apartment in the stroller. Finally, I tried feeding her again, and she fell asleep after only one side.

Fourteen

CRYING ALL THE TIME

ELIZABETH KEPT CRYING. I took her to the doctor for her six-week checkup. My obstetrician's office had given me a list of pediatric practices. Not knowing anyone to ask for a recommendation, I chose the one that was closest to our neighborhood. This was our third checkup. The doctor said Elizabeth was a perfect baby. He asked if I had any questions. I told him that she cried a lot. She looked at the fluorescent lights on the ceiling and studied his hairline. He said maybe I just wasn't used to being around babies. He said, "They do cry, you know," and smiled with one side of his mouth.

"But she cries all the time," I said.

"All the time?" he said. "She's not crying now."

I said, "At home, she cries all the time. Most of the time. Often."

He nodded. "Babies are very sensitive," he said. "It could be that she is picking up some anxiety from you. Are you feeling very stressed or worried about something? Having a baby can cause severe emotional turmoil in some women. Or it could be something else in your life that's bothering you. Is your marriage stable?"

I said, "Yes. It's fine. Great. Fine."

He said, "She's doing very well. I suggest trying to relax. Call me if you have any other concerns. The nurse will be in shortly to give her the immunization."

Elizabeth hadn't cried when the doctor was there, but after the shot I couldn't get her to stop. She was crying so hard her chin trembled. It was difficult to get her clothes back on. I kept dropping her things on the floor, and each one reminded me that I didn't know what I was doing—a sock that never stayed on, a toy she never looked at, a sweater she hated having pulled over her head. It was hard to pick these things up with Elizabeth screaming and wiggling in my arms, and it took a long time to get her dressed. I tried to nurse her, but someone came in and said the doctor needed the room for another patient. I went out to the waiting room. She screamed all the way. I sat in a chair and fed Elizabeth, watching a mother of three read a story to two kids while the third, a newborn, slept on her back in a stroller. I was never going to get the hang of this. Half an hour later, after the second side, Elizabeth fell asleep. I put her in the sling, picked up my bag, and went out.

As I walked, I tried to figure out how I was making Elizabeth cry. I didn't feel tense, but maybe she was picking up on something I wasn't aware of. Nick and I were doing fine, really well, considering. We were finally getting the apartment fixed up. Nick had hired some actors he knew who had started a home-repair business. The bathroom was finished. It had taken only a day. Now I caught my breath every time I went in there, thinking I had somehow walked into someone else's bathroom. There were towel bars and everything. We had a new kitchen floor. The actors had pulled up the rotten floorboards, put down new ones, sanded and polyurethaned them. Before we knew it, we had a smooth, shiny floor that didn't give us splinters in our bare feet or squeak under our weight and threaten to collapse any minute. Soon they would start on the bedroom. Then Nick said that actually we could afford to move now to something bigger in a nicer neighborhood. But this idea of moving to someplace nice seemed too much for us to take in; so far we had not done anything about it.

Nick had done a voice-over for an airline commercial a couple of weeks before, followed by a frozen pizza commercial, then one for a fabric softener. He wasn't very busy, yet it was different from other times when he hadn't been busy. This time he had money. He wasn't fidgety and consumed by self-doubt. He had put himself in charge of our food. He brought home take-out dinners and put them on plates while I fed Elizabeth. Or he got fresh pasta and boiled the water for it. He made sandwiches with plenty of mayonnaise. He liked holding Elizabeth, and if she hadn't cried so much, he would have done it more. He was the one who gave Elizabeth her bath every few days, even though she hated it and screamed the whole time. When she woke up at night, he brought her to me. After he went somewhere, he came back and told me where he had been, what he had done, and what everyone had said. We did not talk much about the time we had been separated or what he had been doing and with whom. Instead, we referred to this period as the time I was living with my grandmother.

Everything was fine with us, really much better than I ever could have hoped. If only it weren't for a few little things, I would have been completely convinced that our troubles were over. First, we still weren't having sex yet, but that didn't necessarily mean anything. It might take some time to get back on track. And there was the thought that kept coming to me about what a good actor Nick was and how he was trained to behave differently from the way he was feeling. I kept thinking that you can never be sure that an actor is sincere. There was nothing about his behavior that suggested he was acting, so I felt awful for thinking this, but I thought it anyway.

The biggest problem was that I couldn't stop thinking about Dan. I couldn't stop thinking about the night he drew the heart in the steam on the car window, when we heard that sad song, when I couldn't help kissing him, the night I stayed with him in his apartment, in his bed. I couldn't stop replaying all that in my mind, recalling every detail I could, trying with all my heart not to forget any of it. Then I tried to push it away, to erase it forever, only to bring it right back the next minute. I would try to convince myself that maybe if I kept rerunning it, the memory would become worn out, like some old home movie watched too many times until it became meaningless, without emotional content. So far this had not happened. Now that I was married, I couldn't talk to anyone about it. I would just have to keep it to myself and hope that it went away.

Once, I almost told Gram about it. She phoned and said, "So how's married life?"

"Good," I said. "It's good."

"Well, things worked out just right for you, then. Just the way you wanted them to."

"Yes," I said, "they sure did."

"And do you ever see Dan? He was in love with you, of course."

"Oh, I don't know about that," I said, flustered.

"Certainly you do," she said.

"You think he was? Maybe."

"Yes, I do. I really and truly do. And so do you."

It was then that I almost said, "I can't stop thinking about him. What's wrong with me? I'm married to Nick. I've loved Nick for the longest time and now we're married and have a beautiful daughter and I'm thinking about Dan so much it's driving me crazy." But I didn't say this. Instead, I said, "How are things with you? I was thinking of coming out for a visit."

Gram said, "Don't you dare. You're newly married. You stay with your husband."

"Oh, God, Gram," I said. "Now you really sound like an old lady."

She said, "I am an old lady. And how do you think I got so old? By using my head and not doing anything stupid. You stay with your husband now, and don't you dare come out here."

I kept thinking about Dan. I thought about trying to see him again, to talk to him and tell him everything that had happened. But of course I wouldn't do this, because I had everything I ever wanted. I would have to be very careful now not to ruin it.

I thought about my mother too. She had had an affair once. One afternoon I found her whispering into the phone in her bedroom. I stood in the doorway and looked at her. "Alley," she said. "This is a private conversation." I was twelve, and I thought she was talking about Christmas presents to my father at work.

That night she came into my room. I woke up. "Hey,

Alley," she said and sat down on my bed. She rubbed my back for a little while.

"Where are you going?" I said. She looked so unsettled, so restless, that I thought she had come to say goodbye to me before she went out to get something that she couldn't be without.

My mother shook her head. "I'm not going to go." She paused, thinking, trying to sum up something too complicated to put into sentences. My question had made her think I knew something that I actually had no idea about. "There's nothing wrong with your dad. It's just that he makes me sad. I don't know why. He just makes me sad." I didn't say anything. I looked at her face and let her go on. "A few months ago, something happened to me, Alley. Do you know what that was?" She was already whispering, but now she leaned down close. "I fell in love," she said. I pictured a girl in rags kissing a prince. "I went to a party and your dad stayed home with the flu, remember that? I fell in love with Charles Morrison." I didn't say anything. I had known this man all my life. He was a dentist we didn't go to. I did not allow my eyes to move from my mother's face. "He loves me too, Alley. That's my secret." Her eyes filled with tears, and she looked away. She kept talking, while I watched her. "I don't know what I'm going to do about it. Nothing, I guess. Sometimes we talk on the phone. We've taken a couple of drives. That's about it."

One of her tears splashed down onto my wrist. She wiped it away and looked at me. I felt terror as cold as a frozen rock in the pit of my stomach. I was afraid that my mother was going to leave, go away somewhere forever and not take me with her. She looked at me, biting her lip, more tears running down her cheeks, her nose starting to run. I felt that it was my turn to talk, but I had to say the right thing, something to make her stay, something that would make her glad that she told me her secret, make her want to tell me more. In the end, I didn't say anything but put my arms up, reaching for her. My mother let me put my arms around her, as if I were offering her comfort. She put her head down next to mine on the pillow and hugged me for a long time. After a while, I moved my legs over on the bed. She kicked her shoes off and snuggled up, falling asleep in her clothes beside me. I found a couple of old doll blankets and covered her.

After that, she began to tell me things she didn't tell anyone else, and I learned how to listen to secrets. As long as I could do this correctly, I knew she would stay; she needed me. I never looked away; I was always careful to keep my face neutral, not allowing the surprise, alarm, fear, or disappointment that I might feel to show in my expression. With practice, listening this way became second nature, and my mother talked to me in my room every night before I went to sleep, in the car on the way to ballet lessons, or as we drove to pick up Laura at a friend's house. Hearing her secrets made me feel special, important.

My father changed. He became crisp and short with our mother and cozy and talkative with Laura and me. He asked us detailed questions about the things we did and the kids we played with.

When I came home from a birthday party once, he played with all the little toys in my goody bag with me, putting a lavender plastic ring on the end of his pinkie and pushing the red and white numbers around in a puzzle, while I tried to jiggle some tiny metal beads into a clown's eyes. I ate a red Pixy Stix, and he started an orange one, staring gloomily into space while shaking the straw's contents onto his tongue. He didn't finish it. "Are you sure that's candy? It tastes like flavored vitamins or aspirin or something. So what presents did Vicky get for her birthday?"

"Horse stuff. A couple of horse books, some riding clothes from her parents. A big hair bow with rhinestones on it in the shape of a horseshoe. She likes horses."

"What'd you give her?"

"I gave her one of the books."

He nodded. Then he sighed and put his face in his hands. "Alley, I don't think your mother loves me anymore." I tried to keep myself from shivering. I looked at his face and waited. But that was all; he didn't say any more. He stood up then and went to mow the lawn.

Once I overheard my father say, "All Charles Morrison cares about is healthy gums and keeping that stupid Cadillac of his from getting dings in parking lots. I'd set your sights a little higher, if I were you. Don't sell yourself short."

It ended finally after what seemed then like a long time but was probably not even a year. Dr. Morrison sold his practice and moved with his family to Phoenix. His wife had allergies. My parents changed again, not back to the way they had been before but happy, silly sometimes, laughing and singing dumb songs that embarrassed Laura and made me grateful that the sad time was over. My mother's business started to take off. My father helped her with it.

There were no more secrets between my mother and me, and I was hurt when she stopped confiding in me. Once her life was stable again, my mother had suddenly left me.

She had my father to tell things to and didn't need me for this anymore. The abandonment that I had dreaded for so long had come in the form of my mother's happiness. I realized now that it must have been the reconciliation with my father more than anything Aunt Louise said that had made me feel deserted by my mother. After the secrets stopped, she hugged me before I went to sleep and whispered that I was her special girl, that she was mine forever and ever. But it wasn't the same. With my father, she had returned to a grown-ups' place that was closed to children and left me alone outside. This was the betrayal that had hurt me so badly the year I was thirteen and made me withdraw from my mother. Then both my parents died, making the abandonment I already felt an irrevocable fact.

Walking home from the doctor's office with Elizabeth still asleep in the sling, I passed Tower Records. I thought again about the song on the radio in Dan's car on the Fourth of July. That seemed so long ago. It was only six weeks. I glanced in the store window, kept walking, then turned around and went back. Inside, I tried to find that tape. There were some X tapes—even a new one. I picked up the tape on top and looked at it. Nothing called "Fourth of July." I put it back and picked up the next one. Nothing. I would have to know at least which album it was on before I could hear it again. If I thought about it enough, I was sure I could come up with someone who would know. I went to the front door and pushed, then stepped back into the store and let it close again. I saw a Tower employee. He was young, maybe twenty. "Do you know anything about X?" I said.

He shrugged. "A little. It's a band? From L.A.?"

I said, "I need a song, and I don't know which album it's on."

"OK," he said. He folded his arms.

I was going to have to sing. I took a deep breath. I said, "It goes like this: 'Hey, baby, it's the Fourth of July.' That's all I remember."

He looked at the ceiling. "Hm. Just a second. I'm going to have to get Dave. Dave's our expert on West Coast stuff. Yo, Dave. C'mere," he yelled. Other customers turned around to look. "Got a lady with a problem here."

A very tall boy walked over and stood in front of me. I had to tip my head back to look up at his face. He had big, dark tattoos of insects on his arms. He put his hands on his hips. He didn't say anything but dared me to speak to him. I said, "I'm looking for a song by X. The band X?" He waited. I sang quietly, not wanting the other customers to hear. " 'Hey, baby, it's the Fourth of July.' " He leaned down to hear me better, putting his ear close to my mouth. I said, "That's all I know."

" 'She's waiting for me when I get home from work, but things just ain't the same,' " he sang to me.

"Yeah," I said. "That one."

He went on singing, " 'She turns out the light and cries in the dark, won't answer when I call her name.' "

I said, "Do you know the name of the album?"

" 'On the stairs I smoke a cigarette alone.' Yeah. *Here We Are.*"

"Oh. Is that the name of the album?"

"Sure is."

"Well, do you have it?"

"Sure don't," he said. "Out of print."

"Oh," I said. "That's too bad."

"I guess," he said. "Cute baby."

"Thanks."

"I love babies," he said. "They're so cuddly, and they smell so good."

I got another X tape instead, which wouldn't be the same.

When I got home, Nick was in the kitchen, talking on the phone. I went straight to the bedroom and stashed the tape in my dresser drawer under a nightgown, as if I had shoplifted it or as if I were not permitted to listen to rock music.

Nick came to the door. "Hi," he said. "How did it go? What did he say?"

"What?" I said, turning around. "Who? Oh, the doctor? He said, well, he kind of suggested that it was my fault that she cries all the time. He wanted to know if I was stressed out or nervous about anything. And if so, he said that might be the problem. She's crying because she's picking up on my tension. But, I mean, of course I'm stressed. I live in the world, for God's sake." I threw my arms up and dropped them. This woke Elizabeth, who started to scream immediately. I held one arm under her while I pulled the sling over my head with the other. Sitting on the bed, I pulled up my shirt and snapped open a flap on my nursing bra. "It's my fault. I'm not calm. I'm not calm at all." I started to cry.

Nick sat next to me on the bed. He rubbed one hand across my back. "Who could be calm, under these circumstances?" He looked at me, as if I might have an answer. "You've never had a kid before, and now, suddenly, you do. You don't know what you're doing, but you're figuring it out as you go along. You hear screaming about twelve hours of the twenty-four. You have to get up four or five times a night, so you're always tired. When she's not screaming, she's either drinking your milk or hanging around your neck in a sling. Who could be calm? I sure couldn't. Geez, this guy doesn't know what it's like. You're doing an excellent job. I mean it. You're a great mother." He put his hand on my hair, stroked it. "I'll take her for a walk when you're done, and you can take a nap. You must be tired; that's why this doctor got to you so much."

I shifted away from his hand and stood up. I didn't want to be this close to him now. Technically, he was saying exactly the right thing, but somehow hearing it made me feel lonelier and more isolated than I had felt when we were separated. "You're being so nice," I said. "How come you're being so nice all the time? You were never this nice. Even before things started to get lousy, you weren't this nice."

"What are you saying?" Nick said. "First you're not happy because I never talk to you, I'm not understanding. Now what? I talk to you too much and I'm too understanding? I'm too nice? What is it that you want, Alice? I'm trying hard to do what you want, and now it seems that once again I'm not able to meet your impossibly high standards. You tell me what you want me to change this time, because I'm really getting confused here." He was yelling at me for the first time in ages.

I yelled back. I regretted what I was about to say before the words were out of my mouth, but I said them anyway. "I just want you to be real," I said. Elizabeth was screaming now, full force, terrified. "I don't want to feel that you're acting in this real-life play all the time, playing this sweet, sensitive husband and father, when actually you wish you were a single, unattached actor a million miles away, with

244 | Heart Conditions

no responsibilities. I just want to feel that you're here because you want to be here, because you love us, not because it's part of some script you're reading from in your head, from some giant commercial for family life that you're starring in."

Nick didn't say anything for a long time. The two of us looked at Elizabeth. I sat on the bed again and put my nipple back in her mouth, and she started sucking diligently. A little dimple appeared in her cheek with each suck.

I thought for a minute that Nick might start to cry, he looked so sad. Then he said, "I might have to go to L.A. I mean, I do have to. Tomorrow. Just for a couple of days. A TV series. A sitcom. I'm not going to get the part. It's just something that I have to do."

"OK," I said quietly. "That's good news. Isn't it? I'm happy for you." He probably didn't believe me, though, because I was crying. I wanted to erase the fight we had just had. I had this feeling that I had spoiled everything, that if he left he would never be back. And I didn't want to be alone with Elizabeth now, even for a couple of days. "I'm sorry, Nick," I said. "I shouldn't have said all that. It was mean. You're right. I'm really tired and behaving badly. You're doing a great job. Really. I know you're trying, and I appreciate it. I see all that. I do. I'm just exhausted and kind of deranged or something. I didn't know what I was saying." I looked at his face. He looked at mine. "If you're not going to get the part, maybe you could stay here?"

He shook his head. "I'm sorry. I know this is horrible timing, but it isn't going to be for long. Even if I'm not going to be in the running, it's important to go. I'll meet a few more people, and maybe they'll think of me for another project. Contacts—you know how it works. Hey, you can come," Nick said. "Why don't you? You can hang out at the beach or shop or something."

"No," I said. "I'll stay here. I don't want to go. I couldn't handle the beach or shopping with Elizabeth. Maybe when she's older. Next time. We'll be fine. Don't feel guilty. My sister will help me." Nick put both hands over his face. "OK, she won't," I said. "But I'll manage." Elizabeth had fallen asleep. I put her down on the bed. I hugged Nick. "I'm sorry," I said. "I'm just feeling very insecure right now because of that doctor. Do you think you could just forget about those things I said?"

"Are you kidding?" he said. "It's forgotten. No one knows better than me about saying the wrong thing. You're talking to the king of assholes here." He kissed my hair.

"You're not," I said. "Stop it, OK?"

"You all right now?"

"Yeah," I said. "I'm fine. You?"

"Perfect," Nick said. He smiled at me. It was the soap commercial smile. "Never better."

I reached for a Kleenex and blew my nose.

Fifteen

A BIG MESS

DREAMED I was still at my grandmother's and she was yelling for me to come and do something for her. "Alice! Alice!" she was saying, but when I woke up, it was Elizabeth I heard. She was saying, "Eh-heh, eh-heh," hungry and wet in her crib, working up to crying. I moved fast to scoop her up.

I fed her. Sitting there, I had a feeling of dread: something bad was happening, something I didn't want to think about, and at first I couldn't remember what it was. Then I did: I was married to Nick; I had a baby who cried a lot; soon I would have to go back to work. Elizabeth drank greedily for a few minutes, then took a break long enough to look up at me and smile, milk dribbling out of the corner of her mouth. "You goofball," I said. "You look so silly." She had smiled at Nick that morning, causing him to pause in the doorway and sigh, torn for a minute about whether to stay or go. Then he ran fast down the steps and outside to get a cab for the airport. He threw us kisses from the window as the cab pulled away from the curb. Now I gave

Elizabeth a little squeeze, and she went back to nursing.

I wanted to know right now what to do about Nick. I did not want to wait and see if this was going to work out. If someone would just tell me what to do, I would do it. I wanted to know what to do about Elizabeth crying so much too, and whether or not I should go back to my old job or try to find something else now. Maybe if my mother were alive, she would tell me what to do. Probably not, though. People never did. They just let you struggle and suffer with some impossible problem until, finally, you figured out yourself what to do. Then everyone you knew told you that he or she had the solution all along and couldn't believe it took you so long to work it out.

I looked around the half-finished apartment. There were drop cloths and paint buckets all over the living room. The actor who was going to paint had gotten a soap-opera audition and taken off suddenly. I wanted to get out of this place. I would go to Gram's to show her Elizabeth's funny smile, which made all the screaming a little easier to take. What was I doing in the city, anyway, with Nick gone? As soon as she had finished nursing, I threw some clothes for us both into a bag. I loaded it with diapers. I put Elizabeth into the sling, picked up her car seat to use at Gram's, locked the door, and went to a cash machine.

On Gram's driveway, there were six newspapers. They were all soggy from the rain the night before. The fact that Barbara was fictitious, completely made up, didn't hit me all at once but dawned on me gradually. The mailbox was stuffed. In the house, I put my things down by the front door. I strapped Elizabeth, sleeping, into her car seat on the floor and went to look for Gram. There were dirty dishes stacked on the table next to the couch. A few had moldy food on them. I said, "Gram? Gram, it's Alice. I brought Elizabeth out for a visit. Gram, where are you?" I went to the kitchen. There were seven grocery bags full of garbage near the back door. Some were the plastic kind with handles, torn and leaking. Others were the paper kind, crumpled and soaked from the inside. The room smelled like a restaurant Dumpster during a garbage strike. In the sink were dirty mugs and glasses with lipstick on them, plates stuck with dried food. A bunch of black bananas oozed on a plate.

I went upstairs. "Gram? Where are you?" She wasn't in her room or the bathroom. I heard her coughing before I saw her. She was in the basement, wearing a nightgown and a dirty white beaded sweater. She was standing next to the washer, holding a hammer and an aspirin bottle. Her hair had not been combed in a long time. She had on a pair of old glasses I had never seen before and wasn't wearing any makeup. "Gram," I said. "Are you all right?"

She jumped. "Well, look who the cat dragged in," she said. "I'm just trying to get this aspirin bottle open. I have a cold. I might be running a little temperature." She coughed hard, holding on to the washer for balance. "Now look," she said, recovering. She wiped her mouth on a tissue. "Push Down and Turn, it says here. And I'll show you that's just nonsense." She put the bottle of aspirin on top of the washer and leaned against it as hard as she could with the heel of her hand. Then she picked it up and turned the cap, which made a clicking sound. "See that? Impossible. Doesn't open. I'm just going to have to bust it." She laid the bottle on the washer and banged on it with the hammer. It didn't break. She hit it again. The third time, the plastic bottle flew across the room and landed, spinning, at my feet.

I picked it up. "I'll open it for you," I said. I pushed the bottle against the palm of one hand, twisted the top. I pulled back the safety seal and removed the ball of cotton. I shook out two aspirin and walked over to give them to Gram. Her hand was icy, and her lips were colorless, with flakes of dry skin starting to peel up. She had a fever. "Let's get you some water for those. You should be in bed. Have you seen Dr. Rikkers yet? This could be bronchitis again."

"Doesn't that just beat everything?" she said, looking at the pills in her hand. "I've been trying to get that thing open for the longest time. I came down here for the hammer. You know, I don't think there's a thing in this world you can't do." She put the tablets in her mouth and swallowed them.

I said, "You just have to push down and turn at the same time. Let's get you upstairs."

"At the same time?" she said. "Now, why don't they tell you that?" She started coughing and had trouble stopping.

"Gram," I said. "This sounds bad."

"I'm glad you're here," she said, "because I've been thinking a lot about you. You know I never tell anyone what to do. People may know my opinions about certain matters, but I never tell them what to do, do I? I have watched people organize all kinds of disasters for themselves and kept my mouth shut about it. I can't tell you how many weddings I've attended, how many gifts I've bought for couples who are obviously dead wrong for each other, just smiling my head off and saying nothing more than 'Congratulations.' And I've seen just as many divorces that are all wrong, men and women leaving everything in the world for nothing at all. But I've never said a word, just 'You're very brave,' or some such crap. Now, I don't want you to take offense at what I'm going to say, because, believe me, when I was your age, I was just as stupid as you are about my own life. It took me years and years to admit to myself that Walker Kincaid was a phony and a cheat and, as an actor, let's face it, wooden. But I would like to believe that all my mistakes had some purpose. I'd like to think that I can save you some heartache. I'm going to tell you the same thing I wish someone had told me. You've got to wake up right now. You're wasting your time with this fellow. He doesn't love you. It's as plain as the nose on your face. You may think I don't know what I'm talking about, but I do. That dentist will leave you high and dry, Carrie, and no one is ever going to love you the way Jack Hammond does."

I called an ambulance.

At the hospital, the doctor admitted Gram right away. She had pneumonia. They started antibiotics through an IV and wheeled her off to a room. I called Nick's hotel, but he hadn't arrived yet. I called my sister, then I remembered that she had joined Mark on a business trip for a few days. There was no answer at my aunt and uncle's house.

I called Dan. I said, "My grandmother has pneumonia. I'm at the hospital, the same one where I had Elizabeth. She told us she had hired someone to take care of her, but she was lying. She made the whole thing up. I got here this morning, and the place is an incredible mess. She wasn't making any sense. She thought I was my mother."

"Where's Nick?" Dan said.

"Los Angeles."

"Is Elizabeth with you?"

"Yes."

"I'll be right there."

"No, I didn't mean you had to—"

"I'm on my way."

"No—" I said, but he had already hung up.

When he got there, he took Elizabeth for a walk. She didn't scream. She stared at the lights on the ceiling, a surprised look on her face as Dan ambled slowly down the hall, explaining something quietly to her. The doctor came to find me. He said, "Oh, good, I see your husband's here." I opened my mouth to explain that Dan wasn't my husband, but the doctor didn't wait. "The three of you should go on home. There's nothing more you can do here. I can't promise anything, but it looks as though she'll pull out of this. She's very strong for her age. We will let you know immediately if there's any change. See you tomorrow." He walked quickly away, as if afraid I might ask a question and detain him.

Dan came back. "He said we should go home," I told him. "He said she will probably be all right."

"Let's go, then," Dan said.

We started for the house. I led the way in my grandmother's car, and Dan followed in his grandfather's. Somewhere along the way, I lost him, but he knew how to get there.

As soon as I arrived at Gram's, I called my aunt. "What do you mean, there's no Barbara?" she said.

"She was completely made up," I said. "An imaginary friend. Gram is really sick. The doctor thinks she'll recover, but she scared me. She thought I was Mom."

"Should I come now?" she said. "Tonight?"

"Why don't you come tomorrow? There's nothing you can do tonight anyway."

"I'll be there first thing in the morning."

After I hung up, Dan arrived. "We'd better get this place cleaned up. You don't want your aunt and uncle to see it this way."

"Don't be crazy. You don't have to do anything else," I said. "Go back to the city. I'm fine."

"I'm not going to leave you to clean all this up by yourself. I'm not leaving you and Elizabeth alone in this mess."

Elizabeth was asleep. I took her upstairs and put her carefully into the bassinet Nick and I had left there for visits. When I came down, Dan was carrying bags of trash outside. I collected dirty dishes from all over the house, threw away old papers and magazines, and cleaned Gram's bathroom. We met in the kitchen. I turned on the dishwasher, while Dan looked for a mop. He found one in a back closet near the maid's room. He rolled up his sleeves and brought a bucket to the sink. "Excuse me," he said, and I moved over so that he could fill it with hot water and Lysol.

"This is my fault," I said. "I abandoned her. I could have figured out that she was lying, that Barbara wasn't real, but I didn't want to know."

"I'm sure you didn't mean—" He tried to break in, but I didn't stop.

"She could have died because of me. I thought I was getting everything straightened out, and now I've got a really big mess on my hands." He got a knife and started to scrape at a big lump of gunk in front of the stove. "Dan?" I said. "I'm sorry." He looked up at me. "I know I hurt you. I didn't appreciate you. I treated you badly."

"About your grandmother," he said after a pause. "You're not the only person in the family who should have been concerned, who should have been checking on her. You had a couple of other things going on. Someone else could have stepped in, but no one did." He went back to the lump, jabbing at it, trying to get it off the floor. He didn't say anything for a long time, scraping fiercely. "You know how I found out you were married? I called you here. I waited and waited to hear from you, and you never called. I was worried. I was afraid that there might be something wrong with the baby. It didn't occur to me that you would just not call. I thought we had something there. I called you, and your grandmother said you weren't here anymore. She said you married Nick. I was surprised, to say the least, very surprised. But I accepted that. I made a mistake about you. I have let it go. It's gone. And I don't want to see you anymore. You've apologized for hurting my feelings, and now I don't want to hear from you. I don't want you to call me up and ask for help with something, then hint that there might be something more between us. It isn't fair, Alice. You've made your decision. You chose Nick. Next time he's out of town, call someone else. Call your sister or your aunt or somebody. But don't call me in to fill some void that Nick has left. This was an emergency; I see that. I'll help you clean up here, but that's as far as it's going to go."

"OK," I said. "I understand."

We stood there for a couple of minutes, saying nothing. Then, because nobody had spoken for such a long time, it was hard to know how to break the silence. He said, "I'll just get this hunk of crap off the floor." He crouched and scraped some more. "What do you think this is anyway? God, it's sticky."

"I don't know. Something with a high fat and sugar content, I'm sure." I went over to look at it. "Yuck. Let's try some baking soda and water. That works on a lot of things." I got the baking soda and another knife. "Let's put more hot water on it," I said. "Maybe we can melt it off." We poured steaming hot water on the glob, and both of us got to work with our knives. It took a long time, but we got it all off, leaving just a few traces, which Dan scrubbed away with a Brillo pad.

When the floor was clean, Dan stood up first. His knees cracked. He said, "Well," and then nothing. He walked to the sink to drop his knife in. "I guess I'll go."

"Thank you for your help," I said.

"Don't mention it," he said. "I hope your grandmother recovers fast."

"Thank you," I said. "She really liked you. And she doesn't like anybody."

"I liked her too. I'm flattered. So long, Alice."

"Bye."

I walked him to the door and watched him get into his car and drive away. Upstairs, Elizabeth cried, and I went to pick her up.

Sixteen

THE QUEEN OF SHEBA

Aunt Louise and Uncle Richard arrived the morning after Gram went to the hospital. When we visited, the nurse told us that the antibiotics were already starting to work. This was hard to believe, because Gram still looked terrible and was too tired to speak to us much. The nurse explained that Gram's confusion the day before was due to the fact that her lungs had been so full of fluid that she was not getting enough oxygen. Within the next few days, we should be seeing a big improvement.

Back at the house, I changed Gram's sheets. When I was finished, Aunt Louise untucked the corners and tucked them in a different way. I did some laundry. Aunt Louise came down to the basement, looked into the washer, and added more detergent. I put away all the clean dishes from the dishwasher, and Aunt Louise took some of the things back out of the cupboards and put them in a box for the Salvation Army. I went for a walk, with Elizabeth in the sling, and tried to stay out of the way.

The third day that Gram was in the hospital, before it

was light outside, the phone rang. I was already up with Elizabeth and answered it in the kitchen. "Hello?" I said.

"I had to let Barbara go."

"Gram," I said. "You're better."

"I'm fine. I just wanted you to know that Barbara didn't work out."

"I wondered why I hadn't seen her."

"I'll tell you why. She broke my best casserole dish, that's why. And she couldn't make salad dressing to save her life."

In a few more days, Gram was well enough to come home. Aunt Louise and Uncle Richard went to pick her up at the hospital, while I went to the 7-Eleven in Gram's car to buy *People*, *Us*, and the *National Enquirer*. I called Mary Lou and asked if she would come over to do Gram's hair. "She won't be able to go out for a while, and I know she's going to be cranky—even worse than usual—if she doesn't have her hair done."

"You're telling me," Mary Lou said. "I'd be glad to do it. And I want to see that little one of yours. I bet she's an angel."

I said, "She screams all the time, but I love her."

I went to the grocery store and replaced the food that Dan and I had thrown out. When Aunt Louise and Uncle Richard got back, we had to figure out how to get Gram upstairs. "You're ridiculous," she said. "I can walk up a single flight of stairs." But she couldn't.

"Indulge us," I said. "Just this once make us feel useful. I've got it. Uncle Richard, grab my wrist." We made a seat the way Laura and I had as children: my right hand held my left wrist; my left hand held Uncle Richard's right wrist.

Gram sat down on our forearms and put her arms around our shoulders. We carried her up.

"I feel like the Queen of Sheba," she said.

Uncle Richard said, "Don't let it go to your head." We set her down on the bed. Uncle Richard said, "I'll see you downstairs, Alice," and left us.

"Oh, my Lord, what happened to my room? Where are all those books and papers I had on the bedside table?"

"And the dust?" I said. "And the candy wrappers and apple cores? Gosh, I don't know. We could call Barbara and see if she knows anything about it."

"All right, Miss Smartie," my grandmother said. I took a nightgown out of her drawer. "No, I don't like that one; the sleeves are too short and the neck is too low. No, not that one, either; I get too hot in that. Where's my Dior? Where's that pretty Dior I like so much?"

I said, "I was going to throw it out. It's torn. It's a rag."

"Well, that's not your decision to make, is it?" she snapped.

I pulled it out of the shopping bag I had stuffed with all kinds of ripped and stained clothing that was beyond hope and had hidden behind the door. As I helped Gram get into her tattered nightgown, I could hear Uncle Richard and Aunt Louise discussing something downstairs; arguing, maybe.

I got Gram into bed and put the covers over her legs. "Don't do that," she said. "I'll cook with all that over me."

"Certainly, Your Majesty," I said. I went to the bathroom and got a glass of water to put next to the bed. I took the magazines I'd bought and put them on the bedside table. I turned on the TV.

"Is it time for Oprah yet?" she said.

I handed her the remote control. "I'll go get you something to eat."

"Well, it's about time," she said. "I'm starved." Then she said, "Alice—wait, come back here." I walked over to the bed. Gram took my hand, squeezed it. "Divorce Nick as soon as you can," she said. "Get yourself out of this before he has the chance to hurt you again. You know I'm just crazy about you. I won't let you get hurt, if I can stop it."

I said, "Do you want a sandwich or cheese and crackers?"

"Cheese and crackers," she said. "And I hope you got cookies."

"I did. Chocolate chip."

"Good," she said. Then, as I was going down the steps, she called, "Divorce him, Alice. Quick."

Uncle Richard was waiting for me in the kitchen. He leaned on the counter as I got the lunch things out and said, "I sent your aunt Louise out to buy Gram some flowers, just a little errand to keep her busy while we talked. I want you to move back here and take care of your grandmother. You can look after Elizabeth at the same time. You don't want to put your baby in day care to go back to some lousy job you never even liked. Now, I don't mean to tear you away from your new husband, but Nick's never home anyway. You can visit him anytime, just say the word." He looked me in the eye. "You know Gram better than anyone now. She trusts you. She adores that baby of yours, thinks Elizabeth takes after her. For your sake, I hope she's wrong there." He laughed. "Now, we'll pay you. Don't think I'm asking you to do this out of the kindness of your heart.

What were you making at that publishing company? If you don't do this, I'll tell you what will happen. Aunt Louise will decide to take care of Gram herself. Gram will be mad at her all the time. Aunt Louise will be in tears every day about your Gram's criticisms of her clothes or the kids or who knows what. And I'll go stark, raving mad hearing about it. I will lose my mind."

I said, "Thanks for the offer, Uncle Richard." I arranged low-salt Triscuits and several pieces of cheese in two semicircles on a plate. "I'll think about it. I'll stay at least until Nick gets back."

Nick called. He had a part in a new television show. He would be staying in Los Angeles to tape six episodes. He said, "You and Elizabeth are coming out as soon as your grandmother's better. I'll get us a place here until we finish these shows, then we'll go back to New York for a while. You're really going to like it out here. I think we both need to get away from that apartment. And you need a break from your family. I'll get us something furnished, with a lot of light. When I'm not working, we can take Elizabeth to the beach. It will be our honeymoon."

That same night, Laura called to ask how Gram was doing. Then she said, "Listen, Alice, I think you should dump Nick and stay with Gram. He cares more about whether he's going to get some cat food commercial than he does about you and Elizabeth. Find somebody nice, with a stable job like Mark's. We'll introduce you to somebody from his office. I'm sure we can find somebody. It's best for the baby. You don't want her growing up in an unhappy marriage."

I was wrong about people never telling me what to do.

And everybody told me what to do about Elizabeth. Now she cried whenever anybody but me tried to hold her. Leaving her for more than a couple of minutes was out of the question. I still had to work hard to get her to sleep. Aunt Louise said, "You're spoiling her, Alice." She shook her finger at me. "Just put her down and let her cry until she falls asleep. And hire a baby-sitter. She'll scream her head off until you're out of sight, and then she'll forget all about you. If you jump every time she cries, she's going to have you wrapped around her little finger by the time she's six months old."

I found a new pediatrician, near Gram's, for Elizabeth's next checkup. I told her about the crying. She said, "Did she cry a lot in the hospital as a newborn? OK, then. Here's the way I see it. One aspect of personality we're born with is sensitivity to stimuli in the environment. At one end of the continuum are babies who sleep through the night at two weeks old, who hear fire sirens and don't even fuss about the noise, and who are happy to be left with total strangers. At the other end are babies like Elizabeth here, who doesn't sleep well, cries about even small noises, and screams if somebody other than one or two familiar people holds her. Make sure your boundaries are well defined. Preserve your sanity. It won't hurt her to cry." She gave me a book to take home about getting babies and children to go to sleep, how to condition them to sleep through the night.

As I was heading for Gram's car in the parking lot, a teenager walking with her boyfriend passed me. She said, "That baby should have a hat on."

I stopped at the grocery store on the way home to buy diapers. When I was paying, the checker said, "You should use cloth diapers. It's much better for the environment."

I read the book the doctor had given me. It said to put your baby into her crib awake and not to worry if she screamed. When she woke up in the middle of the night, I was supposed to just pat her on the back and leave her, even if she cried a long time. This was the way to develop healthy sleep habits that would last a lifetime.

That night when she seemed tired, I put Elizabeth down in her bassinet and said good night. She cried, and I didn't go back to pick her up. I waited outside the door and listened to her miserable scream escalate into a piercing wail that was several seconds long. This was followed by a huge, tense pause. I held my breath until the long wail came again. After a few minutes, she began to hiccup and sob. When I finally went into the room, she was red and hard with tension, her tiny fists clenched, her muscles taut, her mouth a circle of despair. I wasn't sure how long I was supposed to let this go on, but I picked her up. I put her on my shoulder and carried her to the bed to feed her. I said, "Elizabeth, what was I thinking? I'm sorry. I will never do that again." She fell asleep still hiccuping down her milk.

"Jimmy Palladino was the love of my life. I mean that. Seriously." Mary Lou was putting rollers in my grandmother's hair, looking into Gram's bathroom mirror at us as she spoke. I was videotaping into the mirror without being in the frame myself. Elizabeth was asleep in the sling. When Mary Lou had come over to do Gram's hair, I asked if she would talk about her life while I videotaped. She said she would be glad to.

"Jimmy died in Korea. I was pregnant, not married to him, of course, and had an abortion. It wasn't one of these back-alley arrangements you read about. I went to our family doctor. Nothing went wrong. Then I married Vince, who was a friend of my brother's from high school, I went to beauty college and got a job. Never looked back." She paused. As she combed another section of hair to be rolled, my grandmother's head pulled back slightly. "That's not true," Mary Lou said and looked into the mirror. "Not a day goes by that I don't think about Jimmy Palladino. Maybe it wouldn't have worked out. Maybe he would have turned out to be a jerk—like my brother, for example." She let her head drop back and laughed. I got this in a medium shot so that my grandmother's face, listening, frowning, was at the bottom right, while Mary Lou's face was top left, her hand poised for a moment holding a rat-tail comb. She stopped laughing and reached for the roller Gram was holding up to her.

"No," Gram said, getting another roller from the plastic bucket in her lap, holding it up for Mary Lou. "You can tell about people when they're still young. People don't change."

"That's probably why I can't stop thinking about him." Mary Lou took the next roller from Gram, rolled the hair, gathered another section with her comb, took a roller. Then she looked up into the mirror. "I never talk about him, though. I don't know what came over me today." She stopped and wiped her eyes on the sleeve of her pink smock. "Would you look at me? Am I a sentimental idiot or what?" She sniffed and combed a new section.

Later, while my grandmother was asleep, I watched the tape alone downstairs. What I liked was that it showed the intimacy and trust between my grandmother and Mary Lou, built up over years of hair-styling sessions.

While the tape was rewinding, I worried about what I was going to do about being married to Nick, taking care of Gram, my job, Elizabeth's crying. Being told what to do had not helped at all; it had just confused me. Then I imagined my mother, standing beside me in the spangled sweater, a ghost or an angel or a personal adviser. Silently, I asked her, "Mom, what do you think?" The result was the same as every other time I had tried this since she died: no answer; I was on my own.

I was giving Elizabeth a bath in the kitchen sink when I got an idea. Maybe my mother's spirit put this thought into my head, or maybe it came to me because I had been thinking about everything so hard for so long. Anyway, there it was, an answer: I would get the costumes back, the costumes from my mother's business. I would have them sent here to Gram's, where there was plenty of room to store them.

Ten days later, a moving van pulled into Gram's driveway. "Who's this?" Gram said. She was up and around now, sitting downstairs on the couch the way she usually did, watching Geraldo talk to female impersonators. "Somebody's got the wrong house."

"No," I said. "It's for me. It's Mom's costumes from her shop. I had them taken out of storage and moved here." My heart raced at the thought of seeing them again.

"You did what? The costumes? I thought all that was gone years ago. What do you want with that old stuff? And where are you going to keep them, that's what I want to know."

"In your garage. Just for now. I cleared out some stuff, rearranged things to make room."

Gram said, "Where's my car going to go?"

"Your car will be fine," I said. "I promise." I put a pink sweater and hat on Elizabeth, picked up her infant seat, and took her outside.

"Alice Hammond?" the mover said, climbing out of the truck.

"Yes," I said. "We'll be putting the stuff in the garage here."

The driver went to the back of the truck, pulled out a ramp, and opened the door. There were my mother's costumes, all of them, packed in wardrobe boxes. He put two of the boxes on a dolly and rolled them down the ramp. When he reached the bottom, he handed me a clipboard and a pen. "You check off the numbers on this list when I bring them down." He showed me the number on a sticker on the first box. I put a check mark next to it on the list.

There were forty-two wardrobe boxes of costumes and a lot of smaller boxes filled with hats, shoes, and accessories—wands, gloves, crowns, bags. As soon as the mover put down the first few boxes, I flipped the tops open to see what was inside. Many of the costumes didn't look familiar to me. There were three oyster outfits, complete with giant fake pearls in them, that I didn't think I had ever seen. "You've got some interesting things here," said the driver, eyeing the costumes. He called out another number, and I checked it off the list. "Where did you get all this stuff?"

"My mother had a costume business. She died twenty years ago, and it's all been in storage since then."

"You going to open up your own shop? Like mother, like daughter, huh?" said the mover.

He rolled down another rack of costumes and called out

its number. When all the boxes were lined up in the garage, I double-checked the numbers and signed the bottom of the list. I gave the clipboard back to the driver, who tore off a copy for me. I took a bank check out of my pocket and handed it to him. Then he got into the truck and drove away. I looked back at the house. My grandmother was watching, standing by the window in the living room. I waved to her. She waved back and turned away from the window.

I went into the garage to survey the costumes and closed the door. I put Elizabeth in her infant seat on the floor and put her seat belt on. I took off my clothes down to my underwear and pulled a belly dancer's outfit off a hanger. A piece of sequin trim around the top started to come off. That would be easy enough to stitch back on. I put on the pants and found that the elastic had lost its stretch and would have to be replaced. I checked the waistband to see how difficult this would be. Not too bad. I took off the belly dancer's outfit and put on a clown suit. The fabric, which was supposed to be white with big red, blue, and green polka dots, had turned brown. It looked as though it had been soaked in tea. There were five of these costumes, and they were all brown. Bleach might get rid of the staining, I thought, but then the dots would fade too much. Maybe there was something else to soak them in.

Elizabeth started to fuss. I gave her a magician's wand that had rubber tips on the ends. Then I noticed that the tips were cracked, took it away from her, and gave her my keys instead.

I took off the clown costume and hung it up with the others. I pulled out a wolf suit and put it on. It smelled like mildew, and the fake fur was flat where it had been squashed on the rack. I rubbed it to fluff up the fur, but it didn't fluff. I put on the head. There was a moth inside, which fluttered against my nose. Elizabeth cried. I lifted the head off fast and dropped it on the floor. An eye fell out. I opened Elizabeth's seat belt and picked her up. "It's OK," I said. "It's just pretend." She settled, but she didn't want me to put her back in her seat. I took off the wolf suit and put it back on its hanger. I got into my jeans and shirt while still holding Elizabeth.

The costumes didn't look the way I remembered them, the way I had hoped they would. They were old and smelly, torn and stained. I looked through many wardrobe boxes before I found the Cinderella costume, my favorite. I had planned to put this on too, but of course it wouldn't fit me now that I was grown up. I looked at the snaps. Would my mother have used Velcro if she made this dress now? I didn't know enough about sewing to figure out problems like this. I searched for the glass-slipper pocket I had sewn in myself and checked my stitches. They were small and neat; I had done a good job.

My mother would have known what to do with these costumes, but I didn't. She would have gotten all fired up, planning how to get them back into shape, but I wasn't. As her little girl, I would have gone along in her wake, doing the jobs she assigned me, happy to further her cause. Now I had my own cause. I put all the costumes back on the racks, closed the boxes, and took Elizabeth into the house.

On a bright fall Saturday, cars started to line up on Gram's street at seven-thirty, half an hour before my sale was scheduled to start. I had pulled open the tops of all the wardrobe boxes and lined them up in the garage. At quarter to eight, I opened the garage. My first customer, a theater arts teacher at the high school, wanted all five clown suits. "Those are stained," I said. "Maybe you should take them out onto the driveway to look at them in better light."

"No problem," she said. "I'm going to dye them solid purple. That ought to cover everything." She also bought the wolf costume, some of the magician ones, several fancy dresses, and a hot dog outfit.

A teacher from a community college bought the oysters. By ten, most of the costumes were gone. I stayed out until noon, because I had said I would in my advertisements in the paper and in the fliers I had sent out to schools and theater groups in the area. I made a lot more money than I had expected. Laura wasn't going to accept any of it, she said, because I had paid the storage bills all these years. I saved the Cinderella dress for Elizabeth when she was older.

The night of the sale, I served my grandmother a Stouffer's spinach soufflé. "What are you going to do with all that money? That's what I want to know," she said.

"Spend it," I said.

"Well, that's exactly what I would do," she said. "I'd buy myself some lovely designer things. A couple of nice dresses, a suit. Good clothes I could wear for a long time. And some pretty shoes. Italian ones are the best, let's face it. Always make sure your shoes are plenty big, Alice, so you won't get bunions. That's why my feet are so terrible today—my shoes were always too small. And what about getting your hair done? You'll have plenty of money for a cute cut and a permanent. Mary Lou could give you a wonderful manicure, but I know that's too much to hope for." She put her plate on the table next to her. "You can take this now and bring me dessert."

I wanted to talk to Nick, but he was difficult to reach. He was always rehearsing or taping, or it was the wrong time to call California. When I finally did get him, he was in a rush to leave. "Hi," he said. "How is she? What's she doing right now? Has her face changed? Did you send more pictures?"

I said, "Elizabeth's fine. She's great. She makes little noises now."

"Noises? She does? Like what kind of noises?"

I tried to imitate the crowing sounds that Elizabeth made sometimes when she was awake and fed, but it didn't sound the same coming from me. "That's not right," I said. "I can't do it."

"Could you make a tape of it, do you think?" Nick said.

"Oh, sure," I said. "Listen—"

"Shit, what time is it? Oh, no. I have to get to the studio right now. God, I feel like I live there."

"But can I just tell you one thing?"

"Oh, OK. What?"

"You know how I've been trying to decide about—"

"Is that Elizabeth I hear? Is that the noise?"

"What?" I said. "Oh, yeah, that's it. Here, I'll hold the phone up to her." I put the phone in front of Elizabeth in her infant seat, but then she was silent. "Sorry," I said. "I guess having the phone right in her face is too distracting. Anyway, what I was going to tell you was that I got all my mother's costumes moved here and sold them. Now I'm going to take the money—"

"You're kidding. Who bought them? I could have given you money. I have plenty of money. Listen, I have to leave right now. I'm sorry for cutting you off. And could you make a tape of those noises for me? I feel like I'm missing everything."

"I could make a videotape," I said. "I was going to—"

"I'm sorry," he said. "I can't be late. But call me again anytime. Give Elizabeth a kiss for me."

"OK. Bye."

"Bye."

I stood outside a camera store in Midtown. In the last several weeks, I had picked out the equipment I wanted to buy, and I had the money with me in cash to pay for it. That morning I had called Dan and asked him to meet me to get his camera back. I didn't know when I would get into the city again.

I met Dan out front. "Alice, how are you?" he said. "Hi, Elizabeth." She looked at him from inside the sling. He bent down and touched her hand with one finger. She grabbed it, held on. "Look. She's glad to see me."

"Of course," I said. "She's known you all her life. Here's your camera." I handed over the case. "Thank you for lending it to me. It got me started with something I really like."

Dan said, "You don't have to give the camera back now. Why don't you keep it, use it for a while?"

"Thanks," I said. "But I'm getting another one that's much smaller and lighter, with better resolution. It just came out. I'm starting my own business, helping people get their stories on videotape, you know, the way we did with my grandmother that time." The business had practically taken off by itself. I made a tape of Elaine, across the street from Gram. She asked me to make copies for her children. Then Mary Lou's husband, Vince, called. He wanted me to tape him talking about his childhood in Italy and moving to upstate New York as a teenager. Charles and Tom, Gram's costume designer friends from her Hollywood days, wanted me to tape them talking about fifty years of working on movies and in the theater. I was building up a small collection of tapes of people telling their stories, and I had three more people scheduled—a friend of Elaine's and two more of Gram's Hollywood friends. They were going to pay me. I had named a price, and they agreed to it. It was that simple.

Dan took the case from me. I said, "So. Well. I'll see you, OK?"

"Good luck with everything," he said. "Do you want me to go in the store with you? These camera guys can be pretty intimidating."

"No, thanks," I said. "I'm OK. I know exactly what I want. I've bought stuff here before."

"You want me to hold Elizabeth while you're inside?"

I said, "Thanks. I appreciate it. But she would cry. Don't take it personally; she's just sensitive." I turned to go into the store. Then I stopped and said, "Good luck to you too. With everything." He put his camera case over his shoulder and waved as he started walking away.

The store wasn't crowded. In just a few minutes, I had my camera, a tripod, tapes, and a bag. I was finished so fast that I thought I might make it back to the train before Elizabeth got hungry again. But I didn't. I was barely outside again before she began to fuss. I started walking back to my old office. There were two weeks left of my unpaid maternity leave. I had my key with me. At Stringer and Russland, I could sit down and feed Elizabeth before I went back to Penn Station.

By the time I got inside the building and in the elevator, my milk was leaking and my nursing pads were wet. I pushed the button for the ninth floor. The other people in the elevator looked at me out of the corners of their eyes. I was wearing jeans and carrying a crying baby; I didn't fit in here anymore. When the doors opened, I picked up the camera bag and walked to the doors of Stringer and Russland.

Jane was standing near the inside door. Somehow I hadn't expected to see her first. I had pictured visiting Eric for a while, maybe showing Elizabeth to some of the editors.

"Hello, Alice," Jane said. "You're back."

"Oh, I just stopped by because I was in the area and Elizabeth—"

"Good. I was going to call you and let you know that there's quite a bit of fact checking piling up on your desk. You don't want to get too far behind."

"Actually," I said, "I'm not coming back."

"Fine," Jane said. "You can do the work from home for the last part of your leave. But I want you to know that as a staff member, we can't pay you for doing free-lance work. It's against company regulations."

"I don't think you understand," I said. "I'm not coming back at all. I mean, I'm quitting."

Jane pursed her lips. "No, I don't understand. I think we've been very generous with you, letting you just take off and have a baby and keeping your job waiting. Now you're telling me that all of a sudden you've decided to quit. How can you do this? You're leaving us stranded with no warning at all. We were depending on you, Alice. I'm very disappointed."

I said, "It's not all of a sudden, not at all. I've never liked working here." With Elizabeth crying, it was hard to think clearly enough to be tactful.

Jane wound herself up to say more, then didn't. She said, "I'll take your key, then." She held out her hand.

I had already put my keys in my bag and had to fumble around to get them out again. I wrestled the key off my ring, with Elizabeth wailing full force.

Dan heard the crying and came out. "Alice? Everything all right?" he said.

Eric came out. "Hey!" he said, grinning. "The baby! Jesus, is she always this loud?"

"Yes," I said.

Jim and Mary came out. "Oh, it's you," Jim said. "We couldn't figure out what that racket was."

"Awww," said Mary. "What's wrong with her?"

"She's hungry," I said.

Jim said, "Why don't you feed her?"

"I thought I would," I said. "That's just what I was going to do."

They all stood there looking at me. Jane folded her arms. "Was there anything else?" she said, ready to dismiss me from the premises.

"Dan," I said. "I need Dan. I mean, I needed to see Dan about something." I looked at him for help.

"Excuse us," Dan said. I followed him to his office. He shut the door.

It was dark in there, as usual. Elizabeth quieted a little. I put down my stuff, got Elizabeth out of the sling, sat down, and got her started on my left breast. "Phew," I said.

"I just quit my job. Jane was mad." I shook my head. We sat there for a minute, watching Elizabeth.

"What did you want to see me about?" Dan said.

Elizabeth stopped drinking and looked at him, leaving my breast to chill in the draft. She was three and a half months old now. I could no longer carry on a conversation while she nursed. I pulled up the sling to hide behind, but she batted it down again to see Dan.

"You said you wanted to talk to me," Dan said.

"Oh." I looked at him. I said, "I'm in love with you, and I think about you all the time, and I wanted you to know. That's all."

"Alice, you're married," Dan said.

"Separated," I said. "I knew I was doing the wrong thing when I married Nick, but I did it anyway. We're getting a divorce. I told him it wasn't going to work for me, and he got it all organized. It was easier than you'd think. He was relieved, probably, because already he's started seeing the director of the TV show he's in. He's out in Los Angeles, permanently, I guess, except that he's been back twice to see Elizabeth. We're living at my grandmother's. I'm taking care of Gram. Elaine, the lady across the street, stays with her when I have to be away for a couple of hours."

"So what's your plan? What did you have in mind?"

"No plan," I said. "I just wanted to tell you."

We sat there for a long time. I switched Elizabeth to the right side. When she was finished, I changed her on a pad I laid across Dan's worktable. Then I put her back in the sling and picked up my bags. "I'm going to have to go if I'm going to make the next train," I said. "Thanks for letting me use your office."

"You're welcome," Dan said. He stood up as I started out. "Alice?"

"Yes?"

"I'll come with you. I love you too." He smiled. "Well, you knew that. Anyway, I'll come with you now. I can carry this stuff for you." He kissed me, holding me carefully so that we wouldn't squash Elizabeth between us in the sling. Kissing Dan was every bit as good as I remembered, except that Eric opened the door in the middle of it.

"Oh, geez," he said, slapping a hand to his forehead. "Can you believe this? I didn't know. God, I'm sorry. Nobody tells me anything around here. I can come back. It's not a problem." He backed out of the room. "You could have told me, though. I don't like to be the last to know what's going on with my two good friends."

Dan said, "You're the first to know. The very first. Besides us."

"Oh, well," said Eric, smiling. "In that case, congratulations." He shook Dan's hand, then mine. "I've got to go proofread some bullshit now, count characters until my eyeballs drop out of my head. But you two have a good time. Dan, take the rest of the day off. See you guys."

"Oh, my God, look who's here," my grandmother said as the three of us walked in. "It's the Queen of Sheba and her entourage." Elizabeth was crying again.

"Me?" I said. "Are you calling *me* the Queen of Sheba now?"

"Elizabeth," said Gram.

"I thought you were the Queen of Sheba," I said.

"I am," Gram said. "But I'm nearing the end of my reign, and I'm grooming my great-granddaughter to take over the throne. I think she's most deserving of the crown. As a matter of fact, I think she's already snatched the damn thing right off my head. Isn't she a pistol, Dan?"

Dan set my bags down by the door. "She certainly is. But a cute one," he said.

"Where's Elaine?" I said.

"I'm out here in the kitchen," Elaine yelled.

"Elaine is preparing our lunch," Gram said and rolled her eyes.

"Tuna salad. Special recipe," Elaine said. "Very low fat, high protein."

In a loud whisper, Gram said to Dan, "Take my car. Go get me the biggest chocolate bar you can find."

I said, "I brought you some chocolate. It's in one of the pockets in that diaper bag."

"Oh, good," Gram said. "So, Dan. I see you're back in the picture."

"Yes," Dan said. "I'm back in the picture. And what a picture it is."

"Excuse me," I said. "I have to go and change the Queen of Sheba." I went upstairs, put a new diaper on Elizabeth, and walked her to sleep. Carefully, I put her down in her bassinet. But by the time I got downstairs again, she was crying. I turned around to go back and get her.

Elaine was bringing out Gram's lunch on a tray. She said, "Let her cry, Alice. You hop every time she squeaks. You know that, don't you?"

I stopped, turned around, and addressed the room. I said, "She's only three months old. She cries for a reason. When she cries, I try to make her feel better, if at all possible. That's my system. That's the way I'm going to do it. If anybody has a problem with that, just keep it to yourself. I appreciate your support. I really do. But now, everybody, please stop telling me what to do. Thank you."

There was a pause. Then Elaine said, "Well, she's your baby. You're the mother."

"That's right. I am," I said. "I am the mother." Slowly, with some surprise, I had realized that being a mother was something I could do, something I was going to be good at. Maybe I had learned what I knew from my own mother. Though she made the usual number of mistakes, big and small, she always took care of us in her own quirky way, which seemed to work for us, no matter how wrong it appeared to other people.

"Here's your lunch, Mrs. Williams," Elaine said.

"Thank you," Gram said. Then I heard her say to Dan, "Of course you know Alice can't cook to save her life and she never picks up after herself."

Dan said, "But she's kind to babies and old people."

Upstairs, as soon as I picked up Elizabeth, she stopped crying. She smiled, glad to see me, glad I was there.